NAKED STRANGERS

NAKED STRANGERS

ROBERT POWELL

Debonair

Cover designed by Cordero & Davenport Advertising of San Diego

ISBN 0-9651648-0-2

Printed in the United States of America

10 9 8 7 6 5 4 3 2 1

To Alan Harrington, a scholar and a gentleman,
who taught me something about writing a story.

"Think ye that God made the universe,
and then let it run round his finger?"

. . . *Goethe*

A CHRONOLOGY

1971	Kelly joins Navy
1972	U.S. bombs Hanoi and Haiphong
1973	Vietnam War ends
1976	Carter elected President
1978	**Kashan goes to Miramar**
1979	Khomeini returns from exile
	U.S. Embassy in Teheran seized
1980	**Kashan returns to Iran**
	Iran/Iraq War starts
	Reagan elected President
1981	Embassy hostages released
1984	Iran/Iraq fight in Persian Gulf
	Reagan reelected President
1986	Kelly quits Navy
1987	Cessna lands in Red Square
1988	**Kashan flies thru Baja to U.S.**
1988	Iran/Iraq War ends
	Bush elected President
1989	Khomeini dies

PROLOGUE

On May 28, 1987, a young West German pilot, Mathias Rust, astounded the world by flying his small Cessna under the radar screen across Finland and Russia and landing in Moscow's Red Square in broad daylight. Even with the wildest of imaginations, no one could have dreamed such a feat was remotely possible.

The success of this daring escapade was a great embarrassment to Soviet Air Defenses and resulted in heads rolling at the top of their military hierarchy. Regularly scheduled television programs were interrupted by news of the deed; it made headlines in every major newspaper in every country of the globe with the exception of the USSR and some of its satellites. A milkman in Peoria, Illinois dispensed the hilarious news and a few chuckles with every bottle of whole milk, low-fat, or half-and-half he handed to awaiting customers on his route that day. Newspapers sold like hotcakes in Coos Bay, Oregon and in Poughkeepsie, New York and in Waxahachie, Texas. New car salesmen, too engrossed in talking with prospective buyers about Russia's appalling stupidity, forgot all about hustling. The young West German sure put one over on the Russians. They were good at making great vodka from lousy potatoes, but evidently knew precious little about sophisticated radars.

All over the world, people had a field day at Russia's expense. Before the day ended, much beer and alcohol was consumed in saloons and alehouses, cocktail lounges and bistros, and a good portion spilled amid rowdy backslapping, raucous laughter, and inane frivolity.

❦

In the offices of the Iranian Secret Police in Teheran, Iran, two khaki clad officers sat quietly at their shabby wooden desks. One shuffled busily through reports detailing planned student demonstrations and proposed speeches by the ayatollahs. The other officer, a bald-headed, bespectacled man of medium, but muscular, build, sat with his feet propped up reading the morning paper.

"Did you see what happened in Russia?" he said.

A large portrait of the Ayatollah Ruhollah Khomeini dominated the wall over his desk.

"Yeah, the German infidel landed his little airplane in Red Square. But so what?" answered the other with disdain in his voice. "Who cares?"

Several minutes went by in complete silence.

"I wonder . . . ," mused the officer with the newspaper.

"Wonder what?" replied the other, his tone indicating a building irritation with the unwanted distraction.

"Could the same . . . or a similar thing . . . happen . . . say . . . in the United States?"

The officer sifting through the reports stopped at one, focusing his attention to a particular item on it. He wrote with a stubby, well-sharpened pencil and placed the report on a pile to his left. Picking up another, he began reading. "What did you say?" he asked with detached interest as he started writing again.

"Could the same thing . . . oh . . . just forget it."

Almost a year later, the bald, bespectacled man would remember this brief exchange, little more than a monologue. And he would remember it with a smirk on his face.

1

BAJA
Spring of 1988

Flying alone at night in a small airplane is an incredibly lonely occupation. Especially when flying over a barren region of the Earth like the Baja peninsula. Night, ever a pilot's dreaded enemy, drags on painfully eternal, moments linger, slowly the hands of the clock advance. The whirling propeller masks explosions in the cylinders, pounding of pistons, rushing of exhaust gases through the manifold. The appearance of the next navigational landmark seems eons away. Only a dim glow of lights on the instrument panel hints of another world far below where babies cry and adults procreate, where governments wage war and kill, where children laugh and play, where scientists tinker and men deceive. For most, the safety of a warm bed cries out and longing for tenderness of human touch overpowers logic and common sense.

But, Kashan wasn't that kind of person.

From 6000 feet, he could clearly make out the rough shapes of both coastlines of the Baja peninsula, the full moon providing a surprising amount of light. Kashan's single-engine Bonanza cruised effortlessly and gracefully over vast acres of water or cactus and sagebrush. Above, billions of stars glimmered brightly. Below, white crests of long waves breaking on beaches and smashing into cliffs danced like strings of pearls. The outline of an occasional building defined by the moon's harsh shadow crept slowly under his wings.

Scattered ranches and fishing villages dotted the otherwise barren and desolate wasteland of Baja. Baja – the bastard child of Mexico – a 700-mile-long peninsula almost entirely separated from the mainland by the Sea of Cortez. At some points Baja was less than thirty miles wide. Uninhabited with the exception of border cities and a handful of major towns, in most areas the peninsula had no potable water, no radio, no electricity, no telephone. Were it not for the large oil companies who popularized Baja with their annual race, it would still be unknown. Baja was too damn hot and too damn arid. Not even the early Mexican tribes like the Aztecs, the Mayas, or the Toltecs had much to do with Baja. To this day, one finds virtually no mention of it in Mexico City's monumental Natural Museum of Anthropology or National Museum of History. The legendary serpent god of air and water, Quetzalcoatl, evidently had not spread his wings far enough to encompass the Baja peninsula. The bastard child.

Kashan had chosen this night because of the full moon. He knew too that the only clouds this far south of the border were on the western side of the peninsula along the Pacific Ocean, created almost every night by the colder water masses there. He encountered no clouds here and none were expected.

He glanced down at his map. Only 400 miles to go. About two hours.

Flying at night in Baja was illegal. He recalled laughing when he found out this was a joke. The Mexican government did nothing to stop it.

Except for the landing fields at Tijuana, Mexicali and La Paz, none of the runways had lights and only a handful were paved. Most were lousy dirt strips. Kashan had all the available navigation charts, but his destination was not on any of them. That's why he had picked it. He also had a book with photographs of all the landing strips, which he had no intention of using.

He fidgeted and squirmed in his seat, flexed his arms and shoulders and rubbed his eyes. He was a large man for a small airplane but the Bonanza had an unusually spacious interior and he fit comfortably. Besides, flying the Bonanza required a lot less effort than flying the fighter jets he was accustomed to. He checked the charts one more time. *Almost there*, he thought, *almost at Punta Estrella.* The Mexican was called Chicken Bill, he remembered.

His plane was modern and up-to-date with all the latest radio gear. Although it had U.S. registration, the plane had been provided by SAVAK, the Iranian government's secret police under the Shah. SAVAK had also confirmed that the Mexican was still there and that he still sold aviation gasoline.

Kashan's flight began in Mexico City. He had stopped for gas in Mazatlán and waited for nightfall. He did not enjoy his dinner because, he believed, most food except Middle Eastern was barbarian. After midnight he crossed the Sea of Cortez in the general direction of La Paz at the southern tip of the Baja Peninsula, heading north before reaching the outskirts of the city. This might have seemed like an unnecessary risk to some pilots since he crossed over open water for nearly 250 miles. *It's a lot safer than flying over the ocean in a 747*, he thought while planning this flight. And he wanted to get off the mainland of Mexico as soon as possible. It wasn't beneath the CIA to keep a few agents in the northern part of the country. He would arrive at Punta Estrella at first light. That's the way he planned it and that's the way it would be. He could not help but feel elated, though, that everything was working out so well. Kashan admired precision in human endeavor.

⁂

Chicken Bill felt elated too. It wasn't often that a plane came by so early in the morning at such a low altitude. He threw another piece of cold fried fish to Chango, his dog and only companion at Punta Estrella.

Chango had a good ear for airplanes.

Sitting by the old table in front of the window, Chicken Bill poured himself another shot of tequila and lit another American cigarette. Chango had heard the plane when it was well down the coast, much before Chicken Bill, and barked. It wasn't so much a bark as it was a muted yelp. Like most Mexicans,

Chicken Bill did not tolerate barking dogs. He could tell by the sound that it was low and wondered if the plane were going to land. He wasn't expecting anyone. But once in a while a dope dealer or smuggler came in early. Sometimes they were taking guns south and sometimes diamonds or illegal aliens north. He didn't care. Chicken Bill sold his gasoline only to a small clientele, at a handsome markup. Not many knew that a plane could land on the hard sand along the beach.

He didn't have much inside the shack in the way of comfort. A puny little old guy like him didn't need much. Numerous cases of tequila and cartons of cigarettes lined one wall. Most of the boxes contained empty bottles. Old aircraft radios and some spare parts crowded against another. By any standard, the place was filthy. There was scarcely room for a single bed. But, even Chicken Bill had his *macho* vanity. His most valued possessions were his elegant leather boots and belt. Next came the fine black Western hat he always wore. Once in a while, he thought about retiring to Guadalajara or maybe Mexico City. That would take a lot more pesos and American dollars than he had buried outside. And once in a while, he got a little nookie from a local Indian girl. That ate up some of his handsome profits. Outside an old jeep was parked next to the shack alongside a small boat with an outboard engine.

Chango stirred restlessly as the plane drew nearer.

In a lean-to behind the shack, a couple of dozen drums of aviation gasoline sat under an old tarp. Drunken posts and dangling wires hinted of a feeble attempt to build a makeshift fence. Some drums were trucked in. Others Chicken Bill got from passing shrimp boats along with an occasional lobster or red snapper. Chango knew the difference between the sound of a shrimp boat and an airplane. Chango too preferred the *langosta* and *huachinango* to their usual diet of fried triggerfish and cheese macaroni. And Chango had come to relish tequila almost as much as Chicken Bill.

⁂

Finally, Punta Estrella was off Kashan's left wingtip. He had been keeping track of time along the coastline. At first he passed the larger towns of Loreto and Mulegé, then tiny Alfonsina's on Gonzaga Bay and the even tinier little rock in the water called Huerfanito, the Little Orphan. And just before Punta Estrella, the village of Puerticitos. The solar disk began to appear behind his right wingtip.

In a gradual descent since Puerticitos, Kashan was down to 1000 feet and circled over the shack. He had a hard time seeing the runway but was aware it paralleled the beach between the building and the water. He knew exactly where to touch down though, for SAVAK was seldom wrong. Nevertheless, Kashan was not the type to completely trust intelligence. He had been told about Chicken Bill and Punta Estrella during his previous stay in the States. That's why he had a case of tequila and some cartons of American cigarettes in the back seat. He circled the Bonanza out over the water, lowered the landing gear and put in twenty degrees of flaps.

Rays of the sun flowed over the horizon like hot blood.

✈

Chicken Bill did not recognize the Bonanza. Neither did Chango. Chicken Bill smiled and thought about his box with the money buried out back. Some days, little else occupied his mind. Living in Baja wasn't easy. He mumbled something to Chango in Spanish and the dog ran out the door and off towards the sand dunes. He poured himself another shot of tequila and squinted out the window. He had fifteen more minutes before the plane completed circling and went two or three miles down the beach to set up a long, slow approach, land, and taxi back.

Chicken Bill waited in the shack and watched Kashan through the window. Kashan was unloading the case of liquor and the cigarettes when Chicken Bill finally went out to greet him.

"Buenos dias. Yo quiero gasolina. Cien," said Kashan with the few words of Spanish he knew, asking for 100-octane gasoline.

"Good morning," answered Chicken Bill in practiced English. To Chicken Bill, all men were either Spanish or American.

"Mucho Americano dinaro," he added with a grin before Kashan

could reply. "You got? You show. You come inside *mi casa*."

"I've got money," answered Kashan.

Chicken Bill walked around the plane and eyed it with obvious admiration. He got up on the wing and looked inside the cockpit. *Muy bonito!* he thought. He jumped back onto the sand, backed several feet away, then circled the aircraft, all the while grinning a wry grin alternated with a devious smile. Kashan noticed. This was indeed a very, very beautiful airplane, much nicer than any Chicken Bill had ever seen. The elegant V-tail towered over his head. The radios alone would be worth a small fortune. There were many suitcases in the back seat and the luggage compartment held more. This *hombre* didn't look like an American or like the typical Baja bush pilot. Even though his English sounded good to Chicken Bill, this *hombre* was definitely not a gringo.

"Where you come from?" he asked with a look of suspicion.

"From Tijuana," answered Kashan guardedly.

A lie. If Kashan had come from Tijuana, he would have had lots of gas left in his tanks. Besides, Kashan didn't look like a dope smuggler. Chicken Bill knew dope smugglers. This guy was going to pay through the nose for his *gasolina.*

"You wanna give me money, now!" demanded Chicken Bill.

"No," replied Kashan firmly. "You fill the tanks and then I'll pay."

Chicken Bill grinned again. Paying after the tanks were filled was the usual procedure, he well knew.

"Where to you go?" he asked with obvious caution, aware it was not a proper question for a stranger in Baja, especially one who stopped at Punta Estrella.

"I'm going to fish for *totuava* at Bahia de los Angeles," again lied Kashan.

The *totuava* did not migrate as far south as Bahia de los Angeles. It was a stupid mistake Kashan rarely made. He should have said he was interested in whales or turtles or red snapper. That's what L.A. Bay was noted for. Besides, people going fishing usually did not come alone. After the lie, Kashan remembered and felt uneasy. He would not make the same mistake again, he promised himself.

Chicken Bill lit a cigarette and let it dangle from his mouth. Pensive, his mind was busily engaged in converting pesos back and forth to American dollars, wondering . . .

Unnoticed by Kashan, Chicken Bill raised two fingers to his nose and glanced in the direction of the shack. He picked up the case of tequila and Kashan the cartons of cigarettes. Kashan followed Chicken Bill in the soft sand away from the beach towards the shanty. From somewhere, Chango suddenly appeared, woofed once, and scampered behind.

When they reached the shack, two Mexicans stepped out. The rising sun reflected off the barrel of the pistol the taller of the two waved at Kashan.

"Hola gringo," he said. A broad smile beamed from ear to ear showing large white teeth.

The other, more boy than man, edged towards Kashan. Chicken Bill's wide grin grew even wider. It was not the first time they had killed a strange pilot and chopped up his airplane for spare parts. There was good money in that.

"Hola, hola, chinga su madre," laughed the tall Mexican defiantly, not noticing that he was inching dangerously close to Kashan and carelessly waving his gun.

Kashan threw the cartons of cigarettes into the tall man's face. In what seemed like an instant, Kashan produced a stiletto from his sleeve and lunged at him. The man teetered slowly with incredulous eyes staring in amazement, blood trickling slowly out the sides of his mouth. In agony, he reached for Kashan, but was dead before his knees crumpled. The stiletto had made a tiny hole through his chest and found his heart.

At first startled, the boy began to run. Kashan caught him from behind. They grappled momentarily in the sand before Kashan cut his throat. Kashan had some difficulty, the stiletto wasn't designed for cutting. He would have preferred to have stuck him, but the boy was strong and did not cooperate. By the time he was done, Chicken Bill had vanished. Kashan reached down, picked up the gun and stuck it into his back pocket.

Kashan looked at the two bodies with disgust. He did not enjoy killing. It was sometimes necessary, always messy. Still, he felt remorse, largely in that the precision of human endeavor had failed. He could and should have been more careful. He'd be in the future, he told himself. He did not know what he could have done to have been more careful, but, still, he decided to fast for two days as self-punishment.

Kashan found two empty jerry cans and used them to refuel the Bonanza. *An airplane without gas in its tanks is like a mother without milk in her breasts,* he thought. Voraciously, the Bonanza drank in the precious organic liquid. It had been almost 800 miles since he last filled up in Mazatlán. He filtered the gas through a chamois he found in the shack. The plane consumed nearly a full 55-gallon drum and the refueling took more than an hour. All the while, Kashan kept an eye looking for Chicken Bill amid the myriad of sand dunes going off for miles in each direction.

He could not help sweating profusely in the punishing sun. He had dragged the two dead men behind the jeep and thrown the old tarp over them.

Kashan pondered his options. "Pagan thieves!" he said quietly to himself.

Finding rope in the shack, he decided to dispose of the bodies in the water, weighing them down with some rusty old automobile parts strewn around behind the shack. They wouldn't last long in the combination of salt water and hungry sharks. He didn't like the idea of leaving Chicken Bill alive.

It took all his strength to pull the small boat down to the water in the soft sand with the keel digging in when it wasn't supposed to. Finally he managed and rested for a short while before retrieving the bodies and automobile parts. The outboard engine was fairly new and he had little trouble starting it. Even though Kashan was from Iran, he was familiar with boats and engines and, in fact, most mechanical things not commonly found in his country. He had made it a point all of his life to be so.

Without flinching, he walked into the calm chilly water and guided the small craft out until the water was waist-deep along the side of a narrow reef. He reached into the boat and removed the drain plug from the transom, white bubbles of sea water immediately forming in the small hole. He aimed the boat for open sea after securing the engine with a piece of rope. Diving into the water, he was refreshed by the short swim back to the beach. He dried quickly in the hot sun.

All the while, Kashan was concerned about Chicken Bill. Leaving the Bonanza unattended for the brief while had been a slight risk. But most things in life were risks of one sort or another and he had been trained to take chances. There had been no sign of Chicken Bill. Scuttling the boat once it had been loaded with the dead cargo had taken scarcely longer than five minutes.

⁂

Kashan sat in the cockpit, looked over his navigation charts, and contemplated his next steps. Although he had been over them many times, experience had taught him it was always wise to make one final check. The mark of a good pilot.

He had no choice but to be good at most things. His honor and his family's honor in Iran depended upon him being so.

A shot zinged off the top of the Bonanza's cabin and then rang out. Kashan spun his head just in time to see the little dog scamper behind a sand dune. Leaping from the plane, he ran in the direction of Chango. Another shot. This time Kashan saw Chicken Bill's head. With all his energy he raced through the soft sand, reaching into his back pocket for the gun the tall Mexican had been waving at him.

The third shot whizzed by uncomfortably close.

This time Chicken Bill was standing erect and grinning, a cigarette dangling from his mouth. Kashan quickly fired twice and Chicken Bill disappeared. By the time he got to where Chicken Bill had been, there was no sign of him. Instead a small herd of a dozen skinny cattle was milling about. Large clumps of manure were strewn in the sand. Footprints, either animal or human, seemed to be everywhere.

What're cattle doing in this uncivilized place? Kashan wondered.

2

SAN DIEGO BAY

The *Baja Vagabundo* lay at anchor 100 yards off Shelter Island in San Diego Bay. A sleek fiberglass yacht, 42 feet long with a beam of 14 feet, a 40-inch draft, a displacement of 12 tons, she had been built in Bellingham, Washington. Twin Volvo TAMD-60-B 235-horsepower diesels gave her a cruising speed of 21 knots and a range of 500 miles. Although she slept eight comfortably, with two staterooms fore and aft of the salon, Kelly always thought of her as suitable for four. All the comforts of home were aboard, including air conditioning, a microwave, a garbage disposal and AM/FM stereo with a CD player. On the more practical side, she carried two Ritchie compasses, a Sitex 24-mile radar, two Raytheon D-600 depth finders, a Benmar auto-pilot, and two VHF radios.

All this for only $100,000, thought Kelly when he bought her.

The yacht was inexpensive, *compared* to his airplane. With full tanks and a small amount of baggage, the Bonanza could carry only four people, and one of those had to be the pilot. The Bonanza weighed less than one-tenth of the *Baja Vagabundo*, but cost three times as much. But, then, the *Baja Vagabundo* could not cruise at 200 mph nor loop and slow roll (the Bonanza was not certified to do loops or slow rolls either, Kelly had been warned more than once by the FAA).

Jennie sat on the aft deck over the aft stateroom with a sketch pad. The late morning breeze had blown her hair into disarray, exposing her soft, tender neck. Petite, with dark brown hair, Jennie had wide hazel eyes that turned green when she became angry. Her face was delicate and she had an elegant way of carrying herself. At times she was fiery and impulsive, but preferred to regard herself as merely feisty. She longed to be eighteen once again even though she was near thirty.

With a charcoal pencil, she drew the fishing pier on the Coronado side of Shelter Island in San Diego Bay. A group of pelicans coasted overhead. There was considerable small sail boat activity in the bay, but most boats were departing past Ballast Point for the deeper waters of the open ocean. Jets taking off from Lindbergh Field could be seen in the background, their engine noises barely audible. Behind them, an occasional military jet landed or took off from North Island Naval Air Station on Coronado. They, too, were hardly noticeable from where the *Baja Vagabundo* was anchored.

Reading a magazine and sipping a mimosa, Kelly occupied the captain's chair on the flying bridge. He looked down at Jennie and thought how lovely she was in her white shorts and yellow camisole, a large yellow bow in her hair. He always missed her when he was away from San Diego and hoped she missed him as much. This time, it had been six days.

Jennie glanced up, sensing he was watching.

"I was right," he said.

"About what?"

"My intuition told me you were just about to finish your sketch."

With his drink in one hand, Kelly descended the ladder to the deck as easily as if walking down a flight of stairs. He was agile for a man six-foot-one and nearly 200 pounds. He sat on the deck chair next to Jennie. From that point he could watch the motion of her breast as she sketched and could almost see her right nipple as her arm moved across the paper. He enjoyed his vantage point and she was too preoccupied to notice.

"Well, you're pretty clever," she said devilishly. "But not this time. I'm not anywhere near finished," she playfully lied as she reached for a different pencil.

"Intuition isn't an exact science," Kelly replied.

"I'm so glad you called this morning. It's such a wonderful day to be out on a boat. Now, that's what I call intuition."

"A mixture of intuition and ESP glued together with one part love. Every day is a good day to be out on a boat with you."

Smiling, Jennie felt warm inside.

"Did you and Francisco have a good trip to Mexico?"

"Yeah, we did."

"You never talk much about your trips – about what you do and where you go."

"What we do and where we go isn't important – it's getting away that counts."

"Yes, that's what you always say," Jennie answered. She tried to speak without appearing too interested, trying her best to be matter-of-fact.

"You know how I enjoy flying and how it sets me apart from most – how I need to get away from time to time – away from the one-dimensional existence of the masses; away from people living their lives as if in elevators, going up and down, doing one thing at a time, not realizing they have other choices."

A 20-foot catamaran seemed headed for a collision with the *Baja Vagabundo,* but made a last minute sail correction and cleared by a wide margin. Traffic on the bay was building as the day wore on.

"But not all people can live the way you do," Jennie answered. "Some people need to feel they belong to something . . . feel they are a part of something bigger than they are, or bigger than they can ever hope to be."

Still holding several pencils, Jennie stopped sketching, her eyes locked onto his.

"I don't pretend to be like most people," Kelly said. Then he looked out toward the boats in the bay, avoiding her face, as if to hide his, and continued, "But I . . . I did give of myself to something. Don't forget the fifteen years I spent in the Navy defending helpless women and – "

"Why, you fake!" blurted Jennie, angry and raising her voice. Although he was looking away, she could make out the smirk, then could not help but smile. "You weren't *giving* of yourself for one moment. You loved every minute of it. You couldn't have been happier with Uncle Sam spending millions to develop new toys for you to fly."

Pausing for a moment, she asked quietly, "Haven't you ever felt strongly about some cause?"

Kelly thought before answering.

"The truth is . . . No!" he answered. "I don't understand why anyone should be so obligated he *has* to do things for others or to please – especially to the extent he spends his whole life *pleasing* and not *being pleased*. Well, I say to hell with the *Pleasees* in favor of the *Pleasers*. It's our turn."

"You sound like a hedonist."

"What do you want to hear?" Kelly asked. "Do you want me to be like the Japanese who live to work, instead of working to live? There has to be more to life than just work. I'd rather nose dive my V-tail into Mount Everest than go to a nine-to-five job every day."

"But you must believe in something other than boats and airplanes. Aren't causes or ideas important to you?"

The conversation was becoming too heavy and Kelly made an attempt to lighten it. Chuckling, he said, "Maybe I'll take up religion. I'll write to the Pope and become a Catholic – the religion of servants, immigrants and drunkards. I'll become the oldest altar boy in the world. A bellhop from heaven."

Jennie could not hold back a muted laugh. "Don't make fun of others," she scolded, "especially of other people's religions."

"You're too serious sometimes, Jennie."

"I'm just trying to find out more about you."

"I believe the world began the day I was born and it will end the day I leave. There is no history before my birth and there will be no future after my funeral. Make life a ride on a roller coaster, Jennie, and not one on a bowling ball."

"You must believe in something *more*," insisted Jennie for the last time.

"I do. I believe I live to live."

Putting down her pencils, Jennie turned sideways. He gently put his hands on her cheeks and drew her close enough to kiss her lips softly.

"I think you love to live," she said.

"Not quite. I don't love to live." Kelly's hands were rubbing the insides of her thighs, her hands on his elbows, encouraging, guiding him. "I live to love."

Kelly caressed Jennie's breasts and kissed her again. The more affectionate he became, the surer she was that her questions would not be answered until later.

He whispered into her ear, "Speaking of love, would you like to come to my cabin and go over some maps and charts?"

"No. But, I might just come below and check your engine oil."

⚓

Both felt comfortable and uninhibited on the *Baja Vagabundo,* isolated from the routines of daily existence, protected as it were by the vastness of the sea.

Surely, Jennie realized, Kelly, had had other women in the aft stateroom before her. She would have been a fool to think otherwise. After her first night on the *Baja Vagabundo,* Kelly sent her roses, the accompanying card dwelling on her feminine virtues. That afternoon, she sent him a set of new satin sheets and pillow cases.

⚓

It was late afternoon when Jennie heard sounds coming from the galley. The melodic notes of Beethoven's *6th Symphony* echoed in the distance. She made the queen-size bed, showered, and quickly dressed and combed her hair. Kelly was in the salon eating toasted cheese and tomato sandwiches when she peeked her head in.

"I'll have one of those sandwiches, if you please, Captain," said Jennie.

"Comin' right up."

"Thanks."

The sun began spending more and more time behind the billowing clouds. Without the sun, the afternoon was uncomfortably cool, especially after the ocean breeze developed into a mild wind.

"I caught a weather broadcast while you were sleeping. A low is moving in. High waves are forecast in the jetty, so we better head on back."

"I'll drive," offered Jennie, eager with enthusiasm.

Jennie preferred to pilot the *Baja Vagabundo* rather than just be a passenger. She only piloted from the flying bridge, which she called the *command bridge*. She ran the boat in much the same way she drove Kelly's Ferrari – with little regard for the mechanical limitations of either. Although a fast driver, she was careful. Occasionally, however, Kelly found himself wishing there were brake pedals on the passenger side. To Jennie, there was only one way to operate the *Baja Vagabundo's* twin diesels: both throttles full. There wasn't anything to run into on the ocean, she argued, other boats could be seen for miles. Kelly often thought he was fortunate Jennie never wanted to fly his Bonanza.

The *Baja Vagabundo* crept past the submarine base on Point Loma at the agonizingly slow speed limit, past Ballast Point, and along the submerged jetty which goes out from Zuñiga Point on Coronado along Zuñiga Shoals. Passing near a U.S. Navy destroyer heading into the bay for maintenance, Jennie smiled and waved to the sailors crowded on deck. Clearing the shoals, Jennie eased both throttles forward and headed for open ocean. The old lighthouse at the top of Point Loma beckoned farewell. Staying about two miles offshore, they followed the coastline northwesterly towards Mission Bay.

Out that far, the ocean swelled six or seven feet, but there were no whitecaps. Almost broadside to the waves, the *Baja Vagabundo* dove into the valley of one and up the crest of the next. The wind, steadily increasing, threw up a light mist.

Hundreds of gulls and pelicans, flying in formation, were outlined against the now overcast sky. In recent years, seeing seals hunting for food in and near the kelp beds had become infrequent; they were rare now, missed by those who remembered them.

Grabbing Kelly around the neck to keep her balance as the *Baja Vagabundo* bounced and rolled from side to side, Jennie kissed him on the mouth once, in a long kiss, and said, "I love you."

As the Ocean Beach fishing pier began to take form in the distance, Jennie headed toward it, the entrance to the bay being a few hundred yards to the north. When the tower at Sea World loomed off the left bow, they were near the jetty and she eased back on the throttles. They rode *their* wave all the way in, past the large rocks piled on each side defining the channel.

Once safely inside the bay, inching along at the bay speed limit, they crept past the Mission Bay Aquatic Police Station, under the West Mission Bay Drive Bridge, and turned left into Ventura Cove. Kelly's pier lay straight ahead past Vacation Isle and across Sail Bay.

As Jennie backed in slowly, Kelly jumped onto the pier and tied the *Baja Vagabundo* securely at the bow. Jennie threw a second line and Kelly pulled the stern in close, fastening the line to a cleat. After locking up, they walked along the pier to the stairs and up into the villa.

The villa was small but superbly constructed and detailed in classic Mediterranean style. Each of the two stories had large glass windows overlooking the bay. The interior had hardwood floors of koa, butternut, and oak, hand-painted tiles, two fireplaces and imported Italian antique chandeliers in the entry and dining room. The grounds were lushly landscaped and there was a small pool with a spa and a covered *cabaña* with a barbecue. It was an ideal place for an affair.

After freshening up, Kelly lit a fire in the lower fireplace. and inserted a disk into the CD player. The soft opening violin of Saint-Saëns' *Rondo Capriccioso* filled the air. It was dark, the only light cast by the flames. Jennie nestled close to Kelly, they sipped white wine from long-stemmed glass goblets.

"Being back here at the villa reminds me I received a letter from a former student who's going to be in the country for a couple of months," said Kelly. "I'm going to let him stay here."

"Do you remember all your students?"

"No, but I remember this one. Best damn pilot I ever saw. He was the only student to ever shoot me down in a mock dogfight. I couldn't shake him off my tail."

Kelly related the details of that hot afternoon over the Air Combat Maneuvering Range just outside Yuma, Arizona. It was one of the final exercises before graduation. Both in F-14's, Kelly was the defender and Kashan the invader. To score, Kashan needed to penetrate the perimeter boundary, avoiding Kelly's radar lock. In a surprise move, Kashan went directly at Kelly and locked-up. Theoretically, the exercise was over, but for the next twenty minutes, Kelly could not shake Kashan, trying every evasive trick he knew.

"Why's he coming?" asked Jennie.

"Something to do with the International Red Cross. He's setting up a medical program in the remote areas of his country and needs to get more training in flying small airplanes."

"Why would he need that if he were your best student?"

"Flying a Bonanza isn't quite the same as flying a super-duper, high-powered jet fighter. Actually just flying the plane isn't that hard and he can keep up with me right now even in a Bonanza. The only tricky part is when it comes to taking off from short dirt runways like those in Baja. He said he needs to do that, and I plan to take him to Mexico for a week or so. It won't take long before he's a pro."

"I'm sure it won't with you giving lessons."

"I'm surprised he's coming at all."

"Why?"

"I never thought he'd get a visa, but he said he had no trouble through the U.S. Embassy in Cairo."

"Why should he have had any trouble?"

"He's Iranian. Name's Omar Kashan, but he doesn't like the Omar part – just Kashan."

Stunned, Jennie spilled wine in her lap. Her face paled. A thousand thoughts raced through her mind at the same instant. The flames from the fire seemed blinding and unbearable. Seven years passed by in a moment. *What do I do?* Jennie asked herself. *What do I do? I can't tell Kelly that Kashan and I were deeply in love before Kashan went back to Iran to fight the Holy War? I can't tell Kelly that Kashan left me to dedicate his life to his country and to his religion. Do I say anything? Dear God, please help me do the right thing.* She almost did not hear Kelly's words.

"We're going to have a party for him at my place in Rancho Santa Fe. Sort of a welcoming party. I liked the guy and you will too. You can always tell a man's character by the way he flies an airplane. The party'll be on a Sunday evening. We'll go all out. There'll be music and dancing and . . . "

Jennie decided to say nothing, mounting uncertainty gripping her thoughts.

". . . it'll be terrific. Right after Francisco and I get back from Arizona.

3

THE PERSIAN GULF

Merely a few weeks before Kashan landed at Punta Estrella, he had been half way around the world in another aircraft cruising at 1000 feet near Karg Island in the Persian Gulf. A U.S. built F-4 Phantom jet fighter, it bore the markings of the Iranian Air Force. On a reconnaissance mission, the F-4 had taken off from Bushir Air Base in western Iran. The high, white cliffs of Karg Island gleamed in the bright afternoon sunshine, belying the fact that Karg was the location of Iran's largest oil terminal and had been the target of recent Iraqi air attacks.

Below the bubble canopy, the navy-blue fuselage of the F-4 bore the gold-lettered inscription: *CMDR. OMAR AL-KASHAN*. While keeping alert for enemy fighters, Kashan attended to his primary goal, taking note of oil tanker shipping in the gulf. On this particular flight, his secondary objective was photographing Iraqi troop buildup at Basra in the northern end. Flying as far south as the tiny island of al-Arabiyah, he turned back north, remaining a safe distance off the Saudi Arabian coast.

It was 1988 and the fanatical Iran-Iraq Holy War was in its eighth year. Kashan had seen all of it from the cockpit of his beloved F-4. He preferred these reconnaissance flights to the bombings of helpless oil tankers or air-to-ground missile attacks on cities and military installations. War is hell, but still bombing women and children was not Kashan's idea of it. Iran had been doing this in retaliation to Iraq's use of mustard gas and nerve gas on the battlefields.

As the F-4 cruised near supersonic speed, Kashan's thoughts drifted. It was difficult after so many years of war to maintain a perspective in the present, to keep focused on meaningfulness and reality. The hypnotic effect of the sun beaming through the plastic canopy and the paradoxical silence caused by the roaring jet blocking out all other sound played with his subconscious. He thought about how these mystical and mysterious lands of sheiks and shahs, of caliphs and princes, of viziers and satraps had been manipulated into puppets of the world superpowers. He visualized rapacious Mongols upon massive steeds swooping down in destruction of small villages on the high Iranian plateaus. He saw Persian armies on battlefields fighting mighty Tartars in hand-to-hand combat. For a fraction of a second, he glimpsed a detached head with wide-open, gaping and unbelieving eyes, spewing blood like a broken water main. His visions of caravans and camels, of spices and silks, of rubies and emeralds, and *mullahs* and *imams* slowly blurred into visions of tanks and radars, of bombers and SAM missiles, of burning phosphor and napalm, of smoldering oil tankers. How war had changed in a land in which the camel was the main means of transportation just twenty-five years earlier.

Technology was pervasive even in the triumphant return of the Ayatollah Ruhollah Khomeini from his twelve-year exile in France. The writer Mohamed Heikal referred to Khomeini as "a bullet projected from the feudal and religious world of the seventh century into the 20th century world of space travel, nuclear weapons, and the manipulation of genes." Indeed, for his return from exile, Khomeini's followers had chartered a Boeing 747!

"Center calling Blue Banana." The radio speaker startled Kashan. Even though he had helped devise the mission's secret codes, his wandering mind took a long instant to respond to the words echoing in his ears.

"Banana Peel with you," Kashan answered.

"Vector two-alpha-two," replied center and then the radio went dead.

Kashan knew the meaning of the encoded message: *MISSION*

ABORTED. RETURN TO BASE IMMEDIATELY. The F-4 made a steep right turn towards the Iranian coast, and headed for one of the tallest peaks in the Zargos Mountains whose snow covered tops were barely visible on the horizon.

Most Iranian pilots had been trained in the United States prior to and for a period after the revolution ending the Shah's reign. Kashan had spent two years in intensive air combat maneuvering tactics at the Top Gun School at Miramar Naval Air Station in San Diego. This is where he picked up the American jargon he used for the secret codes. Although U.S. presence ended abruptly with the ouster of the Shah, the codes lingered on.

Immediately after the revolution, most of Iran's pilots were imprisoned for suspected loyalty to the Shah. Kashan was at Miramar at the time. In all, more than 20,000 Iranian officers had been sent for training in the U.S. by the Shah during his twenty-five years in power. Mistrust by the new Khomeini government was natural – especially since the daily military and intelligence activities of Iran had been advised and closely supervised by the CIA for such a long time.

Devoted to Islam and to Iran, Kashan's loyalty was more than blind patriotism. He returned from the States shortly before the war began and played a prominent role in rallying the other pilots to support the new government. He was decorated for his bravery during the critical battle of Dezful. With the local commander having only one large gun and six operational tanks, Dezful would have fallen without the support of the Air Force. The F-4's flew wave after wave of air-to-ground attack, many of the pilots going days without sleep. The Air Force had redeemed itself admirably and word of Kashan's role had been passed all the way to Khomeini.

⁂

Kashan taxied off the runway at Bushir, past the rows and rows of F-4's, hundreds cannibalized for spare parts. Only a small fraction of the once totally-American-maintained aircraft was still flying. Iran proffered an open shopping list to the international black market since it's lack of spare parts had become a major problem.

Kashan's ground crew was waiting, the lead man arm-signaled him into his usual parking space. As he cut the engine, one of the ground crew was already chocking the F-4's wheels. A jeep drove up as Kashan climbed down from the cockpit. Commander Abdul Rashid, Kashan's longtime friend and fellow pilot, sat in the driver's seat.

"How'd the mission go?" called Rashid.

"Good. Nothing unusual today. But, my flight was cut short. What're you doing here?"

"Farrazin wants to see you right away. He sent me. That fat goat has something on his mind."

"What's up?"

"Don't know."

"Must be important to rate you as a chauffeur."

"Important or not, hop in."

Kashan set down his white plastic flight helmet, slipped off his parachute, and zipped out of his flight suit. He left these with one of the flight crew.

Not quite six feet tall, Kashan maintained a firm, solid body. His eyes sparkled and his wide jaw showed perfectly formed teeth when he smiled. A thin and carefully trimmed moustache gave him an aristocratic air of sophistication. A slight depression in his chin kept his face from being flawless.

"Will I have time to change?"

"Afraid not. Farrazin's anxious. Something *very* hot must be on the snake's brain."

"Could be he's just showing off his importance."

"I doubt it. He doesn't exactly favor your company."

Kashan hopped into the passenger seat, and the jeep screeched forward as Rashid let out the clutch. They drove along the taxiway paralleling the main runway for over a mile and turned left onto a shorter taxiway. The hot afternoon sun beat on the two pilots and the jeep. Clusters of dates dangled from the dozen tall palms surrounding the Quonset hut containing Colonel Farrazin's office. In the center of a group of seven, the hut sat away from the large hangar used for repair and maintenance.

After being announced by the colonel's aide, Kashan walked hurriedly into Farrazin's office. A ceiling fan turned slowly in a futile attempt to combat the heat.

Short and obese, with a jugular neck and an ugly face, Colonel Kuri Farrazin disliked most people. But he was smart, smart enough to sense the coming downfall of the Shah, and smart enough to switch sides just before Khomeini's return. Mistaken for courage, his good sense of timing resulted in a top Air Force job even though he wasn't a pilot. *He's too short to see over the instrument panel of an F-4* thought Kashan. Still, Kashan stood at attention as they exchanged formal greetings, then sat in one of the leather chairs.

Always nervous, Farrazin began, "Kashan . . . you've been selected for a special mission. I expect you'll accept . . . of course . . . you must be aware that you have little choice. You can't go against the ayatollahs."

"I see."

"Good, good," smiled Farrazin. "Your plane has been reassigned. You won't need it for awhile."

"Wait a minute," protested Kashan. "I'm a pilot and flying is my – "

"It's not for you to understand," interrupted Farrazin. "Maybe you'd better remember who's in charge here and who gives the orders," he shouted.

Farrazin's eyes scanned, searching for any sign of momentary weakness. It was pointless to confront him, more tactful to sit in silence and let him blow out steam.

"There's several obvious reasons why you have been picked. Unlike the rest of us mortals, you went to the Sorbonne." Farrazin glanced up at the fan, appeared deep in thought, and lit a long Turkish cigarette, blowing smoke in Kashan's direction. Sweat and wrinkles permeated his khaki shirt. "We both know, don't we, that you've got some pull with the ayatollahs because your father was a *mullah*," he added quietly.

"Now, wait just a minute," shot back Kashan. "My father's religious affiliations have nothing to do with it, and you know that! Let's not play cat and mouse!"

Taking a long drag on his cigarette, Farrazin sat back and smiled, pleased with himself for unsettling Kashan. He knew Kashan was respected by all the pilots. Farrazin continued to smoke, purposely making Kashan wait. He usually dealt with the other pilots in more or less the same way, not wanting to admit his own lack of virility, taking pleasure in berating. In between puffs, he glanced at the fan occasionally, all the while studying Kashan.

"Evidently, . . . you're going to the States . . . to be with your pals."

Kashan let the insult slide. That well-educated Iranians wanted to spend time in the U.S. was no secret. While generally disliking the U.S. government's policies, many Iranians envied the happy-go-lucky, devil-may-care attitudes they saw in so most individual Americans. They were clever enough to know the whole was not necessarily the sum of its parts; that the American government, and not the people, had supported the Shah and kept him in power. It was also no secret that a lot of Americans disliked the peanut farmer Jimmy Carter. Iranians were disappointed, though, that professedly neutral, the U.S. was morally on the side of Iraq in the Holy War. Here again, many knew this was largely due to the U.S. government's propaganda and the one-sidedness of the U.S. news media. America was not a country whose people had an intense interest in the rest of the world – they were too preoccupied with their own abundances.

Having given Kashan ample time to digest his new assignment, Farrazin's lip started to twitch. He could not resist a parting shot. "You're glad to be going away, aren't you Kashan? The war here's a bloody stalemate. We're using suicidal human-wave attacks with armed children. Tens of thousands have been literally slaughtered. Cities and civilians are being bombed. Women parade the streets carrying automatic rifles to show support for our soldiers. Yes, you're glad to be going away – away from brother killing brother – aren't you? Aren't you? Admit it!"

In a quiet voice Kashan replied, "No, Colonel. It may be difficult for you to understand, but I am dedicated to our causes. I do desire to remain here and fight this war to its end, and am confident that we can win. Nevertheless, I will – "

"That's enough, Kashan! You highly-principled heroes disgust me."

Although lowered, his voice still conveyed anger. His rage having passed, he reverted to his usual bitter self. He stubbed out his cigarette in the ash tray on his desk. He was sweating even more profusely; the odor permeating the air about him.

"Perhaps some day I will become cynical like you, Colonel."

"That's enough, I said." "You'll report at once to Qom for further orders from General Rajavi. Get your things together and be gone within the hour. Your transportation's been arranged and your friend Rashid'll give you the details, which he's reading now. This is urgent. Outside of knowing that you may be going to the States, I know little else. Salaam."

Without saying good-bye, Kashan quickly left the room.

Rashid was waiting in the jeep. Kashan asked him to drive back to the F-4 before going to his quarters to pack. As they retraced their earlier route, Kashan related the essence of his conversation with Farrazin. In turn, Rashid briefed Kashan on the hasty plans for his trip to Qom.

Rashid parked the jeep by the left wing of the F-4.

"I'll be just a few minutes," Kashan said. "There's something in my plane I need to get before I leave."

He climbed up the F-4's ladder and seated himself in the cockpit. He fumbled through his pockets until he found his small pocketknife. With the knife, he unscrewed a small gold filigree locket that had been mounted next to the altimeter.

Inside the locket was the photograph of a beautiful woman.

Opposite the photo was the inscription: *LOVE IS SPLENDOR.*

4

BALBOA NAVAL HOSPITAL

The roar of the Boeing 727's engines was deafening for the few seconds it took the plane to fly directly overhead. The low lying overcast had the effect of confining the noise and reverberations like an echo in a valley. In less than a minute, another jet followed the same course as the first, leaving scarcely enough time for a few sentences in a conversation.

One might have thought this an odd place to locate a hospital – in the normal landing approach to San Diego's Lindbergh Field. However, the hospital was founded long before traffic at the airport became significant. Now a major medical facility, Balboa Naval Hospital grew up just after World War I. In those days San Diego was a small-town neighbor of Los Angeles and air traffic at Lindbergh Field peaked at less than one flight an hour.

This late in the evening there were no visitors left at the hospital. Many of the patients were asleep, although here and there a television set still blared. An occasional corpsman cleaned an empty room. With a handful of interns on duty, only one or two of the staff doctors would be available that night.

Another jet passed overhead.

In the alcove of the intensive care unit, two nurses chatted. The blonde, buxom Lieutenant Commander Ellen Anderson, did most of the talking while Lieutenant Jennie Ross listened.

"Admiral Homely is going to be transferred to a regular ward tomorrow," said Ellen. "I'll be glad to get rid of *him*. The lieutenant with the teeny weenie is kind of cute and I hope he stays around for awhile. I'm rooting for Captain America to have a quadruple bypass . . ."

Transferring pills from bottles to small paper cups, Ellen was preparing sedatives for the patients she knew would become restless during the night. Jennie studied some charts.

Ellen Anderson became a dedicated career nurse when she decided long ago that she rather liked the unquestioned authority military rank offered. Her large bones and plain features suggested a hint of masculinity. Too domineering, Ellen never thought of being married, but dated often.

Jennie was single too.

The similarity ended there.

⚘

The prospects of adventure and excitement lured Jennie to become a Navy nurse Sadly, she soon found that being a nurse was definitely not what it was cracked up to be. At times it was dirty work and at other times it was outright depressing. She never could get used to watching patients suffer and die. After the novelty wore off, she despised the formalities of military rank. Her stepfather had wanted her to become, like him, an attorney. But, at that time she was not ready for the rigor and demands of law school; instead she hungered for travel. Equally important, her stepfather lacked the passion and desire that, for her, made life worthwhile. If that's what law school did to people, she wanted no part of it.

The mischievous side of Jennie's personality came from her mother. With roots in Mobile, Alabama, and a natural feeling for fine clothes and social graces, her mother was highly desirable as a young woman. Nevertheless, she chose poorly and her father deserted the family when Jennie was a baby. Fortunately, Jennie's stepfather was loving and caring and she had had a relatively happy childhood in Cleveland.

The independence Jennie acquired from her stepfather drove

her to join the Navy against his wishes. "Before I get married, I want to go places and see things," she had said. "No daughter of mine is going to join the goddamn Navy!" he had protested. But the day she left, he kissed her good-bye and told her how much he loved her and respected her decision. He wrote frequently and visited whenever his law cases took him to her part of the country.

"What's the matter, Jennie?" asked Ellen, "You've been so pensive all evening."

"Oh, nothing."

"Nothing, my eye. I can tell that there is."

"You know how I dislike working PM's," Jennie partly lied.

"Yes, but once a month ain't so bad. Is it kiddo? It's something else, isn't it?"

"Well . . . ," Jennie paused. "Yes, but I don't feel like talking about it."

"Hogwash!"

"Please, Ellen."

"How's Kelly?" Ellen went on, not making any attempt to change the subject. "He's a hunk," said Ellen, a twinkle in her eye.

They had known one another for several years and there were few secrets between them.

Jennie had also known Kelly for several years. They had met at the Officers' Club at Miramar Naval Air Station in San Diego. FIGHTERTOWN, U.S.A. THE HOME OF TOP GUN AND THE FINEST FIGHTER PILOTS IN THE WORLD, the sign outside the Officer's Club read. Balboa Naval Hospital was her first assignment, and then, at her own request, she spent two years on Okinawa. At the time, Kelly was a flight instructor in the Top Gun School. Jennie knew that that meant he was one of the very best. Kelly had quit the Navy two years ago.

"Kelly asked me to marry him."

"Well, jeepers creepers! Are you going to?"

"I *don't* know Ellen."

Jennie stopped what she was doing and looked at Ellen. "At times, he makes me feel so wonderful. Then, again, at times he seems so distant and far away, and I hardly know who he is. I feel like a wind chime blowing in the breeze. Sometimes I strike another chime and there is sweet music. At other times, the wind just carries us close and there is nothing."

"Do you love him?"

"We thought we were in love. I know I love him. How much, I don't know. Basically, he's a wonderful person." Now she had a dreamy look in her eyes. "He has a thing about the stars."

"What do you mean."

"Oh, it has to do mostly with navigation. He's sometimes a romantic. Navigation intrigues him. Wonders how Columbus could have found his way with such primitive instruments. Things like that. But, I'm worried he thinks too much only of himself."

"You'd better be sure about a thing like marriage."

"Kelly went to Mexico for a few days. To fish."

"Damn fool," said Ellen without thinking.

"Kelly still likes to fly," said Jennie in defense. "And his fishing is just an excuse to fly somewhere."

"Still a damn fool if you ask me," Ellen protested. "A lot of successful men in this world think mostly of themselves. Maybe that's the secret to success. But, he sure goes fishing a lot, and that smells fishy."

Ellen finished preparing the evening's medications and walked down the hall to check on some of the patients. Although Jennie was alone, Ellen's words were still penetrating and Jennie could not get them out of her mind. *Sure goes fishing a lot*. She had wondered herself about Kelly ever since he left the Navy. Kelly was extraordinarily successful. He owned, among other things, an airplane, a boat, a Ferrari, a small villa on Riviera Drive in the Crown Point area of San Diego overlooking Mission Bay, and a large lavishly furnished home in Rancho Santa Fe, the second wealthiest community in California. Yet, he did not seem to spend much time with his *investments*. That caused Jennie to wonder more than she liked.

Ellen walked back into the alcove and said, "Jennie, the nurse on duty in the emergency room on one came up to tell me they just received a call. A helicopter is on the way. Can you go on down to the emergency ward by the heliport and make sure everything goes alright? You can never trust these damn interns."

Shortly after 10 p.m., Jennie went down to the emergency ward taking some charts with her to work on. The ward was bleak. Decor would have been wasted since most patients brought in by helicopter were immediately rushed to other parts of the hospital. There was a wooden desk, a chair behind it upon which Jennie sat and a half a dozen metal folding chairs scattered about, some with tables and lamps. All of the furniture was scratched and outdated and the lamps needed new shades. There were no curtains on the windows. A gurney sat along one wall, next to a long table with emergency supplies stacked neatly on it.

As stark as any military institution could possibly be, the hospital had high ceilings and exposed pipes and hanging ducts. Everything was painted the same drab shade of gray. In many places, the paint was peeling. Most of the nurses wore sweaters because the building was inadequately heated. There were no pictures on the walls and the rooms were poorly lit with the fluorescent fixtures being up much too high.

Normally, Jennie would have enjoyed the silence and relished the time alone. But, Ellen's words kept nagging at her. Could she be wrong about him? When she actually thought of it, she really did not know that much about Kelly. She started to think about someone else she had known before she met Kelly – someone she had known before she went to Okinawa. She found herself staring at the pages in the charts and not seeing the words or numbers. She started to think about the past. *No, no,* she thought. *I must not think about that again. That was a different life.* She tried to force herself to study the charts, but the harder she tried, the more difficult it became. She was more interested in herself. *What am I doing here in the Navy? I don't want to be a robot. I want to . . . No, no, I must not think of those things. The past is gone.*

Jennie went to the window and watched the landing jets fly over. In a couple of hours, the evening curfew would take effect and the flights would stop until seven in the morning. Soon, there would be total quiet in the hospital.

She glanced down at the traffic on Park Boulevard which ran between the hospital and Balboa Park. Balboa Park was one of San Diego's premiere attractions and Jennie often walked there after a hectic day. It was the home of some of San Diego's theaters, art and history museums, one of the world's finest zoos, the aerospace museum where she and Kelly had gone countless times, and the outdoor restaurant, *Cafe del Rey Moro,* where they often dined. Jennie thought of the jugglers who performed on weekends, riding unicycles and tossing fiery objects into the air, of the self-styled preachers who gave impromptu sermons, of the roller skaters who frequented the park, and of the fountain with its jets spewing water twenty-five feet into the air. Had it been daytime, she could have seen the fountain from where she stood.

Jennie was distracted by the two young interns, Doctors Healy and Sutton, who stepped off the elevator across the room and sat on chairs near doors that led to the heliport. Their clothes were disheveled and they looked as if they had not slept in days. Sutton, visibly nervous, smoked a cigarette while Healy toyed with a button on his coat.

"Any word on the chopper, Jennie?" Sutton asked in a loud voice from across the room.

"All they say is that it's on the way," answered Jennie.

"Probably some general's wife who belched instead of farting," offered Healy. "Goddamn stupid reason to keep us from our work. Where's the chopper comin' from?"

Doctors are crude, Jennie thought, and then answered, "They never tell us until they get here."

Jennie went back to studying her charts. Healy turned to Sutton and began conversing in a monotone without enthusiasm.

"I hope it's not too bad."

"What?" asked Sutton.

"The helicopter case."

"Must be somebody important to rate a chopper."

They sat and listened to the sounds of the overhead jets. A siren coming closer and closer could have been a fire engine or a police car, but they knew it would be an arrival at the emergency room. Sutton crushed out his cigarette and thought about lighting another, but walked over to the window instead. He glanced out for a moment, walked back and sat in his chair. Healy was still playing with the button on his coat.

Jennie lapsed back into her reverie. Her thoughts were troubling but she did not seem to have full control. First Kelly's proposal and then Ellen's vexatious suggestions. *You're the prettiest girl in San Diego . . . Don't go . . . Stay . . . the prettiest . . . in all . . . Don't go . . . stay and . . .*

⸙

Both Healy and Sutton jumped when the telephone rang. Jennie said a few words into the mouthpiece but listened mostly for several minutes. Then she turned in the direction of Healy and Sutton and said, "They're having some difficulty in communicating with the helicopter. They're in Mexico and there's been some sort of accident and a lot of bleeding. They're advising us to have an operating room ready."

"Holy shit," said Healy, "I'll probably miss breakfast."

"Better get hold of a resident and have him check on an OR," said Sutton.

"There's always one on five," said Healy. "They'll be ready to let a butcher scrub up in a couple of minutes after the patient gets here. We'd better stay and make sure he's handled out of the chopper OK. Must be some VIP."

⸙

It could have been imagined because it was ever so faint at first. But there was no mistake. The rhythmic *whop, whop, whop* of the rotor blades grew louder and louder. Healy and Sutton went quickly through the swinging doors followed a few seconds later by Jennie. The three of them stood by the doors and looked up but could see nothing through the overcast. Jet traffic at Lindbergh had apparently been delayed or put in holding patterns to give the helicopter enough time to land. Healy was the first to see the bright spotlight overhead and slowly the helicopter began to take shape as it descended through the mist. When it was down to 100 feet, they could see it was a U.S. Coast Guard helicopter and not the U.S. Navy one they expected. As the helicopter lowered, the wash from the rotor blades at first lifted, and then blew away a small cloud of debris. Jennie thought about going back inside, but instead grabbed a door handle with one hand and put her other over one ear to partly block out the roaring noise.

As soon as the helicopter touched down, two corpsmen jumped out and opened the wide cargo door. They had the patient out and onto a gurney they carried and were buckling the last strap as Healy and Sutton arrived. Healy took over pushing the gurney while Sutton guided it past Jennie, through the double doors towards the emergency room.

With the patient on his way to surgery, Jennie felt momentarily let down. The pilot of the helicopter waited by the telephone on the wooden desk. He held his flight helmet like a star fullback holds a football. He was young to be a pilot, thought Jennie, and looked more like he should be cutting hay on a Nebraska farm.

"Evening Ma'am," said the pilot.

"Good evening, Lieutenant," answered Jennie.

"Hope I don't get into a heap a trouble over this."

"What do you mean?"

"The patient, Ma'am."

"What about the patient?"

"He's a Mexican, Ma'am."

"What?"

"Yes, Ma'am. We were south of the border checking on a fishing boat out over the ocean – had a bad engine. The boat was OK and we were heading back when we heard this message that an American was injured in Baja and needed immediate help. We normally don't fly into Mexico without permission of the Mexicans, but decided to make an exception. We've been doin' this more and more in support of the president's good neighbor policy with Mexico. The radio message said a couple of bikers found an injured dude on a beach that was on our map and so we decided to have a look-see. When we got there, we found the Mexican."

"Why didn't you call the Mexican government?"

"We tried to, Ma'am. But the Mexicans don't have any helicopters and the poor guy would of died by the time a truck or a jeep got to him. So, we took him and were going to take him to a Mexican hospital in Tijuana. The hospital said they didn't want him."

"What? Why not?"

The pilot shifted from one foot to the other and appeared uneasy. He hesitated before answering.

"Because of the injury, Ma'am. They're not equipped to treat him, they said."

"What kind of an injury?"

"Gunshot wound, Ma'am. In the head. Hope I don't get into no trouble for what I done."

The pilot made a call on Jennie's phone to Coast Guard Headquarters. He was correct in suspecting he might be in hot water. It was one of those situations bureaucracies are not equipped to deal with, one of those out of the ordinary situations for which no rules had been written. This was certainly out of the ordinary – landing on foreign soil and picking up a foreign national and taking him across an international border. All would have been overlooked, though, and the pilot a mini hero had it not been for the bullet hole in the Mexican's head. The pilot could not help but wonder why the patient could not simply have had a heart attack or perhaps cut his hand off in a motorcycle chain or anything besides a gunshot wound. When the call was finished, he made another to air traffic control to get a clearance to leave. With a quick "Bye, Ma'am," he made a hasty departure and the helicopter took off within minutes. The overcast was starting to break up.

⁂

Emotionally exhausted by the long night and the excitement, Jennie sat down once again at the desk, crossed her arms in front of her and put her head down. *If I could only close my eyes for a moment . . . You're the prettiest . . . in the . . . hold me . . . war . . . everything is immaculately beautiful . . . there are flowers everywhere and fruit trees and ponds and flowing water . . . the sun is radiant and warm and the sky ever so blue . . . there are white clouds but the sun seems to be shining through them and around them and under them and over them . . . my dress is long and flowing and white like snow . . . the clouds tower over like a vast cathedral with hundreds of hidden passageways and thousands and thousands and thousands of arched windows letting in the bright sunshine . . . it's peaceful and serene . . . I'm alone but I'm not lonely . . . I feel happy and content . . . look! . . . here comes an airplane . . . it's so quiet and it's moving so slowly . . . all white and made out of cloud . . . it's slowly moving around and through the passageways and the windows . . . I'll wave and maybe the pilot will see me . . . he's dodging the columns and has disappeared behind a towering cloud . . . a towering cloud within the vast dome under another towering cloud inside yet another vast cathedral . . . each cathedral is as bright as if it had its own sun . . . a million cathedrals one within the other harboring a million suns and a million towering cumulus clouds . . . a boundless eternity of space . . . an infinity of curves each converging one upon the other into nowhere . . . he sees me! . . . he's waving back! . . . he's going to land! . . . oh, how happy I am! . . . he has landed nearby . . . he's getting out and coming over to me . . . how dashing he looks all dressed in white . . . a white silk scarf . . . white boots . . . a white helmet . . . he's taking my hand in his and his hand feels so warm . . . it's difficult to believe that this is all really happening . . . I'm high and dizzy from excitement . . . if he would only take off his helmet so that I could see his face . . . please take off your helmet . . . please take off . . . please . . .*

"Jennie, Jennie, Jesus Christ, wake up!"

Jennie opened her eyes to find Healy standing over her.

"The Mexican is still in the OR. A neurosurgeon is coming in to work on him," said Healy. "Jennie, are you OK?"

"Yes, I'm alright. I had a strange dream . . . I'm not sure if I was dreaming about someone who is very close to me . . . or about someone I haven't seen for a long time . . . dreams are sometimes so confusing and mixed up."

"Dreams are a waste of time and energy," said Healy as he

strutted away.

5

QOM

The Holy City of Qom was an unlikely place for a meeting of the directors of SAVAK.

On the high desert sixty miles southwest of Teheran, Qom abounded in a cosmic sea of dust, sandy powder covering all in the paths of its capricious swirls. The scrawny sheep and goats, the shanties at the outskirts of the city, the walls, the leaves on the trees, the square clay-brick houses, the one-pump gasoline stations – all were defiled by the erratic wind.

Qom had been a place of pilgrimage for over a thousand years, and the center of Islamic learning for centuries. Here was the shrine of the tomb of Massoumeh, sister of the eighth of the twelve early religious leaders of Islam. From miles distant, its graceful dome rose out of the dust, surrounded by minarets, gleaming in the bright desert sunshine, dominating the flat and barren plain. At night, the dome and minarets were lit by floodlights. Qom was where Khomeini retreated after his triumphant return to Iran.

The capital of Iran, Teheran was New York City and Washington, D.C. rolled into one, the home of the highly centralized government, the palaces of the Shah, all Embassies, the central offices of every business and bank. Cosmopolitan with modern freeways and tall buildings, Teheran was where SAVAK should have been meeting and not Qom, the religious capital.

Disbanding SAVAK was one of the first objectives of the revolutionary government after the overthrow of the Shah. When it was formed, SAVAK was essentially a branch of the CIA, later becoming the Shah's private enforcement and execution squad. SAVAK was responsible for spying on all branches of the military and coordinated all Iranian intelligence, both domestic and international. The organization topped the revolutionary hate list with Khomeini's own son being one of its countless victims. Originally, SAVAK was to be eliminated; however, the religious leaders soon realized that no modern government could function without some form of intelligence-gathering, undercover agency. And so SAVAK was reborn under the more palatable name of the *Iranian Islamic Information Service*. Few paid much attention to the new name, and for all practical purposes SAVAK survived, with two distinctive changes: the former director was shot after a quick trial, and the CIA was booted out. The new agency was led by General Mosbah Rajavi. Although not totally justifiable, the religious leaders recognized the need to deal with unbelievers in unconventional ways. Even the Prophet Mohammed killed rebels and destroyed pagan idolatry. The more modern world required new methods and techniques – like those known to and practiced by SAVAK. Nevertheless, the existence of the transfigured SAVAK was not well publicized.

General Rajavi brushed the dust from his khaki uniform and from the leather holster on his belt containing his 9mm Beretta automatic. He strutted into the large sand-colored building, walked past the guards without a nod. The building was a mini-palace which the Shah had constructed for the times when a visit to Qom might be necessary in order to meet with the religious leaders. Although the exterior was plain by design, the interior was ornately decorated with panels of marble, ivory and wood inlay, and the stairways were lavishly mirrored.

Rajavi passed a half-dozen, high-ceilinged reception rooms and offices and walked up the wide, sweeping stairway to a large room on the second floor. Already seated around the enormous circular mahogany table were his aides, Colonel

Alam, Colonel Badri and Major Muluk. On the table, an old, well-worn slide projector sighted its lens at a silvery screen hung from the ceiling against the wall. A guard stood outside the door embracing a Uzi submachine gun.

Setting his briefcase on the table, Rajavi looked out of the arched windows at the bright sun, paying no attention to the three men sitting behind him.

Tall for an Iranian, Rajavi was just over six feet, with a large head. His wide, square face had stone-like features and deep-set eyes.

Remaining standing, he regarded the three sitting behind him, as he did most, with scorn. Rajavi was irritated by Alam incessantly stroking his black-gray beard. When looking into Alam's pale blue eyes, one had the impression of being able to see straight into his head, where instead of a brain there was an empty cavity. *Colonel Alam would have made a good college professor,* thought Rajavi.

Heavyset, Badri's large mouth turned down at the edges, making him look grouchy and dogmatic. *He has some good points, but is too old-line.*

Not a large man, Muluk could not have weighed over one hundred and sixty pounds, all muscle and no fat. He wore wire framed glasses on his gleaming bald head with large ears and an aquiline nose. Many women found him appealing. *Muluk should have been a pimp,* Rajavi said to himself. But, Rajavi was wrong about Muluk, for he did not know that Muluk's body contained the mind of a nuclear physicist and the heart of a raging bull.

After several minutes, Rajavi began, "Gentlemen, over the past weeks, I've had frequent discussions with the ayatollahs. As we know, they've no desire to be involved in the day-to-day operations of the country. But, when things aren't going well, the ayatollahs feel that some help from them is in order. The war with Iraq has become a drain on our economy, has slowed the Islamic reformation. It's been sapping our national morale. We've lost many in the struggle. We don't appear to be making headway in achieving the ultimate goal of total victory. In short, the advantage we have by our larger numbers is balanced by Iraq's superior equipment. The time is ripe for a final, devastating attack."

"But, General, we've heard that story before," interrupted the sarcastic Badri. "We're still a long way from total victory."

"Unfortunately, you're correct," answered Rajavi. "But, after months of meditation and prayer, the ayatollahs have some new ideas and want to approach the situation from a new angle."

"Haven't we tried everything?" asked Badri.

"We haven't tried miracles yet – nor divine intervention," answered Rajavi. "More precisely, what I mean is we haven't tried symbolic acts that might appear to our people and the rest of the world to be miracles of sorts – signs from Allah – signs to rally our people and inspire our fighting men. I'm not sure I agree completely with the ayatollahs. I, for one, have always been in favor of emphasis on aircraft and missiles, and less on things like divine intervention. However, the ayatollahs have given me orders to come up with a plan, and so we're here to discuss ideas."

"Divine intervention, bah!" exclaimed Major Muluk in a deep, strong voice, with authority. "What we need is some help from the Russians. The Russians can be our divine intervention. They'd be delighted to give us a hand – especially since the U.S. has been more than kind to Iraq. I don't know why everyone is so worried about the Russians coming in and helping out. We don't have to sell our souls to them."

"Your point of view isn't very popular," countered Rajavi. "And, if I were you, I wouldn't spread it around outside this room. You should know the ayatollahs' feelings about mixing communism with Islam."

Muluk answered, "Of course, but as a temporary measure to get us out of this dilemma that the ayatollahs are responsible for, we could – "

"No! We can't waste time on such foolishness. Foreign assistance isn't what we're here to debate. We need something from within – something we can have national pride in."

Pausing for a moment, Rajavi was angered, but did not show it, and continued: "If Iran can demonstrate its strength and power to the rest of the world, this will have a demoralizing effect on the Iraqi troops and would be inspirational to our own men. We must somehow punish the imperialists for toying with our sovereignty for the past hundred years. Showing our power to the world is tantamount to showing the light of Islam. Clearly, we must punish the United States. The sit-in at the Embassy was child's play. We should have executed the infidel hostages to repay the Shah for his attempts to make us like the capitalists that kept him in power – the Shah and his whore of a sister, Princess Ashraf, the Black Panther bitch."

"Maybe Colonel Khadafy had the right answer all along," interjected Alam, sitting to the right of Muluk. "Maybe terrorism *is* the way to go."

"We've tried terrorism in the past with our Revolutionary Guards," said Badri, talking down to Alam. "We've got terrorists camps where we're training men now for future activities."

"That's not what I had in mind," returned Alam. "We need something on a world-wide scale. We need to get involved in skyjacking airplanes, in bombing trains and airport terminals, in destroying atomic power plants. We need to frighten the world, teach them that Islam can bring a halt to international travel. Some of our Arab friends have the guts, the know-how, and the means to help us with a program like the world has never seen. We should turn to them for help. They've offered, but we've never paid attention to them. Why not try something like this?"

"Well . . . maybe," added Badri with disgruntlement.

Rajavi pounded his fist on the table from his still-standing position. "Gentlemen, gentlemen, gentlemen," he cried with impatience, "The purpose of terrorism is to terrorize. Must I remind you of that? Terrorism hasn't gotten terrorists anywhere. They let off a lot of steam, but the rest of the world sees them as psychopaths. We have a long and proud history. SAVAK cannot condone nor propose acts like smuggling plastic explosives in women's panties aboard international airliners."

"But", came back Alam, "You must admit the bombing assault on the U.S. Marine barracks in Beirut was effective. America suffered great humiliation by the loss of three hundred of its best fighting men to the loss of only a single Arab. There are many groups that can help us with projects of this sort – Palestinians, Germans, Italians. Why even the Irish go around blowing up one another. The Israelis were certainly humbled by Black September and the massacre of their Olympic team. America was further embarrassed by the bombing of their Embassy in Lebanon. The Americans are vulnerable with embassies all over the world. We can – "

"No! No! No!" shouted Rajavi. "Terrorism is out of the question, and will not be considered by the ayatollahs. We must keep public reaction in mind. And then again, there is secrecy. The rest of the world is fed up with terrorist activities, and is going to retaliate more."

"How can anyone retaliate against terrorism?" asked Muluk. "The whole notion is absurd. Fight terrorism with terrorism? That's ridiculous. The rest of the world is too sane to fight terrorism with terrorism. They'll do what they have always done, make endless speeches – bellow at the United Nations – talk tough. Maybe an occasional air strike. Maybe – "

"Allah hear me!" screamed Rajavi. "Terrorism is out of the question and we won't discuss it anymore. Now just relax. I'm going to give you an idea of what the ayatollahs have in mind. It'll take awhile."

Badri lit a cigarette. Alam rubbed his eyes and stroked his beard. Muluk did not move nor did the expression on his face change.

Rajavi finally sat down, opened his brief case and took out some papers. Looking across the table at the three aides, he began, "In spite of our feelings towards the U.S., many of our best students are still going there for university study, and, you might be surprised to learn, many are still getting scholarships and financial aid from the stupid Americans.

"One student in particular was studying for a doctorate at an American university called George Washington University in St. Louis, a city of about a million in the central part of the U.S. The city sits on the banks of the Mississippi River, and on one bank a very large arch, over six hundred feet high, has been constructed. The arch is to proclaim the city as *The Gateway to the West*, the way to the American frontier, or some such nonsense."

Rajavi took a box of slides from his briefcase, loaded some into a tray, and turned on the projector. The first slide showed the arch. He waited to let the others absorb the details, then went on, consulting notes from his briefcase, occasionally glancing down.

"The archway is of extreme emotional value to Americans. They take pleasure in creating such useless edifices as symbols of the success of capitalism, while we all know that capitalism has succeeded only by repressing the poor. But, that's besides the point. The arch wasn't even designed by an American.

"Getting back to the Iranian student, his doctoral study was concerned with a computer investigation of the arch. He was studying civil engineering, and was calculating what are called *the modes of vibration* of the arch. Evidently, such studies weren't possible at the time the arch was constructed because modern day computers weren't available.

"The student apparently discovered, much to everyone's chagrin, that the arch has certain catastrophic modes which might lead to its own self-destruction. The student concluded something like, *If ten strong men were to push at precisely the right places along the periphery of the arch at exactly the same moment of time, and in exactly the right directions, the whole arch would be set into a growing, unstable oscillation, and would fall apart in a short time*."

Rajavi went on, "Instead of ten strong men, ten one-pound charges of high-explosives could accomplish the same thing. The arch has a walkway inside which can be used to access any part. It would be a simple matter for SAVAK to recruit the student, find out where to place the charges, and have our agents in the U.S. take care of the rest.

"Think of the impact!

"One of America's cherished monuments is destroyed by the forces of Islam!

"It's not an act of terrorism, but rather an act of humiliation. No one is injured and, in the eyes of the world, Islam is humanitarian by destroying idolatry without sacrificing life."

Of course, the whole idea was perfect. It was terrorism without terrorizing. It was terrorism without violence. The ayatollahs had much more wisdom than they were usually given credit for. Whoever said they were religious fanatics was stupid.

Being the first to speak, Muluk said: "But, the Americans will never admit we had anything to do with their precious arch falling down. They'll cite the work of our student and blame the destruction on natural causes. They 'll never admit to being vulnerable and humiliated by us."

"Of course, Major Muluk," said Rajavi. "The ayatollahs considered this possibility and dismissed the arch as an interesting exercise in logic. But the idea might provide some insight into another possibility, something with the same emotional impact, something undeniable. Our job is to suggest these alternatives."

"Forget the silly arch, let's go for the Eiffel Tower," yelled Badri, excitedly, with a grin exposing his black teeth.

"That's out," advised Alam. "With all the terrorists running around Europe, the French have been searching visitors to the Eiffel Tower for years."

"We must concentrate on America," Rajavi ordered. "It's the Americans who have taken over from the British as the world's masters of imperialism. We'll concentrate on America."

Just before sunset, a holy man climbed up into one of the minarets of the nearby mosque visible from the second-story windows. In a powerful and penetrating voice, he cried out the evening call to prayer:

God is most great.
I testify that there is no God but Allah.
I testify that Mohammed is God's apostle.
Come to prayer.
Come to security.
God is most great.

If it had been morning, he would have added

Prayer is better than sleep.

Being more important than the call, their meeting went on. Rajavi made repeated references to the notes from his briefcase. He gave examples and showed many slides of structures, buildings and monuments that symbolized America. He had slides of the Statue of Liberty, the Golden Gate Bridge, the Empire State Building, the Astrodome, Mount Rushmore, and the *Spirit of St. Louis*. There were more than fifty. The last several showed Independence Hall, the frigate *Constitution*, London Bridge and the *Spruce Goose*.

They talked at length about the number of atomic power plants in the United States, water treatment plants, electric power stations, hydroelectric stations, subways. They considered the locations of the U.S. Mint, the Library of Congress, and satellite tracking stations. They wondered about railroad systems, ferry boats, oil refineries, and universities. Rajavi even had figures on the numbers of miles of overland high-voltage transmission lines and the number of acres occupied by the movie studios of Hollywood. It was obvious Rajavi had spent a long time in the library at the University of Iran.

Even the shuttle space program was discussed from the standpoint of American emotional pride. If America could not keep its own space program going without periodic disasters, they speculated how interference by SAVAK might further deter progress.

❦

It was after midnight and they had not stopped for any meals.

"We've been over a great deal today. Perhaps it's time for contemplation," intoned Rajavi. "I can't be emphatic enough about the need for absolute secrecy. All western countries have new programs for covert military action, for infiltration of terrorist organizations, and for infiltration of intelligence agencies such as SAVAK. They spy on one another. Now, they're being more overt in their policies of *preventative assassination* which, as we know, the CIA has practiced for years. Secrecy in the present matter is of utmost concern. You're not to discuss our meeting with any of your staffs, or seek their assistance in any way. Any research to be done, you'll do yourselves.

"Although we haven't come to any definite conclusions, it's

clear that America has many symbols of national pride. A matter of this importance can't be rushed. For a successful operation, we need patience.

"I've already taken the first step in persuading the ayatollahs to reassign five of our top pilots to help with our mission. Each has an impeccable dossier, is unquestionably loyal, and has a distinguished battle record. They'll be sent to the United States with cover alibis. All have trained there. They'll return to the places they'd been, to rekindle old friendships. I want them to fit in, as they once had, not to arouse any suspicion. When we're more definite about the goals of our mission, they'll be ready and waiting."

"Why are all five pilots and not other professionals?" asked Alam. "We must have had students in all disciplines trained there."

"We did," responded Rajavi, "But pilots give us the most flexibility."

The others seemed to accept his answer and there was no sign of disagreement.

"Before anything's done, we'll have more meetings" concluded Rajavi.

6

ARIZONA

"Buenos dias, Padre," shouted Kelly.

"Buenos dias, Señor Kelly. Buenos dias Señor Diaz," answered Father Miguel.

Father Miguel's old one-and-a-half-ton pickup truck had pulled up next to Kelly's plane at the Douglas, Arizona airport. Three Mexican boys occupied the front seat with Father Miguel and another half-dozen scampered off the flatbed as the truck came to a halt. The niños, ranging in age from five to eighteen, wasted no time in encircling Kelly and Francisco Diaz who passed out Hershey's chocolate bars and packs of Wrigley's gum. All boys, the children laughed and yelled, pushed and shoved in the jest of a mild pandemonium. This was Kelly's monthly visit to *La Casa de Niños de Agua Prieta,* an orphanage located just below the border in Mexico.

"Glad to see you! Did you have a good flight?" asked Father Miguel.

"*Perfecto,* as always, Padre," said Kelly.

"*Muy bien,*" said Francisco Diaz.

"We were able to bring along some good two-by-fours. And a couple of ninety-pound sacks of cement," said Kelly.

"I'm grateful, Kelly. Bless you!" said Father Miguel.

"It's nothing, Padre," said Kelly. "We were also able to get you the nails and screws you wanted. And, this time, we brought some pencils, crayons, and paper. And chalk and erasers."

"The niños will make good use of them," said Father Miguel.

As Kelly and Father Miguel chatted, the children encircled the baggage compartment of the Bonanza. It was packed to capacity with used clothing, cases of canned goods, assorted tools, two small saw horses, several fifty-foot extension cords, medicine, blankets and four pillows. Francisco Diaz passed the items to the awaiting arms of the boys and everything was packed neatly behind the cab on the bed of the truck. Kelly had weighed it all to insure that his Bonanza would not be overloaded. It came to nearly five hundred pounds. Everything had been donated by the parishioners of the Church of Guadalupe in south San Diego.

"You and Señor Diaz must be our guests for lunch. We have a special treat today," said Father Miguel.

Kelly and Francisco Diaz climbed into the front seat with Father Miguel and the children sat on boxes or stood and held onto the wooden frame enclosing the bed.

After passing the American Border Patrol Station at Douglas, the truck was waved on by the Mexican Border Guards. They all knew Father Miguel.

The orphanage was located nine miles west of Agua Prieta on a bumpy and dusty dirt road. Another twenty-two boys impatiently awaited their arrival outside the three buildings that comprised the tiny settlement. Some had been playing baseball and others soccer. On the edge of land owned by a rancher, the orphanage consisted of one large dormitory for the children, a modest two-room house for Father Miguel and a small chapel. One wall of the dormitory was open during the day, the side where the building was being added onto. At night the opening was covered by sheets of plywood. Various building materials were scattered about, mostly used and salvaged by whatever means Father Miguel could manage. Several large picnic benches under a thatched palm patio, which also sheltered a gas stove, beat-up gas refrigerator, and assorted wooden tables, served as the kitchen and dining facilities. Behind the stove and refrigerator sat a one hundred gallon liquid natural gas storage cylinder. Alongside a large water tank painted green was an enormous two-part sink in which the food and dishes were washed. A lean-to attached to one side of Father Miguel's house functioned as a pantry and storage shed. At the rear of the house was a tiny pottery shop in which he made statues of the Virgin Mary, crucifixes, and other religious artifacts which some of the boys helped paint.

This was home to thirty-one children. Supervised by Father Miguel, the older boys did the cooking and the laundry. Sunday Mass service was held outdoors because the chapel was not large enough to accommodate everybody. Of necessity, school classes were also conducted outdoors, mostly under the patio. Everyone worked in the large vegetable garden tending the carrots, tomatoes, lettuce, beans, corn, and other vegetables. A dozen trees bore lemons, oranges, grapefruit and avocados.

Father Miguel had started and run the orphanage for more than ten years. In his early forties, he could easily have had a regular congregation in one of hundreds of small Mexican villages, not to mention a more comfortable position in Nogales or San Luis. He was a quiet man with a purpose, unassuming, forthright, and even forward when necessary to get something he badly needed.

There was more hustle and bustle when the truck pulled into the orphanage, and more chocolate and gum to be passed around. Every boy without exception had said he wanted to be a pilot when he grew up, just like *El Piloto Señor* Kelly. To signal Father Miguel that they were arriving, Kelly dive-bombed over the orphanage letting the Bonanza get up near red line and pulled out just over the tree tops. It was exciting to the kids.

As much as Kelly was admired, it was Francisco Diaz who was their secret hero. He was one of them. He was the Cisco Kid they had seen in old television movies. A burly, well-built man, with jet-black hair and a handle-bar moustache, he exemplified the strong Latino male personality. Being self-centered and opinionated gave him cause to be proud. The oldest of nine children of illegal alien parents, he had grown up in Los Angeles speaking English and Spanish, each without the slightest trace of an accent.

Francisco Diaz played soccer with several of the niños while lunch was being heated by two of the teenagers. Father Miguel and Kelly strolled about the orphanage, Father Miguel enthusiastically telling Kelly of his plans for a new dormitory and showing him where he planned to build it. If he could only get twenty-five head of cattle. That would be a godsend and provide an income that could go a long way. If they could only get a new commercial-type oven to bake bread. If only they had a large drill press to make some furniture.

"I brought you two boxes of .22's," said Kelly.

"Thank you my friend. We need them. Every once in a while we see rattlers around here," said Father Miguel.

"And, I also have an unabridged English dictionary for you."

"*Muchas gracias!*" said Father Miguel.

Father Miguel was interested in learning new words, words that he did not hear in everyday conversation, abstract words like "infinity" and "coscinomancy" and "obloquy." Unusual words like "discombobulated," "Jabberwocky," "flibbertigibbet," and "oxymoron" fascinated him. Father Miguel studied and read philosophy every night before going to sleep.

Father Miguel's special lunch was *camarones rancheros*, ranch-style shrimp cooked in a spicy sauce of onions, tomatoes, green peppers, celery, chilies and cilantro. A nearby rancher had bought more shrimp than he could use at a ridiculously low price on the black market in Hermosillo. He had donated the excess, that which he couldn't jam into his freezer, to the orphanage. It was a delicacy they could never afford on their own resources. Father Miguel had saved the shrimp especially for Kelly's visit. There were at least a hundred tortillas and numerous bowls of fried rice and refried beans to go along with the shrimp.

Kelly felt slightly guilty in eating food he knew was needed by the orphanage. He accepted the hospitality as Father Miguel's only way of showing his gratitude. Both he and Francisco Diaz had second helpings. Father Miguel gave Francisco Diaz an ice-cold bottle of his favorite beer, *Carta Blanca*. Kelly and the children drank milk.

Francisco Diaz laughed with the children and told jokes in Spanish. He made up fantastic stories about how his distant relatives had been in Spain during the Spanish Inquisition and how one of them had been an executioner who cut off heads every day before breakfast. He told about the freeways in Los Angeles and about growing up there as a child, all the stories embellished in one way or another with grandiose lies. He had a vivid imagination.

Disappointment filled the air in the late afternoon when it came time for Kelly and Francisco Diaz to leave. Above mild protests, the truck, with a different set of young bodies in the back, headed back towards Agua Prieta on the bumpy, dusty road. Also in the bed of the truck were three boxes containing statues of the Blessed Virgin.

Long accustomed to Father Miguel's frequent trips across the border, his truck was passed through without an inspection by U.S. Border Patrol agents. All the guards had seen his statues many times before. One of the boys told the inspector to "Stick 'em up, buddy!" as the truck rolled by.

The boys insisted on staying and watching Kelly's plane take off, but Father Miguel knew that Kelly often had people to see in Douglas before he left. Besides, Kelly would make a low pass over the truck which was much better and more exciting than a takeoff. They could watch other planes takeoff, but none of the them was going to make a low pass over the truck. "Just like in the war movies on TV," Father Miguel had explained.

Kelly carefully loaded the boxes with the statues in the baggage compartment of the Bonanza, lashed them down with a piece of nylon rope, and locked the door.

Francisco Diaz watched him turn the key and exclaimed, "Momma's gonna love me tonight." He affectionately referred to his 200-pound wife as *Momma*.

About half the statues contained hidden medicines.

This setup had been arranged by a friend of Kelly's at the Pentagon who had a connection in the Surgeon General's Office. Some of the medicines were manufactured in Mexico, others in Central and South America. Some were exact copies of drugs manufactured and sold by the big drug companies in the United States claiming exclusivity under the protection of U.S. Patent Laws. Others were drugs widely used in many countries but not yet approved by the agonizingly slow processes of the Federal Drug Administration. A few were experimental.

Frequently, Kelly and Francisco Diaz picked up the medicines in Baja. On the way back to San Diego they would then fly ten or so miles out over the Pacific Ocean at twenty feet altitude to insure they passed undetected under the radar screen. The U.S. Coast Guard, of course, denied that this could be so easily done. But it could. It worked fine and they had been doing it for the better part of two years.

"It'll be a snap, Pachuco," Kelly had said to Francisco Diaz before their first flight together. And, it was.

It was no secret, Kelly felt, that the large American drug companies made enormous, unjustifiable, and unregulated profits in the sales of many medicines and drugs. He maintained the big drug companies doled out large sums of money to fund Political Action Committees, had little difficulty in convincing politicians to go along under the rubric of Public Safety. It was a disgusting situation, he thought, that had been bitterly debated for as long as anyone could remember. Still, the drug companies always seemed to twist things in their favor and win out.

Kelly had been assured by his friend in the Pentagon that all the medicines he brought across the border would ultimately find their way to those who needed them at prices far below what the big drug companies charged. Kelly had no idea who the woman in the Surgeon General's office was, nor did he care. He had been told that she headed a complex underground of hundreds of participating physicians and surgeons, hospitals, and medical research institutions. It was the type of thing that many were aware of but few discussed. The big drug companies knew. They were reluctant to openly raise the issue for fear of public outcry against them. By comparison to their huge profits, this was peanuts anyway.

Some of the drugs were in short supply, Kelly was told, like the one used to treat degrading lung tissue, alpha-1-antitrypsin, made by purification of blood plasma extracts. Another, Hepataxin, an extremely rare drug was used to treat the brain disease spinocerebellar ataxia, was made from the venom of the South American anaconda snake. Since the venom was hard to get, it cost thousands of dollars for one ounce. Kelly knew from a class he took in genetics that there were some five hundred diseases, mostly rare, which could be transmitted genetically from parents to children, and each of these could be potentially treated with medication. In some cases, the medications had yet to be discovered. A lot of money was still to be made by the big drug companies.

At some point, Kelly knew, it would be necessary to tell Jennie everything. Being a nurse, how could she not understand? She had been becoming increasingly curious about his absences from San Diego, and rightly so. Although he never lied to her, he could not overcome his feelings that he was still being deceptive.

Kelly had once smuggled diamonds across the border for a rich real estate broker in San Diego, and another time a rare jeweled Mayan statue for a wealthy collector in New York. He was younger then, wilder and more cynical, but still had an empty feeling each time. Helping the sick, the old, and the poor was different and gave him great satisfaction. He was well paid for what he did. This he justified by the chances he and Francisco Diaz were taking

As for Father Miguel, a practical man, he realized he was participating in an activity that was, strictly speaking, illegal. The money he received from Kelly was welcome. Thirty-one boys consumed nearly three hundred and fifty gallons of milk alone each month. Although he prayed every night for God's forgiveness and Kelly's safety, he was not about to question the mysterious ways in which the Lord sometimes worked.

Most bars in the border towns are dingy and smell of stale beer and whiskey. This one, in Douglas, Arizona, was no exception. However *Taverna Hernando* was the accepted place for doing business in this part of the country. Carlos Alvarez, a Chicano who lived in Douglas, had called Kelly two days before and requested a meeting.

"Hola, Carlos," said Kelly.

"Hiya, Kelly," Alvarez replied, not bothering to acknowledge

Francisco Diaz.

The dimly lit bar had no windows to the outside world. They sat in one corner at the back separated from the bartender by a wooden dance floor. Behind them was the bandstand from which a mariachi band played each night. A small man with an enormous belly, Alvarez toyed nervously with his beer bottle, digging one fingernail into the edge of the label.

"'Fraid I got some bad news for you," said Alvarez.

"How's that *amigo*?" asked Kelly.

Alvarez was not one to play games and Kelly liked this about him. "Got word from Sancho in Mexico City that we'll be making a small change."

"*What?*" asked Kelly.

"Well, you know . . . how it goes. "One of my cousins is going to do your job at . . . at half the cost to Sancho. Sancho's agreed." Alvarez smiled cunningly.

Francisco Diaz grabbed Alvarez with both hands by his shirt collar and lifted him out of his chair. "Why you double-crossing greedy motherfucker, you cocksucker, I'm gonna bash your fuckin' head in!" he said.

Before Francisco Diaz could throw a punch, Kelly grabbed his wrists and he let go of Alvarez. Alvarez slumped back into his chair.

"No rough stuff, Pachuco," Kelly said quietly. The man has delivered his message. Let's get out of here."

When they got back to the plane, they found the baggage door open and the boxes of statues stolen.

After taking off and setting course for San Diego, Kelly put a CD into the player he had had specially installed. The French horns of The Vienna Philharmonic, with Werner Hauptmann conducting, announced the start of the first movement, the allegro non troppo, of Tchaikovsky's *1st Piano Concerto*. Rudolph Serkin was the soloist.

Kelly forgot to buzz Father Miguel's truck.

7

RANCHO SANTA FE

There are not many places in the world where the rich tend to congregate. Rancho Santa Fe, California, situated about thirty miles north of San Diego and five miles inland from the Pacific Ocean, was one of them. The people who lived there, previously lived there, or aspired to live there called it, affectionately, *The Ranch.* To everybody else, it was *Rancho Santa Fe.* In Hemingway's short story *The Snows of Kilimanjaro,* the protagonist, Harry, believed *the very rich are no different from you or me, they just have more money.* Evidently, Harry had never set foot in Rancho Santa Fe.

In a special election, the voters of *The Ranch* actually vetoed the pedestrian concepts of assigning addresses to residences and having mail delivered. Instead, boxes were provided at the post office in the *Village,* the center of town, necessitating a daily stop there to pick up mail. In spite of the inconvenience and traffic jams in the inadequate parking lot, the residents cherished these diurnal outings as opportunities to flaunt new prized possessions, like, typically, Rolls Royces and Ferraris.

Unfortunately, going to the post office was more like attending a meeting of the local geriatric club than a social event. One might well have come to the erroneous conclusion that Rancho Santa Fe was the home of pot bellies, wrinkles, face lifts, fat asses, double chins, and ex-movie stars.

There were virtually no ordinary *houses* in Rancho Santa Fe and an estate on *The Ranch* cost anywhere between three-quarters of a million dollars to upwards of ten million. These modest sums bought groves of orange trees, lemon trees, macadamia trees, acres of horse corrals, groves of eucalyptus trees, swimming pools, guest houses, putting greens and tennis courts. Some of the other necessities of life included imposing gate entries, unsurpassed country views, terraces, private lakes, circular driveways, whirlpools and saunas. Above all, a membership in the governing body, *The Association*, was thrown in for free. The majority of the non-WASP community one saw were Mexican gardeners employed in droves to keep the estates well-manicured. In addition to its own private police and fire departments, Rancho Santa Fe boasted the largest horse population per capita in Southern California. A local real estate magnate, after six martinis, was known to slap prospective buyers on the back and exhort, *"Why, we got more horseshit here than in Colorado!"*

This was where Kelly lived.

When Kelly bought his house at *The Ranch,* it came with two twelve-foot-high ceramic olive jars which highlighted the entrance. The first night there, drunk on Jack Daniels whiskey, Kelly shot those pompous jugs with his .38 so many times there was little left but tiny pieces. When replacing them, he had difficulty in deciding between two lions or two naked virgins. The ten-foot tall virgins won out.

Kelly liked living in Rancho Santa Fe. The rolling hills, colorful groves, white-fenced pastures and generously-spaced estates gave a feeling of openness and freedom. Here, tucked away in the northern part of San Diego County, the residents were almost totally isolated from the stresses of the outside world. Coyotes chasing foxes cried out like babies from the canyons at night, hawks kept watch over the rabbit population from the tops of tall pines and eucalyptus, and snakes feasted on rodents in the rolling sage. It was a fine place to live. Private and quiet, the solitude appealed to Kelly.

Kelly's house, off Paseo Encantada, was of traditional Spanish landmark design built in the 1930's and had over 6000 square feet of living area. It sat in the middle of four and a half acres, completely encircled by a six-foot-high adobe wall. There were five bedrooms, seven baths and a four-car garage. His favorite room during the mornings was the second story *el mirador* which overlooked the entry on one end and the patio and pool on the other. The rest of the house was on the ground floor. Much of Kelly's leisure time was spent in the high-vaulted family room or on the patio.

The Ranch contrasted sharply with the high barren plains around Rock Springs, Wyoming where Kelly grew up. They lived in town because his father was a coal miner, as his father before him had been. As a young boy, his summer days were filled with trout fishing in the Green River, shooting rabbits in the foothills of the Great Divide Basin, and riding horses on the local ranches. The bitter Wyoming winters provided ample instruction in the hardships of life.

Planes landing at the Rock Springs Municipal Airport often descended on final approach directly over town, only a few precious feet it seemed to young Kelly, over buildings, power lines and the church steeple. With landing gear extended, flaps down, and engines throttled back, they appeared as quiet, giant eagles, majestically swooping down on unsuspecting prey. "I'm goin' to fly one of those someday," he boasted once to his three brothers. "Coal miners don't fly airplanes, you idiot," his oldest brother ridiculed, "Ya can't fly an airplane with coal dust in yer eyes."

Kelly began spending whole days at the airport, just watching at first. Then, slowly, he started asking questions of the pilots and the crop dusters. He began doing odd jobs at the airport when he was fourteen and later worked weekends driving the gas truck. In exchange for washing an airplane, helping do routine maintenance, or changing a tire, he would get an hour here and an hour there of free flight instruction. He earned his private pilot's license before graduating from high school. Working at the airport had a second advantage: he saved enough money for his first year at the University of Wyoming in Laramie. The remaining years were covered by a football scholarship. Then, he joined the Navy and entered flight school. Although he fancied thinking of himself as a "cowboy," he was sure he would probably never again live in Wyoming.

Jet training came easy for Kelly; he was the first in his class to solo and the first to land on an aircraft carrier. He flew A-7's during the last year of the Vietnam war off the *USS Enterprise,* making air strikes on Hanoi and other targets in the North. After a tour with the Pacific Air Fleet, he returned to The States. Other tours of duty took him all over the world. With an exemplary record, he was selected to be a flight instructor at the Top Gun School at Miramar Naval Air Station.

❦

The invitations to the welcoming party for Kashan were printed and said simply:

Please Come to a Party Next Sunday Evening
Burton Kelly
Between the Nude Virgins on Paseo Encantada
Rancho Santa Fe

These were mailed the previous Sunday evening. Purposely, there was no mention of a reason for the party, the dress or the time. Kelly did not like to tell people what to wear or when to go home. To say the party was being given in Kashan's honor might have embarrassed Kashan. Anyone who knew Kelly would know the party would be informal, have a distinct Spanish flavor, last from eight till one or two, and any type of dress would be acceptable. Kelly was not a black-tie enthusiast. He'd probably wear a cowboy shirt, Levis and leather boots.

Two Latin trios alternated with a mariachi band to provide constant entertainment and the dancing on the patio never stopped. The evening was warm for spring and the moon full.

The caterers set up bars and buffets, one each inside and outside the house. Largely for show, fountains at each end of the pool sprinkled champagne into the air. Waiters circulated with trays of margaritas, daiquiris and hors d'oeuvres. Bowls of rum punch shared the buffet tables with plates of fresh lobster, crab, shrimp, oysters and assorted cheeses. These were complemented by fresh pineapple, grapes, papaya, and coconut. A Mexican, wearing a large chef's hat, roasted bite-size chunks of beef and pork over an open fire.

More than a hundred guests attended including pilots from Miramar, local politicians, a state senator, a San Diego Charger football player, an interior decorator, a judge, doctors and staff from Balboa Naval Hospital, Francisco Diaz's relatives and friends and Kelly's business associates.

Jennie was striking in a Peter Popovich vivid red, blue and yellow stained-glass-crystal pleated top and matching flounced skirt. With gold bracelets on each wrist, large gold hooped earrings and shocking red lipstick to match the red in her rayon challis, she could not have looked more Spanish or more appealing.

Mostly, the women were smartly dressed in festive skirts and gala blouses – all originals from the shops of La Jolla, Fashion Valley and Rodeo Drive. The men were more casual. Most wore sport shirts and dress slacks, a few had on coats and ties, and some came in jeans.

Ever since that night in front of the fireplace at the villa, Jennie felt ambivalent about seeing Kashan again. Terribly hurt and disillusioned when he left, she questioned her own ability to love for longer than she cared to remember. After returning from Okinawa and meeting Kelly, her life changed radically to a semblance of what it had been with Kashan, some of the fire and passion returned, she was certain. Did she want to face Kashan? Could she? At moments, she did not see how she could withstand the memories of the old emotional pain. At other times, she was excited with the prospect of seeing an old friend, an old lover. After vacillating back and forth, she decided the evening would not be easy, but she made up her mind to force herself to be an amiable hostess.

"Is something troubling you, sweetheart," asked Kelly when they had a few free moments together.

The question caught her off balance. She thought back to the hospital. "Oh, I can't help but think of that poor Mexican that was brought into the ER last week. He was found at a place called Punta Estrella down in Baja with a gunshot wound in his head. You ever go there?"

"Not any more. Haven't been there in years. The runway isn't any good." In an effort to change the subject, he added, "Cheer up, honey, Kashan'll be here soon."

"When'd he get in?" asked Jennie.

"Yesterday afternoon."

"Did you get a chance to talk?"

"Not much. He was tired from the trip."

"How's he going to get here tonight?"

"I asked Laura Denton to pick him up."

"Kelly! You didn't!"

"Yeah, I did! Told him I was busy with a lovely lady."

There were the usual small groupings of two, three and four save for an occasional lost soul. Jennie and Kelly circulated to make sure they spoke to everybody, but often became separated. There was much of the good-natured joking that goes on at parties when people have not seen one an other for long periods of time and do not know each other that well. As the champagne and other drinks loosened their tongues, everyone seemed gay. The mood was festive and people did not take each other seriously. There was continuous motion within the large group, like bubbles in a boiling pot, to renew old acquaintances, make new ones, refresh empty glasses, and to fill voracious appetites. This atmosphere compelled some to try to be verbally clever, cute or smart and considerable small-talk and corny witticisms dominated many conversations.

Occasionally, the men were jokingly flirtatious, like Kelly's chunky stock broker. A little drunk, after several abortive attempts, he finally cornered Jennie just inside the living room.

He said, "My portfolio is so *beau-tee-ful,* and I could buy this joint and everybody in it."

"Why don't you?" asked Jennie.

"I'd rather spend it on you. Come with me to St. Thomas for a week."

"Get your *beau-tee-ful* portfolio a new bikini and take *it* to St.

Thomas for a week," she laughed.

Jennie knew these men, knew it was their naive way of being flattering to her. Normally, she would not have tolerated this type of conversation. These were Kelly's friends and Jennie had long since accepted them and their boisterous ways. Once in awhile, though, she was still taken by surprise – like by the young naval pilot who asked her to dance. Boasting new wings and the only guest in uniform, he crowed for several minutes about his natural flying abilities then hinted, in no uncertain terms, that he was good at other things. Finally, deciding that subtlety was not going to get him anywhere, he said, "I'd sure like to get into your pants."

"There are four hundred and thirty-seven ahead of you," Jennie came back quickly.

"Jesus Christ, I'll be an old man by then," the lieutenant blurted.

"Oh, too bad," kidded Jennie.

Although not many of the women had much to say to Jennie, Kelly was also sought out by the men. One of Rancho Santa Fe's leading realtors patiently waited for the mariachi band to finish playing *La Cucaracha,* turned his eyes to Kelly and, in a robust tone, said, "The music never stops playing and the booze never stops flowing at Kelly's house."

Jennie did not see Kelly lean over and whisper in his ear, "And the girls never stop fucking."

Francisco Diaz and Momma and their friends from South of the Border had lain siege on one of the champagne fountains. But, at the same time, they kept a waiter busy providing fresh margaritas to wash down the champagne. Francisco Diaz jested with a Tijuana businessman who had a margarita in one hand and a glass of champagne in the other. Setting down one of his drinks, he picked up a piece of lobster and nibbled on it as he talked.

"With my brains and your friends, we could go places, eh, compadre?" the businessman said.

"You'd have to learn to wear shoes," roared Francisco.

"Tienes un hermano mayor?" asked Francisco Diaz. Do you have an older brother?

"Si tengo, muchacho," answered the businessman.

"Entonces tu eres el hijo de chinga su madre." Then you are the son of a motherfucker. "Ha, ha, ha!"

Eager with anticipation, the evening began dragging for Jennie. She wondered what Kashan would say now that over seven years had passed and how she would react. Would any of the old feelings return when she saw him?

Jennie noticed Kelly off to one side of the pool talking with three men in dark suits and ties – men she had never seen. None were drinking or eating and their conversation, from a distance, seemed to be serious, not at all light-hearted. One was waving a finger in the air as he spoke. As a group, they moved further away when the mariachi band began playing *Spanish Eyes*. The one waving his finger continued to do most of the talking.

Flash cubes blinked as a photographer darted from group to group like a honey bee from flower to flower. This was an *Event*, and the locals would find out what had happened in the next issue of the weekly Rancho Santa Fe newspaper.

Glancing away from the group with Kelly, Jennie was caught by surprise, seeing Kashan standing on the patio just outside the doorway. Her hand on his arm, Laura Denton listened intently while he talked.

Jennie's pulse quickened. Her first thought was to run across the patio and throw her arms around him. The sweet memories came back, the painful ones pushed off somewhere into a corner. Jennie struggled to keep her composure.

Kashan hadn't changed, thought Jennie – he looked as if he could have been a sheik or a desert crown prince in his dark maroon blazer with a white shirt and white bow tie. Kelly had a ruggedness about him which contrasted with Kashan's stately presence. They were both masculine, but in vastly different ways. Each commanded respect, but again for different reasons.

Kelly was tough-minded around other men and gave no quarter. But Kashan was sensitive. Jennie had loved that sensitivity. He commanded others by showing he cared and understood their problems. Was it possible for Jennie to feel love for both?

A would-be socialite who migrated to California in her early thirties, Laura Denton spent several years in Los Angeles before discovering Miramar Naval Air Station and Navy Pilots. Real or not, she portrayed a royal air and was always dressed well by any standards. Never out of place, her blonde hair hung straight down just barely touching the tops of her shoulders. Her Russian heritage showed in her determined walk. Laura was five-foot-three and small in stature with adequate breasts. Her face never tanned, she would have been more at home back in Boston. Her cheeks were smooth and her eyes appeared to be two different shades of brown. She seemed to know what she wanted, but had not yet found it. Only her excessive use of eye makeup hinted at a defect in her personality. She wore high heels and a distinctive, elegant Braemar patch round-neck pullover. She kept a shapely figure and was still appealing.

As soon as he saw them, Kelly abruptly excused himself from his conversation with the three men and went to greet Kashan and Laura. He escorted them to where Jennie was standing.

"I'd like to introduce Jennie Ross. Omar Kashan. Please call him Kashan."

"I'm delighted," Jennie replied.

Kashan reached for Jennie's hand, bowed over, and kissed it, holding it longer than he dared. Both felt the energy surge between them, rippling along their arms, racing through their fingers. "It is my pleasure, mademoiselle," he said, his voice conveying a vastness of words unsaid, his eyes much more.

"Why don't you two get to know each other a little? C'mon Laura, I want to introduce you to a handsome Texan who's got lots of oil wells. I need to talk to him too. Kashan, you and I'll have plenty of time to catch up on old memories when we go to Baja."

Suddenly, Jennie and Kashan were alone. He guided her over to the wall across from the pool and took her hand in his. The first words came automatically.

"I've missed you, Jennie"

"And I you. I can't help it. I tried but I can't ever forget you."

"It's been an eternity," said Kashan.

For a moment there was silence, neither quite knowing what to say.

"Kashan, why didn't you write?" Her voice was tender. She tried to hold back but could not keep tears from forming.

"I tried . . . I tried . . . I tried many times . . . but the words just wouldn't come . . . "

He thought of the locket in his plane, her picture, and how he had yearned then to see her once again. Now it was happening.

The distinguished, tall, silver-haired judge saw them along the wall and strolled over. He extended his hand to Kashan and interrupted with, "Name's Willoughby, Judge Willoughby. Hear you're from Iran m'boy. How's the legal system over there after the revolution?"

Kashan spent twenty minutes answering questions. The judge was in no hurry. He carefully phrased each question and made sure that he understood each answer. Kashan assured him housewives and little children were not being executed by firing squads, Iranians had more freedom under the ayatollahs than under the Shah, and the legal system was alive and breathing.

"Maybe so, maybe so," the Judge said when he had heard enough. He turned and walked away as if he did not believe a thing Kashan had said.

Before Kashan could speak to Jennie, they were interrupted again, this time by a doctor from the hospital.

"Hey, hey, here's the man of the hour!" "I'm Doctor Charles Adams. Hear you're setting up a medical program in Iran like our Flying Samaritans. I'd like to hear about it."

"That's right. I'm here to learn more about them and their operations in Baja. There's a similar group in Australia called the Royal Flying Doctors."

"Yes, yes, I've heard of them too."

"Our basic idea is to get more service to the remote areas of my country. We have over thirty-seven million people and only twelve thousand doctors. There are over sixty-four thousand villages without even running water."

"Marvelous, marvelous that young chaps like you should be dedicated to helping your fellow man. My hat is off to you."

From across the room, a middle-age brunette called "Charlie," and, as quickly as he had come, the doctor said, "See you later," and hurried away.

Jennie started, "Do you want – "

"Hey Kashan," Kelly called from across the pool. "Come over here a minute please. There are some people I'd like for you to meet."

"I . . . I'm sorry Jennie . . . I can't refuse . . . I'll talk to you a little later," Kashan said as he backed away leaving Jennie alone.

Everyone wanted to meet Kashan and there were only seconds between the time he extricated himself from one conversation to the time he was captured and engaged in another. It was useless to think they were going to have more than a few minutes alone. Jennie was frustrated in being so near and yet so far from Kashan. She could not fight the human tidal wave.

She and Kashan had to be alone during their first meeting.

Nothing else was acceptable or possible. The thought pounded relentlessly in her head.

With the time nearing midnight, she had to get away. Now, *think,* she said to herself. *Oh, there's Doctor Birch and his wife. I'll ask them to give me a ride home. They must be leaving soon.*

"I'm sorry about your headache, Jennie," Kelly said with disappointment. "I understand. The party'll be over soon. Go ahead and go on home with Doc Birch and I'll call you in the morning."

Jennie did not try to say good-bye to Kashan who was hopelessly entangled with the medical needs of Iran, explaining them to an affluent Rancho Santa Fe woman who had traveled widely in the Middle East.

⁂

The valet brought the last car to the front of the house and went home. Begging exhaustion after his supposed long flight from Iran, Kashan had left shortly before with Laura. Kelly bid goodnight to Francisco Diaz and Momma and they drove away. He went out to the patio and sat down for the first time all evening. He was not tired and had drunk very little during the party. He decided to have a nightcap before going to bed.

✤

Laura drove her yellow Corvette with one hand and sipped from the champagne bottle with the other.

"It was sure a swell party," she said.

"Yeah, Kelly's quite a guy," said Kashan.

"He's not at all like you. Why, you're straighter than Gary Cooper," she giggled. "So, you've got Kelly's villa all to yourself. That sure's nice of him. But, I'll betcha he won't let you use his boat. He's got a thing about that hunk of plastic. That's his floating sex palace, you know."

"You're wrong, Laura. He gave me the keys to the boat *and* the keys to his airplane. He wants me to have a good time while I'm here."

"You've got to be kidding!" said Laura.

"Why would I joke about a thing like that?"

"Well then, goddamn, honey, let's go flying. Want a little sip?"

"No, I don't drink," he said. This was only partly true. Although drinking was forbidden by the Koran, Kashan sometimes drank a little wine to be sociable, but never around other Iranians. "We can't go flying. It's too late."

"Never too late." Laura kissed him on the cheek.

"You're being illogical, Laura. It's too late."

"What's the matter. You forget how to fly?"

"You never forget how to fly."

"You owe me a favor. Pay up. You thanked Kelly for having me escort you to the party. You never thanked me. Well, now I *want* to go flying. Pay up your debts, welsher."

Kashan did not answer.

"What's a matter, you Iranian big bluff? I know where Kelly's hangar is and that's where I'm headin'. I want to go flyin'. Kelly'll never know"

"I'm afraid I can't do that."

"You can do anything you sweet little heart desires, Mohammed. If you don't take me, I'll make up some nasty story about you. Like how you tried to seduce me."

"There's no need for that," Kashan laughed.

"Just try me." Laura was determined.

"You've got your mind made up."

"Yessiree! Well, then take me flying – now!"

"It's crazy this time of night." Although he had been protesting all along, the idea actually appealed to Kashan the first time Laura mentioned it.

8

MT. SOLEDAD

They talked more about the party and more about Kelly during the rest of the drive to the airport. After Laura parked next to Kelly's hangar, Kashan rolled open the metal doors and pulled out the Bonanza. Seconds later they were taxiing and a few minutes later they were airborne. The tower was closed and there was no other activity.

"I brought along some champagne in a bag," said Laura.

As the Bonanza climbed, Laura sipped the champagne and giggled. The bottle of Dom Pérignon sat on the floor in an ice bucket next to her feet.

"Are we flying yet, Captain?" she giggled and took another sip.

Reaching 4500 feet, Kashan trimmed the plane for a 15-degree bank so it would continue to circle in a one-mile radius over Mt. Soledad. From there, they could see the lights of Del Mar and Solana Beach and all the way to Oceanside in one direction, the lights of La Jolla, Pacific Beach, Mission Bay and Point Loma as they circled left, and the lights in the tall buildings which defined downtown San Diego. Above the downtown area was the faint glow of Tijuana, and in completing the circle, there were the lights in the inland areas of Mission Hills, Mission Valley and Clairemont. Several airport beacons blinking white and green came and went as the plane rotated like a toy bird on a string.

Laura knelt on the passenger seat and kissed Kashan on his neck and lips and in his ears, whispering with a slight slur, "Are we flying yet, Captain?"

"We're up there," answered Kashan. "Aren't the lights gorgeous?"

Slowly, she unbuttoned his shirt, kissing his nipples while helping him slip out of it. Kashan started to get excited. Laura unzipped his pants grabbing his throbbing penis. She bent over and encircled the end of it with her moist lips, feeling his power hungering for an outlet. She knelt erect and kissed him on the lips and in his ears, knowing that the temporary respite would excite him more.

"Are we flying yet, Captain?" she giggled and teased.

"Yes, we're starting to fly!" Kashan exclaimed.

"No!" protested Laura. "Not yet!"

She reached down and took off his shoes and socks.

With his left hand, Kashan found the release handle for the seat, pulled it, and let the seat slide slowly to its rear-most position. From there, he could not reach the rudder pedals, but no longer cared. He could reach the yoke with his arm not quite fully extended.

Laura undid Kashan's belt buckle and helped him slip out of his trousers and shorts.

Kashan was naked.

"Are we flying yet, Captain?" Laura giggled cheerfully.

Laura sipped from the champagne bottle, then lifted it to his lips and fed him a long gulp.

After pulling her dress over her head, Laura undid her bra, and slipped out of her lace panties. She flung everything on top of Kashan's clothes on the floor, then kissed Kashan again on the mouth and rubbed her breasts in his face.

"Laura, I can't see the instruments," Kashan said with mild reluctance.

A look of mischief in her eyes, she licked his belly and thighs. "Now, we're going to fly, Captain," she said with a drunken laugh. Her hair in her face, she threw her head back and from side to side to shake it away.

Bending down, she took him in her mouth. He was ready.

He moaned soft sounds of ecstasy and pleasure. The sounds came faster and louder and he screamed her name before exploding.

After a long silence, Laura asked coyly, "Kashan?"

There was a broad smile on his face, his eyes were closed. He was spent and sat languidly back in his seat, trying to summon up reserve energy but, all that would come was a weak, " Yes . . . what do . . . you want?"

"NOW WE'RE FLYING, CAPTAIN!" she shouted.

James Crawford sipped coffee from a paper cup and smoked a cigarette in front of his cathode ray display at San Diego Air Traffic Control Center. "Hey, Arnie, c'mere a minute."

Arnold Benson, another air traffic controller, walked over.

"Look at that target over Soledad, Arnie," said Crawford. "He's been circling for forty-five minutes . . . keeps going up and down in altitude one or two hundred feet . . . like a yo-yo."

"Just a student practicing turns at night," answered Benson dryly as he walked away.

They were both naked and exhausted. Kashan taxied in front of Kelly's hangar. He smiled at Laura and was about to say something when she opened the door and jumped out with all their clothing.

Laura darted to her Corvette and threw the clothes in. She hopped in and drove away.

Kashan watched curiously from the Bonanza. Then he reached down and picked up the Dom Pérignon. He thought about taking a long drink, but decided against it. Instead, he laughed, and said aloud to himself, *"Why didn't you use the infidel's autopilot, you stupid goat?"*

Dressed in a pair of Levis and a sport shirt that Kelly kept in the hangar, Kashan was about to call a taxi when he heard the distinctive rumble and roar of the Corvette's engine. With yet another bottle of champagne, Laura was laughing and still naked. "How did you ever – " he started to ask but she interrupted.

"It's been said that I think with my pussy. So, let's go back to Kelly's villa and you can screw my brains out. They're right here between my legs."

Once Kashan shut the passenger door, Laura jerkingly let out the clutch and the Corvette screeched away.

9

RIVIERA DRIVE

When they awoke in the morning, Laura looked haggard and ten years older than she had the night before. Years of liquor were starting to have a deteriorating effect on her body. Kashan could not help but think she did not have many good years left.

❧

At times, Laura Denton felt exhilarated about life and compassionate towards people. These moments did not happen often. At age four, she began playing the piano and took lessons in tap dancing. At age seven, she began riding horses. Just after turning thirteen, her parents enrolled her in finishing school in Boston. She was a cheerleader in high school and won a beauty contest at seventeen. When she was eighteen, her father raped her.

She tried to maintain a fake aura of nobility, and did well for a time in New York as a fashion model. Repeatedly showing up for assignments inebriated, her reputation gradually dwindled and she found herself drifting from city to city and then from state to state to find new work. Perhaps to appease his conscience, her father, a state representative, sent money on a regular basis. She had numerous affairs and lived with many men, her drinking in spite of her denial always being responsible for the inevitable unpleasant end.

The discovery of Los Angeles was a bright spot in her life. The supply of available males seemed unlimited and the perennial party atmosphere suited her well. But it was only a matter of time before she found herself driving south on the Coast Highway towards San Diego.

"Where's my tomato juice?" Laura asked. "Aren't there any servants in this joint?"

"Don't get overexcited," said Kashan.

"I need some tomato juice."

"You'll get it. Be patient."

"What a hangover."

Kashan put on a robe and slippers. He brushed back his hair with one hand, then stretched out both arms.

"What did we do last night?" Laura asked.

"We visited a mosque."

"You smart ass. When am I going to get that juice?"

"Just a minute."

Laura's hair was messed and her make-up had worn off showing lines at the corners of her eyes.

Kashan returned from the kitchen with two glasses full of ice and a large can. He poured the juice, added a small amount of salt and pepper and offered one to Laura. She took it and he sat on the edge of the bed.

"Where's your girlfriend this morning?" Laura needled without provocation.

The question caught Kashan by surprise. He did not answer, but gazed quizzically at her.

"What's the matter, flyboy? Don't you know?"

"It's none of your concern, Laura!"

"How the hell did you ever learn to fly an airplane? You're awfully damn stupid sometimes."

"You'd better stop."

"What about it? Flyboy? How about it, jet jock?"

"I'm warning you."

"Didn't you see how she looked at you, you dope? Don't you know anything about women?"

Kashan grabbed the covers and pulled them off, exposing Laura's naked body. He thought for a moment about dragging her out of the bed. Instead, he picked up her dress and flung it at her. "You're a trouble maker. You don't know what you're talking about. Get dressed and get out of here," he said icily. "What's your game, Laura? What's in those bottles you guzzle – liquid viciousness? Is whatever man you happen to run into on any particular day all you're after? That's why they call you a pussy, because you're owned and operated by a cunt."

Laura was astonished by Kashan's evident familiarity with the English language. She quickly recovered.

"That's why they call you a stud, because you're owned and operated by a prick," she shot back. "What makes you think that you are such a holy roller? You sure had a good time last night."

"Get out, heathen woman!" Kashan shouted.

"It's a terrible thing to waste a brain on a man," rifled back Laura. "You're not a bad fuck," she added as she headed for the door. "I've had better and I've had worse. You're really not a bad . . . "

10

BALBOA NAVAL HOSPITAL

No one paid much attention to the heavy-set old lady wearing a tan raincoat, buttoned up with a scarf pulled over her head. She carried a large armful of flowers – so many that her face was barely visible. Anyone noticing might have wondered why she was wearing dark glasses. She walked slowly, partly hunched over because she was so tall, partly dragging her feet covered with gray, scuffed tennis shoes on the tile floor. She stopped outside one particular room, looked up and down the hall, and went in. She swung the door behind her but did not close it completely.

A jet landing at Lindbergh Field momentarily blocked out all sounds in the hospital.

A bottle containing I.V. solution dangled from a stainless-steel stand and a plastic bag, half full of urine, hung from the side of the bed. A television set, perched high on the wall across, tilted down in such a steep angle that it looked as if it were going to plunge to the floor at any moment. The set was turned off and the room was bare of flowers and greeting cards or other signs of life from outside the hospital.

The patient lay quietly on the bed. A plastic tube carrying oxygen was taped to one nostril. A myriad of tangled wires went to the monitoring equipment on the table along the wall behind the bed. Digital displays flickered with periodically changing red and white and black numerals. A bright dot danced on a small screen and a recorder scratched a paper chart with a randomly fluctuating trace, never lifting its marker. One of the boxes emitted a just audible *beep* every few seconds.

The old lady stood more erect.

She waited for the pass of the next landing jet.

It took less than a minute to force a cyanide tablet into Chicken Bill's mouth. He made a small murmur in protest and tried feebly to lift his arms. In a few minutes the coating on the tablet would dissolve, Chicken Bill would never again drink tequila, smoke an American cigarette, or get a little nookie. His pillow was arranged neatly under his head and the plastic oxygen tube properly in his nose.

The old lady gathered up her flowers, hunched over slightly, and left, slowly shuffling down the hall in the direction from which she had come.

11

QOM

The large round mahogany table on the second floor of the mini-palace was set again with pencils and yellow tablets, water glasses, a pitcher and ash trays. In the way they had been during their last meeting, the slide projector sat on the table with the screen off to one side. Several boxes were stacked against the wall next to the screen. The same guard was stationed outside the door with his Uzi submachine gun.

Rajavi stood behind the table in his position of command and eyed his three aides as they entered. A tireless worker, Rajavi had gone over their dossiers in painstaking detail since the last meeting. He was more optimistic than he originally had been that they might be of value in helping formulate a plan which the ayatollahs would approve. Alam, Badri and Muluk certainly did not *look* like much, but their records were mildly impressive, especially those of Muluk who had developed contacts deep within the CIA and Mossad, the Israeli intelligence service. The professorial Alam was a specialist in matters of international oil cartels and banking. He had directed the assassination of two Saudi Arabian sheiks who had been pushing for a reduction in Iran's share of the world oil market. And, he had done a clean job. The career of the avuncular Badri primarily involved security matters within the military.

Rajavi did not waste time on greetings. As the last of them was seated, he abruptly began business.

"Gentlemen, I would first like to give you an update on the five pilots who have been dispersed to the United States. You may still be wondering why pilots were chosen. I can only say that I personally regard them to be the most versatile because of their flying skills. Versatility is what we need since the exact nature of their assignments hasn't yet been determined. In addition, I've always felt pilots are far above average in intelligence which is, of course, a necessary requisite for them to succeed in their difficult training.

"I must confess I had some concern when we last met that we'd be able to get our men past United States immigration and customs and into the country in the first place." There was a slight grin on Rajavi's face, but he would not let it develop into a complete smile. "Once again, the stupidity and soft-heartedness of the Americans has helped us greatly in our efforts.

"The first pilot chosen, Major Shaphur Azhai, turned out fortuitously to have joint Iranian-American citizenship. His father was an American businessman by the name of Collins and his mother the daughter of an Iranian millionaire who sold boots to the military. Major Azhai was born in South Carolina and educated through high school in the United States. His father died when he was five-years-old after which he was reared a devout Moslem by his mother and her brother. He attended the University of Teheran, earning a degree in economics, and joined the Iranian Air Force upon graduation. I have no doubt about his loyalty whatsoever. As a citizen, it was a simple matter for him to go back to the United States under the pretext of purchasing a shoe factory. He's gone to Pensacola, Florida, not far from Eglin Air Force Base where he spent over a year in helicopter training.

"Captain Ali Mossa, the second pilot, is a veteran of over four hundred combat missions against Iraq and was shot down twice. He has a doctorate in electrical engineering and, at one time, was a Professor of Electrical Engineering at the University of Teheran. Through its extensive network of American contacts, SAVAK agents located an Iranian engineering professor who has been teaching for twenty years at Rice University in Houston, Texas and has worked his way up to being chairman of his department. It was a simple matter to arrange for him to give a Visiting Professorship to Captain Mossa and to expedite all of the paperwork. Captain Mossa spent two years studying manned spacecraft at the Johnson Space Center just outside Houston.

"Our third man, Captain Farhad Kavtazi, is posing as an interpreter with our delegation to the United Nations in New York City. Captain Kavtazi has a distinguished combat record and was wounded recently in bombing raids over Baghdad. His wounds were not serious. It wasn't possible, in this one case, to get the pilot any closer to Andrews Air Force Base where he'd undergone training. Although SAVAK's efforts may be viewed as slightly less than successful, we must remember they were operating under extreme time pressures. Captain Kavtazi's strategic location in New York City far outweighs other considerations."

Rajavi paused and looked around the room as if expecting to see dissension on at least one of the faces. There being none, he went on.

"Strangely, as these things often are, our fourth pilot, Commander Omar al-Kashan, has perhaps the most valid reason for being in the United States. His cover, thanks to the cleverness of Major Muluk, was provided by the International Red Cross. Through suitable channels, the representatives of the Red Cross in Geneva were made aware that Iran has less than one-seventh the number of doctors per capita than most industrialized countries, and is badly in need of expanded medical facilities everywhere outside our major cities. With that groundwork, it was a simple matter to find sympathetic ears for our need to have a program based upon flying medical personnel to the outlying areas of Iran. Similar programs currently exist in Mexico, Australia, Africa and South America. Commander Kashan's father was a *mullah* and Kashan is one of our most experienced pilots. He is currently in San Diego near the Miramar Naval Air Station, the base at which he trained for almost two years.

"Getting our fifth man, Lieutenant Mohammed Kurdi, into the United States was a definite challenge and, I am most pleased to say, that SAVAK outdid itself in this case. Lieutenant Kurdi has been one of SAVAK's agents in the Air Force, under the supervision of Colonel Badri, and has served well as watchdog in some of the northern provinces. During that time, he cultivated agents of the Israeli Mossad under the pretext of becoming a double agent. He has convinced Mossad of his sincerity and they, in turn, have assured the CIA that he's decided to sell out Iran for money. After his *defection* to Israel, it was a simple matter for him to get an assignment in the United States. Lieutenant Kurdi is in Chicago which is nearby Glenview Naval Air Station where he spent eighteen months.

"All of the pilots were thoroughly briefed before leaving Iran. They've been given ample funds and each has been assigned appropriate SAVAK contacts in the United States. Emergency lines of communication have been established through our own Embassy in Mexico City, and, of course, through our delegation at the United Nations."

Rajavi paused and Muluk took the opportunity to ask a question. "General, our men seem to be well distributed throughout the United States with the exception of the northwestern part of the country. Are they – "

"Excellent observation Major," interrupted Rajavi. "That part of the country is sparsely populated and not considered as important as the other more established areas."

"Are any of the pilots married?" asked Badri.

Rajavi was taken aback by the insipidity of the question. Before he could respond, Alam broke in. "I've heard it said that pilots are sometimes irresponsible because they'd sooner go flying than do anything else. Also, it seems to me that they can be great risk takers."

Silence permeated the room. Rajavi was noticeably disappointed and could not hold back his feelings of animosity.

"Gentlemen, please do not ask such mundane questions or make such stupid comments," Rajavi said in an irritated tone. "As I told you already, *all* the pilots are unquestionably loyal. There's no concern about anything."

Badri lit a long cigarette. Coming on the heels of a stupid question, this further annoyed Rajavi, who did not smoke. *Some day, I'd like to break all of his fingers for smoking so much,* thought Rajavi. Alam also annoyed Rajavi by incessantly stroking his beard and Rajavi's mind went on, *after Badri's fingers, I'll break*

Alam's too. Glancing at Muluk, he thought, *He may be smart, but I'd still enjoy greasing his little bald head and sticking it up an elephant's . . .*

The white cloud caused by Badri lighting his cigarette diffused, but the acrid odor persisted. Looking at Badri, Rajavi continued, "Now, gentlemen, there's work for us to do which I expect will keep all of us quite busy. Each of us is going to engage in a program of self-education about America. We need to become experts and know more about the United States than ninety-nine percent of the American citizens. But, our knowledge is to be of a special nature. We need to know about communications, information dissemination, transportation, law, and history."

Rajavi pointed to the boxes on the floor against the wall next to the projector screen. "I've assembled a variety of information resources in these boxes. We'll each take one and study it day and night. Three days from today, we'll exchange boxes. In this way, the contents of the boxes will be known to each of us in twelve days. After that, we may continue to exchange boxes when exactly what information we need becomes clearer.

"One box contains three volumes of United States history and selected legal journals and Supreme Court rulings. The second is filled with travel brochures collected by our agents all over Europe. The brochures are, of course, about every conceivable part of the United States. Also in this box, are several *Almanacs* and *Statistical Abstracts* which give general information about the United States. The third box contains complete sets of aeronautical and navigation charts of the United States, Mexico and Canada along with all flying regulations published by the American FAA and all boating regulations published by the U.S. Coast Guard.

"The fourth box is, perhaps, one of the most interesting. It contains a dozen books dealing with security, intelligence and subversive activities within the United States and abroad. One of these is the book written by the CIA agent Kermit Roosevelt called *Countercoup* which deals with the CIA's role in the attempted overthrow of the Shah back in 1953. Another is the book *Counter Spy* which tells of CIA activities all over the world and has a chapter about those in Iran. Another was written by a former director of the FBI and is called *Masters of Deceit*. Books such as these should be helpful in giving us a view into the American mind – into the mind of the devious, the deceitful, the corrupt. These are the tools the American imperialists used to carve their greedy unfair share of the world's wealth, and it is in such tools that we must find a way to fight back and to defeat them."

Rajavi had let himself get carried away. He did not seem to notice that Alam, Badri and Muluk were quietly clapping as he spoke.

❧

The son of a peasant farmer, which he never completely forgot, Rajavi was born in a small village in eastern Iran. Almost as soon as he could walk, he began showing disrespect for all forms of authority. He often refused to play or eat or pray. Punishment made him increasingly rebellious. After mercilessly beating one of his teachers, he ran away when he was twelve and joined the army three years later. Driven and motivated by those early years of poverty, he read voraciously and, after a slow start, rose quickly in the enlisted ranks. He became an officer when his own commander was found shot in the back of the head. Just as Rajavi had planned, no one else had been immediately available to fill the vacancy.

When he was finally court-martialed for brutally killing another officer, his talents did not go unnoticed by a senior member of SAVAK. In lieu of a long prison term, he was soon directing weekly murders of the Shah's enemies. He also took full advantage of this unique position to eliminate a lot of his own personal foes or those who he perceived as standing in the way of his career advancement. How he survived the purge when Khomeini returned was a mystery.

12

BAJA

It had been a long time since Kelly had ridden in the passenger seat of a V-tail Bonanza. Kashan was one of the few he rarely let fly his airplane. "Airplanes are like cars," he commented somewhat pedantically to Kashan before they took off. "If you fly one, you can fly them all."

I know all that, Kashan thought to himself and fought to keep from laughing.

If Kashan had needed to practice being a bush pilot, this was the right place. There were hundreds of dirt runways in Baja. Most were short and not well maintained. Many were built for fishing or mining camps and fell into disuse once the camps were abandoned. These were potentially the most hazardous. Some were used regularly at bona fide settlements but, even on these, unseen dangers lurked- rocks, bumps, ruts and dips. Cows were common on runways near ranches and, in one case, a house had actually been constructed right in the middle of a runway after the local townsfolk decided they did not need the runway anymore. Only a dozen or so runways over the entire 700-mile length of Baja were paved.

They had left Montgomery Field after a leisurely breakfast, stopping first at Tijuana Airport to clear customs and immigration and to file a Mexican flight plan for their flight to Gonzaga Bay. Kelly selected the south end of Gonzaga Bay, a place called Punta Final, as their base. Here, Kelly knew of a sheltered cove, with good fishing, where they could camp. The National

Oceanic and Atmospheric Administration aviation chart for Baja showed twenty dirt runways within 100 miles of Punta Final and Kelly knew of a dozen or so more not on the chart. He planned to have Kashan land at all as well as on a few roads. An additional feature of Punta Final, besides its beautiful setting, was the availability of aviation fuel at Rancho Santa Ynez, twenty miles inland by air but a day's trip by jeep.

One hundred miles southeast of Tijuana, scattered farms composed the landscape of Ojos Negros and Valle Trinidad, broad valleys nestled between high mountains to the east and west. The heavy fog along the coast never appeared this far inland. Visibility was unlimited.

"This country looks a lot like Iran," said Kashan.

"Yeah. Baja is a lot more mountainous than most people think."

"That peak ahead's higher than we are."

"That's *Picachio del Diablo*, the Devil's Peak. It's over ten thousand feet high. We'll pass by just a few miles from it and the ground will be only a thousand feet above sea level. That's why we came this way. It's quite a sight to go right by the face. The mountains in Colorado might be higher but the ground there is a lot higher too. I don't know of any place there where there's a nine thousand foot fall in such a short distance."

When the peak was off their right wingtip, The Sea of Cortez was visible to the left. Kashan started descending. By the time they reached the coastline south of San Felipe, the Bonanza was down to 500 feet.

"We'll follow the coast down to Gonzaga and Punta Final," said Kelly. "Let's stay at this altitude so we can get a good look at the settlement at Puertocitos and at Islas Encantadas – the Enchanted Islands. One of them is called the Island of the Dead because the current goes around it in the wrong direction. The Spanish who named these were both superstitious and romantic."

I know where Puertocitos is popped into Kashan's head. Thoughts of Kelly and Jennie together began to irritate him.

Arriving at Punta Final, the wind was mild and off the water.

"The runway is short," said Kelly. "Make a nice long approach with full flaps. Take it easy and slow and you'll have no trouble. We don't need much more than a few hundred feet since the dirt causes a lot of drag on the tires. Keep the yoke all the way back until we stop rolling."

⁂

Several trips to the cove were necessary to unload their gear. The most important items they carried were two sleeping bags, two folding beach chairs, a large cooler, two fishing rods, personal clothing, and fifteen gallons of water. A mechanics tool kit and a survival kit were left on the plane.

Over the years, a dozen trailers had been brought into Punta Final over the treacherous road from Laguna Chapalla. All sitting to the north of the runway, they were used by Americans as weekend hide-a-ways. Kelly and Kashan were alone and odds were that no one else would show up this early in the week. The cove was situated to the south of the runway, well away from the trailers. A peninsula, which culminated in a forty-foot high sand dune, separated the cove from the rest of Punta Final. Some called the peninsula *The Island* because it was cut off from the mainland at high tide.

After making camp, Kelly and Kashan explored the beaches and fished. They caught three small groupers and one trigger fish for dinner, then bathed in the cove in the late afternoon sun.

Kelly seasoned the filleted fish with salt, pepper, rosemary and bay leaves and fried them in a small amount of peanut oil over an open fire of manzanita stumps. The white wine they drank with the fish warmed their bodies as the early evening breezes from the mountains began to cool down the cove.

A school of porpoises, fins bobbing in and out of the water, chased its evening meal of sierra into the bay. They did not seem to mind sharing the fish with pelicans who dive-bombed from thirty or forty feet into the water. The setting sun dragged down the last vestige of light to reveal a plethora of stars in the dark sky. Kelly and Kashan sat by the fire, watched and talked.

"This is a lovely place," said Kashan.

"It's my favorite in Baja."

"It's so peaceful."

"Right. No telephones, no television, no electricity and no people. That makes a good combination every once in a while."

Kelly added more stumps to the fire and more wine to their glasses. When Kelly wasn't looking, Kashan spilled most of his in the sand. They talked about old times and their flying experiences when Kashan was in training at Miramar and about mutual friends. Jennie's name never came up. Then the conversation turned to more serious matters.

"How's the war with Iraq going?" asked Kelly.

"Killing every day. It's a stalemate."

"How come you're not still in it?"

"I flew over a thousand missions. I was given the option of retirement even though good pilots are in demand." Kashan could not tell the truth, even to Kelly, and this sounded like a reasonable answer.

"How did such an ugly war get started?"

"It's a long story . . . Kelly . . . and goes back a long way."

"Well, I'm interested. And we do have the time."

"OK. I'll tell you. But, I have to say at the outset that I may say some unkind things about your government in the process – not anything hostile, mind you – but what I perceive to be the facts." Kashan looked directly into Kelly's eyes.

"Facts never bother me, Kashan, as well as any truth which follows from them."

"It's basically very simple. The war against Iraq is a holy war, a *jihad*. After people have been oppressed for centuries, they often turn to religion as an outlet. In this case, my peoples' hatred for the Shah and our desire for freedom led us to turn to our religious leader Khomeini. The holy war developed because no one could stop the inertia of the religious momentum."

"What's this about oppression for centuries?"

"The Shah was the last of a string of a hundred and thirty kings who ruled over Iran. He was one of the worst – a ruthless despot and a dictator. He ran the country with an iron hand for over thirty years. There were thousands of murders by his secret police, and the Shah and his family were notorious for corruption. Except for very brief periods, the people of Iran have never had free elections or democracy."

"I thought there was an elected parliament."

"Yes, but only one political party was permitted and the candidates had to be approved by the Shah. What kind of an election is that when there is only one candidate? Would you consider such an unfair system in the United States?"

"Of course not!"

"Do you know what the word *shah* means in English?"

"King, I think."

"That's right. And in 1967, the Shah decided to crown himself. He had a crown made of over three thousand jewels and crowned himself at a gala ceremony. He proclaimed himself to be *Shahinshah* which, of course, means King of Kings. He also crowned his wife as Queen and his son as Prince. He was a powerful egomaniac. He dictated that he wasn't to be criticized by the press and that his picture *must* appear on the front page of every newspaper every day."

"Every day?"

"That's right – every day – day in and day out, year in and year out."

"I don't think we would look kindly upon our president's picture appearing on the front page every day."

"It was well-known throughout the world that the Shah and his family were robbing Iran blind. Iranians were sick and tired of having a merciless, cruel, thief of a king forced upon them. They badly wanted democracy." Kashan was speaking with anger in his voice which must have carried a half mile in the clear crisp air. "The sad thing is the Shah was kept in power with the help of the CIA – that America was a partner to keeping Iran under suppression by a dictator – a partner to keeping democracy from Iran."

"Now, wait a minute Kashan. That's hard to believe. We want everybody to have democracy just like we do. But not everybody is ready for it. Why would the United States keep democracy from Iran? I thought our presidents encouraged the Shah for years to implement freer elections."

"It wasn't so much a conscious desire to keep democracy from Iran, but rather a desire to keep the Shah in power which had the same effect. The fact is that Iran is one of the most strategically located countries in the world, having a common border with Russia. Besides having vast oil deposits, the CIA regarded Iran as its looking glass to Russia during the cold war. The Shah gave the CIA what it wanted and so the CIA reciprocated and helped keep him in power by helping him run the country on a daily basis. It was a question of the security of America. To hell with the Iranian man on the street. America's security was placed before Iran's democracy. No one wanted to rock the boat and no one was sure what would happen if the Shah were thrown out. Expedience was more important than the freedom and equality of the people." Kashan had been maintaining his same feverish pitch.

"Relax, Kashan! There may be some truth in what you say, but don't forget that the United States went into Iran in the first place to help keep your country from getting overrun by the Commies. You might have become another Afghanistan, but twenty or thirty years earlier."

Kashan seemed to ignore this and kept going, "Every Ambassador to Iran for twenty-five years worked for the CIA. In 1973, Richard Helms quit his post as director of the CIA to become Ambassador to Iran. Now, tell me that those are just coincidences!"

"No, they aren't. Everybody knows the CIA supported the Shah. That's old news. But, while we were busy seeing to the security of America, we were also seeing to the security of Iran."

"You know as well as I do the United States has supported dictators all over the world when it was convenient to do so. There was Batista in Cuba and Marcos in the Philippines, just to name two."

"You're right. We have made some mistakes, but all governments make mistakes from time to time. Nobody is perfect."

"Anyway, the sentiment was that you and other foreigners who wanted Iran's oil were playing with us like a toy. We became tired of being humiliated by foreign interference. We wanted to rule our own country. We wanted democracy."

Kashan seemed to be cooling down. Kelly sensed it was time for a break and stood up. The waves gently sloshed up on the sand. The crackling of the fire was the only sound disrupting the quiet night. Kelly added more manzanita and stoked the coals with a stick. He poured another glass of wine and took the opportunity to stretch his legs. Kashan was content in front of the warm fire. Kashan waited until Kelly sat down before going on.

"The people wanted democracy *so* badly. Why wouldn't the United States help them?"

"Kashan, the United States can't go around the world and tell each country how to run its own internal affairs. You know that. You had a Shah when we first came on the scene. It wasn't up to us to throw him out. Our feelings were that a stable government of any sort was better than no government at all. We didn't know what the alternatives to the Shah were, if any. We didn't want total chaos in such a strategic place. If we pulled up and left, the Russians would surely have come in. We helped Iran arm itself and we helped train its armed forces so now your country is strong militarily. But, you weren't not that long ago. Didn't the Shah do some good things? Didn't he have programs going toward modernization of the country? Programs for making it more Westernized?"

"I suppose even the greedy tyrant did some good. But there was window dressing and facade also. There was so much money from oil that he saw it in his heart to do some good. But the real issue was the total absence of any attempt by him to involve the people in any form of representation. And, yes, the Shah wanted to make Iran more Western. He wanted, in particular, separation of church and state. This was his biggest mistake. In a Moslem country like Iran, there is no such thing as separation of church and state."

"What do you mean?"

"Islam is much, much more than just ceremony and prayer like Christianity. Islam tells its followers how to live life on a daily basis. The Koran specifies religion should order *every* aspect of society – man's relations with his fellow man and with the state, and the state's relations with other states."

"Judaism is a little like that."

"That's right, but there is no comparison – Islam is so much more so. In Moslem countries, for example, the mosque is sacred and is one institution government cannot reach. Sanctuary in the mosque is, by and large, respected by most governments. In the few times it wasn't, the governments had to deal with mass rioting. Furthermore, the ayatollahs are isolated from the government in Iran since they get their money directly from the people – one-fifth of each person's income. In fact, there is an old Persian saying about it being OK to cheat your tax collector but not your ayatollah."

Kelly laughed. It was about time for a little humor in their conversation. "I didn't realize the ayatollahs had such power."

"Yes. Under the Shah's repressive policies, the ayatollahs were really the only ones who had any way of speaking out against him. Khomeini did this often in sermons, which probably explains why he ultimately was exiled. But, Khomeini did more. He wrote a book called *Islamic Government* which discussed in clear terms things like imperialism, foreign exploitation and American influence. His book stressed hostility towards the United States. The introduction had a passage from the Koran which said something like, '*If kings enter a village, they will rape it and loot it and turn the villagers into slaves.*' So, you see, as the people turned more and more to religion, the Shah became more and more repulsive to them."

"So, this is about where Khomeini entered the picture."

"Sort of. He had been waging and planting his seeds of revolution for over twenty years."

"What do you think of Khomeini?"

"Iranians literally consider him to be a saint."

"You really mean that, don't you?"

Kashan's voice was now soft. "Absolutely. And when the saint spoke, the people listened. When you think about it, Khomeini did a remarkable thing. He overthrew the Shah, a formidable foe with a large army, without firing a shot. He believed the pen is mightier than the sword, and it worked. He was a patient man and it did take a long time, but it worked. He essentially persuaded the army to lay down its arms and side with him."

"How did he do that?"

"Modern communications technology. Khomeini sent weekly

cassettes from exile. These were reproduced underground by the tens of thousands and distributed all over Iran. Khomeini preached a passive revolution. '*Appeal to the soldiers hearts even if they fire upon you and kill you,*' he would say. And, '*It is your brothers and sisters who will receive your bullets, but they will be praying forgiveness for you,*' or '*You kill us but we forgive you.*' This was powerful medicine coming from a holy man and it sunk in with the people. Soldiers began deserting, a few at first, and then in larger and larger numbers. Being a soldier was not a very popular thing to do. Khomeini had no army – he had his cassette recorder instead of a gun. He used it to wage a successful revolution from thousands of miles away."

"So, that's how it happened."

"When Khomeini returned to Iran, he didn't need body guards. No one would hurt the man they regarded as a saint. The people shouted throughout the streets, '*The doors of Paradise have been opened again*'."

"We sure don't have that picture of him in the States."

"No, Khomeini was wrong in keeping the hostages so long. I'll admit that. As a result, American propaganda isolated Iran and made Khomeini look both ruthless and incompetent. But the facts are there and are really quite simple. The people hated the Shah. The people desperately wanted democracy. Their saint, Khomeini, preached freedom and the people followed. Hence, the revolution succeeded."

"You're damned right Khomeini shouldn't have kept the hostages so long. A week or two might have been enough. If he was so smart, why did he make ordinary Americans pay for the mistakes a few of their leaders might have made? Marcos was dumped in the Philippines, but the new regime is friendly with us."

"As I said, Khomeini made a mistake."

"So, that brings us to the last topic – the war with Iraq."

"There's really not too much to say. The Koran literally preaches that infidels should be destroyed. '*Strike off their heads, maim them in every limb,*' it says. Khomeini regarded the Iraqis as infidels because they practice a different form of Islam. They're Sunis and we're Shiites. Also, they're Arabs and we aren't.

There were some minor border disputes which set things off and before anyone knew it, a full-fledged war was in progress. Mohammed led armies in battle and, I suppose it's fair to say, Khomeini was looking for a chance to lead an army against infidels to satisfy his ego and fulfill what he perceived to be expected of him by the holy book."

"And in the process, he gets millions of people killed. He sounds like a fanatic to me. Are you sure that the Iranians are better off with the ayatollahs than they were with the Shah? Trading a dictator for a fanatic doesn't sound like a very good deal to me."

Kashan looked as if he were going to say something. Instead, he paused as if collecting his thoughts and finally said, "You're probably right."

They sat, both staring into the flames, for several minutes without exchanging a word. Finally, Kashan yawned and said, "It's been a long day. Why don't we turn in for the night?"

"Good idea," answered Kelly.

Kelly added more wood to the fire and the sleeping bags were set on each side of it.

Kashan laid for a long time looking at the stars and thinking. *That infidel Kelly. What does he know of Iran and its people? What does he know of kings and queens and what it's like to live under their rule? How dare he speak of our saint as a fanatic! Kelly's ignorant! I'd pray for him but I don't like him and he's not deserving of my prayers. He's one who has heard and has decided not to follow. There's no hope for him. He's doomed to eternal damnation. How can Kelly understand a jihad? It is important that we destroy as many infidels as we can. I wish I were there now helping my saint to destroy the infidels. I'm needed there but I also have an important mission here. I'm glad I'm here if that is where my saint wants me to be. I will serve my saint. I'll give my life to my saint. The life to come holds a much richer prize than the present life.*

Only a few feet away, Kelly lay looking up at the same stars. He was wondering why Kashan could not comprehend the fanaticism of the ayatollahs. *Could Kashan expect his country to go around the entire world and kill everybody who did not believe in Islam? Surely a well-educated man like Kashan could see the unreason-*

ableness of that! The sheer folly! Holy Wars were thousands of years out of date! We'll talk about it more around the fire and Kashan'll agree. Surely, he will . . .

⁂

They slept well and late. When they awoke, the fire was brought back to life and hot coffee brewed. Like a sheet of glass, the surface of the water reflected the sun's rays with a blinding brilliance. Gulls called back and forth with the morning's latest news.

Kelly planned spending the entire day at Punta Final, concentrating on short field takeoffs. Other strips would be visited during the remaining days and some business taken care of.

"When taking off on a short dirt strip, Kashan, you have to do a lot of things at once. It's important to minimize drag during the take-off roll. First, you pull all the way back on the yoke to take the weight off the nose wheel. After you start rolling, the nose wheel will come off the ground. Then you ease forward on the yoke and try to hold the nose wheel a few inches above the runway. Too much yoke and there's too much angle of attack and unwanted drag by the wings and airframe. Not enough and the nose wheel hits and digs a furrow like a plow. It's got to be just right. Then, after you're going about forty miles an hour, you want to put in twenty degrees of flaps. You don't want any flaps before you start rolling – this'll just be unwanted drag. So, you have to reach over and hold your hand on the flap switch and look out on the wing until you get twenty degrees. All this while you're concentrating on keeping the nose wheel off the ground and trying to keep the plane going straight down the runway. If you don't check the flaps, you run the risk of getting too much. You don't want more than twenty degrees. Sounds like there's a lot to do, but you'll get used to it.

"Remember, on a hot day, you'll need a lot more runway. Same is true from a high altitude field. Always check your density altitude. The airplane manuals have accurate performance charts and they don't lie." Then, remembering some comment that Kashan had made the previous night about cheating your ayatollah, Kelly added, "You can cheat the tax collector, but you can't cheat your Beechcraft manual."

Kashan laughed, sincerely for the first time since they left San Diego.

"Once you're airborne, get the gear and flaps *up* and put the nose *down* to pick up some airspeed. There was an old lady at a small airport in National City a long time ago who used to tell pilots in her squeaky voice,

When in trouble,
When in doubt,
Nose it down,
And fly it out!

Just remember that and you won't have any trouble."

The only trouble Kashan had was in keeping a straight face. He did so well, in fact, that Kelly could not suppress a fleeting impulse of suspicion.

After flying, they relaxed on the beach and spent a few hours going over flight manuals, concentrating on anything related to short fields, high altitudes and high temperatures.

⁂

Fish and wine were the main staples at dinner around the manzanita fire. They again talked well into the night. But, it was different. Kashan steered the conversation away from anything to do with Iran. He was eager to talk about world politics, but not when Iran was part of the discussion. He was willing to talk about religion, but shied away from Islam. Kashan asked many questions about the United States. He even seemed interested in football and baseball, which surprised Kelly. They also talked of history and philosophy. And, of course, they talked airplanes – a pilot's favorite subject – mostly about military aircraft and new advances in navigation equipment and weaponry. When they crawled into their sleeping bags, there were positive outward feelings between them. They were both exhausted from the long day and neither thought much about anything before falling asleep.

❧

Part of each day during the rest of the week was spent going from dirt strip to dirt strip until Kashan had mastered them all to Kelly's satisfaction. The rest of each day was taken up with fishing, swimming, long walks on the beach, and hikes into the canyons and foothills. A few times they landed at small settlements with restaurants – some with only one or two tables – and they would stay for lunch while Kelly conversed at great length with the local Mexicans in Spanish. Kashan did not like being left out of the conversation and showed his irritation visibly, but Kelly did not seem to care. He went on as if he were after some vital information. The evenings were all the same – dinner around the fire and talk of airplanes and moments shared in and around them. Neither seemed to tire of this routine.

One night before turning in, Kelly told Kashan he had an early *business* meeting in the morning, and suggested Kashan not bother getting up because it would just be boring. The Bonanza left at daybreak and returned four hours later.

Kashan did not know that Kelly had gone to visit a small Spanish orphanage. Nor that he had picked up some medicine.

While Kelly was gone, Kashan took the opportunity to pray, kneeling on a towel in the sand in the direction his best guess told him was toward Mecca.

The flight back to San Diego was uneventful.

13

SAN DIEGO

Jennie turned off Sea World Drive onto Ingraham Street. This would take her through Mission Bay Park and to Riviera Drive where she would turn left. She knew where she was headed. She was going to Kelly's villa while Kelly was out of town again "on business."

It was late Monday afternoon and had been over a week since the party at *The Ranch*. She had not seen nor heard from Kashan. Knowing he had been in Baja with Kelly did little to ease her burning desire to see him. Thinking back to the party, a feeling of disappointment came over her. It had been so awkward. All those bodies, the pawing at the women, the inane conversations, the crude and not-funny jokes.

Kashan yearned equally to see Jennie. Soon he would. But, it was necessary to first carry out several of Rajavi's instructions. One meant going to Baja with Kelly. Then there were several meetings later that day. He had to be cautious, being impatient now could well ruin his cover.

Jennie hoped Kashan would be alone at the villa. She had several minutes in which to invent some excuse for "dropping by." As she drove past, the yacht dealer at Dana Landing Marina was totally absorbed in washing down the hull of a slender 30-foot blue sailboat perched high on wooden horses in the parking lot. From the corner of her eye, she caught *MY SEXRETARY* lettered in script on the transom and a smile came to her face. In a minute, the Vacation Village resort on Vacation Isle loomed off to her left like a miniature city under a Christmas tree, carefully laid out on a green felt blanket. Instead of concocting plausible white lies, Jennie's thoughts drifted back more than seven years to the beach at Del Mar . . .

It was overcast in the early morning. Arm in arm, they walked along the beach just south of the main part of town. The apartment they shared was just off 5th Street on Stratford Court. Each morning they strolled the beach to have coffee at one of the restaurants near 14th Street. Signs of new erosion were visible every few hundred yards on the high sandstone cliffs which blocked out the sun. The tide had begun the first of its two daily journeys to the cliffs; soon the entire beach would disappear under the millions of gallons of salt water ushered in by the sea. The beach was desolate so early in the day.

Stopping, Kashan put his arms around Jennie's waist. "You are more beautiful each day, and I haven't told you yet this morning," he said.

"My beauty only reflects your love."

"Then I'll love you more and more. I love you now with all my heart and soul. I'll find a way to manage more."

"I'll love you always Kashan."

Jennie wore only a cotton sun dress without a bra and Kashan only a bathing suit and a red sweat shirt. A shocking contrast to their military uniforms, this was their informal garb. They were two jewels aptly disguised to fit into the beach community. They wanted to be unnoticed, to be ignored by the rest of humanity, to concentrate wholly on one another. While the world whirled by they stood barefoot in the sand.

"The war between Iran and Iraq can't last more than six months," said Kashan. "Probably just a few glorified training exercises and it'll be all over. Just a show of strength. I wouldn't take it seriously."

"But I'll worry about you."

"When I return, I'll interview with several airlines. Prospects are good for a job as copilot. That's how worried I am about the war."

"Darling, I know you can do it. I'll be so happy when you get back."

Kashan smiled, and every time he did Jennie wanted to kiss him. "It won't be more than six months."

"I worry about you every time you fly. If anything should happen to you, I would – "

"There's nothing to worry about."

"I love you so much that if you should die, I would want to die at the same instant – to go with you and share the next life – to go hand in hand."

"The only place we're going to go, Jennie, is on our honeymoon."

Jennie laughed. She reached down into the surf for a handful of salt-water and scooped it towards Kashan before she dashed off playfully down the beach. He ran after, dodging the debris and kelp left by the previous day's high tide . . .

The driver in the car behind Jennie beeped his horn several times. She had been sitting at the green light. She turned onto Riviera Drive and headed for the villa.

Kashan had not returned in six months, but had been gone more than seven years. At first there had been a few letters. She still cried when she thought of the last one telling of the hopelessness of the holy war – *'I love you dearest Jennie, love you so much that you must forget me and find another. The casualties are so high that I will surely be dead within a year. Forget me.'* Shortly thereafter, Jennie requested a transfer to Okinawa.

ꕤ

At the villa, Kashan was deeply in thought at the coffee table on the deck. A large umbrella hovering over him blocked the bright sunshine. A number of aircraft navigation maps were scattered on the glass table top surrounding his coffee cup. He found stacks and stacks of maps in the first cabinet in which he looked. One did not need to be a psychic to find maps in a pilot's home. He paid little attention to the activity before him on the bay, and was totally absorbed with a yellow pad of paper which stood out from the maps. On the pad were the two words he had written in large letters,

WHISKEY HOTEL

He did not want to write the words down, but some inner force drove him. In a minute he would burn the paper, but for the moment it might help clarify his thinking.

Going into the kitchen, he saw telephone hanging on the wall and a fleeting thought of calling Jennie struck him, but his mind was too preoccupied. He went back to the deck and picked up the yellow pad. *WHISKEY HOTEL*, he thought, *code-name for the operation. What operation? What kind of an operation? What'll I be expected to do?*

Kashan recalled the brief meeting two nights earlier.

When he arrived at the villa, they had been waiting in the shadows at the side of the house. Typically Iranian, both wore dark suits and had sallow faces and thick moustaches. One spoke in Farsi.

"We must talk."

"Who're you?" Kashan asked, also in Farsi.

"We're members of the *Brothers of Islam*. Remember, prayer is better than sleep in the morning."

'Remember, prayer is better than sleep in the morning' was the phrase he had been told to expect.

"Quickly, let's go in . . .

Inside, the meeting lasted only minutes. The *Brother* who spoke originally did most of the talking.

"General Rajavi sent us. You'll go to Tijuana next Tuesday, a week from tomorrow. Next to the Jai Alai Palace is a bar named *Tijuana Tillie's*. From there you'll be taken to meet a representative from the Iranian Embassy in Mexico City who'll give you further instructions. In the meantime, continue to familiarize yourself with flying in America. Study all the aircraft maps you can get. The code-name for this operation is *WHISKEY HOTEL*."

Kashan's thoughts vacillated between the party at *The Ranch*, Jennie, and now *WHISKEY HOTEL*. He was having a difficult time concentrating. He decided to let his mind get lost in the pile of maps. An avid pilot, Kelly had maps of the entire United States. There were three or four dozen Sectional Charts – the ones pilots usually use to fly by. In addition, there were Terminal Area Charts for every major metropolitan megalopolis. A complete set of Instrument Charts showed all the invisible highways in the sky. Another set of Instrument Approach Charts showed the delicate and intricate maneuvers necessary for making blind landings at over a thousand cities. There were military maps. To his surprise, there were many foreign maps also, maps of Europe and South America, maps of Iran, Iraq, Syria and Israel.

. . . Now, let's see. Iran is about the same size as Alaska . . . Iran's highest peak, Mt. Damarand, is just over 18,000 feet . . . Alaska's Mt. Whitney is just a little over 20,000 feet . . . that's interesting . . . Israel sure is a small country . . . poor, tiny Israel . . . Israel is only twice the size of Los Angeles County . . . we could fit about . . . hmmm, let's see . . . about seventy-five Israels into Iran . . . in a Bonanza, I could fly all the way across Israel in less than thirty minutes . . . Israel is but a light bulb in a sea of discontent . . . Colorado must be a beautiful place with all of its mountains . . . Kelly mentioned Colorado during our flight to Baja . . . the Appalachian Mountains are just foothills in comparison to the mountains in Colorado . . . I must go to Colorado with Jennie . . . I wonder how far it is from Chicago to New York City . . . hmmm, Mississippi, what an unusual name . . . that's a long river . . .

Footsteps coming up the stairs to the deck distracted Kashan. He looked over the railing to see Jennie's dark hair and thin frame covered in a brightly-colored dress. A small purse dangled from one shoulder and bobbed up and down like a ping-pong ball as she bounced up the steps. Even from this odd angle, he could see the sensuous movements of her body. Just before the top step, some feeling compelled her to stop.

Their eyes met.

No words were spoken.

As Jennie continued, Kashan stepped around the railing. Before she knew what was happening, they were in each other's arms. Finally, she caught herself and said, "No, Kashan. This isn't right."

Kashan had had no intention of saying them but the words popped out. "I love you Princess."

Jennie did not respond.

Kelly and Francisco Diaz met in Kelly's hangar at Montgomery Field. This was about as safe a place as any to talk since the hangar was made entirely of corrugated metal and had no windows. Anyone approaching could be seen for a great distance through the wide double doors. There was not much activity at the airport on a Monday morning. Most of the aircraft owners were at work endeavoring to earn enough to pay for their expensive hobby – they only had the luxury of playing with their winged toys on weekends.

In coveralls, Kelly was busy changing the Bonanza's spark plugs. The Bonanza sat majestically and dominated the hangar. She was all white with blue trim on the leading edges and tips of the wing and along the fuselage. Several gold stripes hinted at a machine fit for royalty. Her registration number N77BK was neatly lettered on the fuselage near the blue rudder just below a small painted American flag.

Francisco Diaz pretended to be helping Kelly and they conversed in subdued voices with their heads close together. Every now and then, Francisco Diaz would walk to the hangar doors and look left and right and up into the sky as if to be evaluating the weather.

"That fiasco in Arizona, Pachuco. It's not over yet. I've got a call in to back East," began Kelly.

"The next time I'll shoot the fucker," answered Francisco Diaz.

"No way, Pachuco. Let's get serious. You know I'll never be a part to murder. The next time you even think of pulling a stunt like that, I'll kick your ass from here to Mexico City."

"OK . . . OK . . . Since the medicine deal looks dead, maybe we should get involved with real dope."

"No! That's not for me. You know me better than that. It's repulsive to me – especially when I think of all the poor kids who end up using the junk. I don't buy the argument that if we don't do it someone else will. I had the same feelings when flying in Vietnam. I pushed a button or pulled a lever and bullets flew or bombs dropped. By the time the crap hit, my jet was miles away. Being a fighter pilot is sweet and clean. You never see the blood and guts and havoc wreaked by your guns. While the poor bastards are writhing in agony, you're miles away sailing through the clouds."

"The medicine deal was sure sweet and clean."

Kelly took a new spark plug from its box and checked the gap with a feeler gauge. While he did, Francisco Diaz looked outside the hangar. He walked back in, picked up a socket wrench, and went on. "Maybe we should start running guns. There's a good market for 'em in Mexico. The government is hyper about guns. Always has been after all the revolutions – "

"No! I don't go for that either. Listen to this though. Here's an idea. I've got a banker friend in L.A. who tells me that he and Mexican bankers are always interested in sending large amounts of cash back and forth across the border. And certain kinds of securities. With the dough, it's legal to take ten grand in or out, but no more unless it's declared to customs. Working with the banker could be almost as sweet and clean as the medicine deal. It's just a thought."

"Yeah, but I'll bet a lot of that dough comes from dope or other things like guns."

"Not necessarily. Bankers don't want to get involved with junkie types or gun runners. There are a lot of wealthy people who have lots of reasons for wanting to take cash in or out. We'll be dealing directly with the banker and will take it for granted that he's legit. Sometimes big business deals need to be closed quickly without the delays caused by red tape. Besides, half the foreign governments in the world are crooked anyway."

Kelly held up a spark plug he had just removed and examined it closely in the sunlight coming in through the hangar doors. This was the only maintenance he personally did on the Bonanza. *It's like a man having six hearts,* he once told Francisco Diaz, *and being able to take them out one at a time and look them over. Everything about the condition of an engine can be told from the spark plugs. Too bad God didn't give us six hearts with each one screwed in with a three-quarter inch wrench.*

"On second thought, even though the banker deal sounds good, I'm not going to go for it. Just because other people are crooked, doesn't mean we have to be. We'll just have to be patient," said Kelly.

Kelly took another new plug from the bench.

"Was out at your place at *The Ranch* a couple of days ago, and a wetback pulling weeds across the way told me a couple of guys been snooping around. He said they was dark like Mexicans but didn't speak Spanish. He said they looked like some kind of foreigners because of their clothes."

"That's all?"

"Most of these *peons* don't have much education, but they do see a lot of television all over Mexico – a lot of American stuff – and he says these guys looked like foreigners – that's all. But, he was sure they weren't Latinos. He sure as hell woulda known if they were chinks. And, definitely they weren't black. What's that leave?"

"How about European?"

"Naw. He said they had thick moustaches."

"Maybe they were Iranians – some friends of Kashan looking for him?"

"If they was friends, they wouldn't a been snoopin' around."

"Are you sure they were snooping?"

"Yeah. Wetbacks do a lot of snoopin' – they would know when somebody else is doin' it."

"Better keep your eyes and ears open," Kelly said with determination in his voice. Kelly thought back to Baja and the fleeting suspicions aroused by Kashan's expertise with short runways. He could not help but wonder what Kashan's real reason was for being in the United States.

"I don't like this Kelly," Diaz added.

"Neither do I, Pachuco."

Kelly looked absently puzzled and said no more. Francisco Diaz went outside the hangar to look around. When he returned, Kelly was closing the cowling of the Bonanza.

Kelly wiped his hands with a red rag. "Pachuco, I need to go to a meeting in L.A.," he said. "We'll worry about the Iranians, if that's what they were, later."

"It's been such a long time," said Jennie. "You'll never know the suffering and agony I went through. How despondent I was when I realized I'd probably never see you again. I had such high hopes back then. You were my entire world. I don't completely understand why I came. All I know is I had to see you."

"It was difficult for me too, Jennie. I didn't enjoy fighting the war against Iraq. But, my country needed me. Try to understand."

"I think I understand, but there's a difference between understanding and accepting. The mind can't always control the heart."

Kashan decided not to tell Jennie how insanely jealous he felt towards Kelly. Or that there had been numerous women in Iran during the war. Attracted to beautiful women, pilots seldom spent evenings alone. The fact that she had come gave him reason to think their relationship was not totally over. He decided to take a chance.

"Why can't we put all that behind us? I'm back now. We can make new plans. I can still get a job with the airlines, just like before. It doesn't have to be any different."

Am I hearing him correctly? thought Jennie. *How can he expect me to forget the past seven years?*

"Things *are* different, though," said Jennie. "I remember reading something once which has always stuck with me, something about how one can glue the pieces of a broken cup back together, but never get rid of the cracks."

"If we love one another, we don't have to care about those things. You've continued to be my whole world. I've thought of you each day for the past seven years. You're not like Iranian women. They exist only to serve their men, are told what to do and obey. You're fiery and impulsive. You're different. That's what I've always loved about you."

There is something distinctly different about him, she thought. *Maybe I should not have come. He has changed. He was never so patronizing.*

"Kashan, if we had gotten married, what would your family have said about me? How would they have accepted a woman who didn't fit their stereotype of an obedient slave?"

"If we had stayed here, it wouldn't have mattered."

"Yes, but would you have expected me to go back to Iran with you at some point? What would have happened then? I know that women in Iran aren't even allowed to drive cars. What about your religion? Would you have expected me to convert to Islam? By your actions, you made it clear that your concern for your country was, and probably still is, more important than an abstract idea like love. I still care a lot for you, but it can never be the same as it was seven years ago."

"Those are tough questions, Jennie. We can still work everything out. Just give me a chance."

"No, Kashan. There is something that can't be worked out."

"Everything can be worked out."

"That's what you say. But, I'd wager that you'll probably go back to Iran again."

"Maybe just one more time. For a short while."

"That's what you said seven years ago."

"Things are different now, Jennie. Everything can be worked out," Kashan repeated.

"No. It can't!" Jennie said emphatically. "Right or wrong, you let your duty to your country destroy what we once had. I don't hate you but I can never rekindle those old feelings. Maybe I never quite fully realized it until now how much Kelly is an important part of my life and I'm very much in love with him."

They did not come as a total surprise. Still, her words hit like a hammer. He decided it would be best to back off. Maybe he was being too hasty.

"You're going to think this crazy, but I've got a great idea. Let's spend an hour or so at the beach, for old time's sake, just like we did when we lived in Del Mar," said Kashan. "It's a beautiful day for a swim. There are lots of things I want to tell you about."

Old friends are still friends, Jennie thought. *Moslems especially are noted for it. They have high standards of friendship. Why not? We've gotten over the hard part. It's been a long time since I've seen him and it would be pleasant to visit for a while.*

Jennie changed into a bathing suit she kept at the villa. Kashan looked through several drawers before finding a pair of shorts and one of Kelly's sweat shirts. She went out to the deck to wait while he put them on.

"Looks like you're planning a trip. I've never seen so many maps on one tabletop," said Jennie.

"I was just playing with these maps killing some time. He picked up a handful. Now I've got something much better to do."

Jennie looked inquisitively at Kashan. "What's this on the yellow pad, Kashan? It sounds strange."

Kashan had forgotten all about the yellow pad and the words *WHISKEY HOTEL*. He did not know what to say. Momentarily ignoring the question, he glanced at one of the maps he held. He was groping for an answer. Finally, he found one. "Oh that! It's the name of a horse racing on a European track. A friend called and suggested I bet on it."

Jennie was not sure she believed him.

He gently took the yellow pad from her hand, tore off the first sheet and crumpled it in his fist, and then threw it through the doorway towards the fireplace. The yellow ball fell short of its intended target, landing on the floor. Nonchalantly, he added, "That's that. It's of no consequence."

Kashan began to worry.

It wasn't like him to be evasive. There *was* something distinctively different about Kashan. Perhaps he was more cynical than she had remembered. She could not quite put her finger on it. If he loved her as he claimed, there was no reason to go back to Iran. He had done that once before and not come back as he had said he would. Besides, she knew Kashan wasn't a gambler. Her thoughts went to Kelly.

They took a blanket and towels and went down the stairs to the beach.

Laura stepped out from the doorway behind the kitchen holding a bottle of champagne by the neck. The bottle was uncorked and she drank from it. She leaned against the door jamb to steady herself, humming all the while, looking around the room.

Aloud, she said to herself, "Before, it was just a wild stab in the dark – an educated guess – woman's intuition. Now I know for sure! Tell Kelly? No! Have a much better idea – much better."

Laura stumbled from room to room, stopping in each to look around and sip from her friendly companion. In the bedroom, her eyes eagerly searched before finding Jennie's lingerie on the unmade bed. She reached down and picked up Jennie's bra. After setting the champagne bottle on the dresser, she took an end of the brassiere in each hand and stretched it out. Again she spoke aloud, "Not bad for a Navy nurse bitch." She threw the bra back on the bed and took another swig from the bottle. Suddenly, she became furious and kicked the mattress. "I'll show that bitch. Laura didn't just get off a pumpkin truck. By hook or by crook, Kashan hasn't seen the end of Laura Denton." Then she grinned.

Laura danced out of the bedroom and into the living room with new vigor. She saw the yellow ball lying on the floor and almost stepped over it. At the last second, she bent down and picked it up. Without looking at it, she put it into her purse.

⁂

By the time Jennie and Kashan came back to the villa, it was beginning to get dark and the spring air was cool. Kashan had his arm around her shoulder to keep her warm. They did indeed have a pleasant visit together.

Jennie went to the bedroom to change. They talked through the door while she added fresh lipstick and combed her hair.

"Jennie, I need to go to a meeting in Tijuana in a couple of days. Why don't you come along? You can shop while I'm busy. Kelly's still gone. Why not get away for a day? I remember that you liked to shop there. I don't know my way around anymore. You'll be a big help. Please go with me."

At first she declined, but he was insistent. Reluctantly she agreed. He was right. She did enjoy shopping in Tijuana and hadn't been there for some time.

After walking her to her car, he stood and watched while the tail-lights disappeared.

Back in the villa, Kashan looked on the floor and what he had expected to find was not there. For an hour, he searched the room, moving each piece of furniture. Then, systematically, he went through the rest of the house.

14

OCEAN BEACH

"Give it to her, Johnny! Atta boy!" yelled Francisco Diaz.

Johnny, an obese black man whose belly contained all of the extra sixty pounds of fat his body could tolerate, was on the bed with Laura. Francisco Diaz roared with laughter and filled the shot glass with tequila from the jug on the floor. He stumbled over to the bed, squeezed several drops from a lime segment into Laura's awaiting mouth, and poured down the golden liquid. Laura swallowed and screamed, *"Chinga, chinga!"*

They were in a cheap, sleazy motel in San Diego's Ocean Beach community on the Pacific Ocean waterfront. Johnny and Francisco Diaz planned to lunch at the restaurant on the Ocean Beach Fishing Pier to discuss a possible marijuana deal. Even though Kelly was not interested, Johnny was highly recommended by friends in Los Angeles. Most of the time, Diaz did as he was told. But, since the medicine deal was in limbo, he might need to make some quick dough on his own without Kelly knowing about it. They were in the right place. Ocean Beach had the reputation of being the home of San Diego's derelicts, and the acknowledged center for anything and everything illegal. The vast majority of an evening's police calls came from Ocean Beach. Before they had a chance to discuss business, they came across Laura, drunk as usual.

Francisco Diaz poured himself another shot and downed it without the lime. Opening Laura's purse, he took out a packet of the white powder he had given her earlier. Gingerly, his large fingers tapped its contents onto the underside of a glass ashtray and, with the blade of his pocketknife, divided it into four equal parts – as equal as any drunk was capable of ascertaining. He sniffed one part of the cocaine with a cut-off straw. His nostrils and sinuses burned with excruciating pain, and he thought his brain was going to explode. Then supreme ecstasy overcame the masochistic torture and his whole body basked in glory.

Johnny got up. Laura still wore her Bonwitt-Teller pearly shift though it was hunched around her breasts. Her hair was messed and there was a far-off glassy, trance-like look in her eyes. She smiled, giggled and laughed repeatedly.

"Coke break," announced Francisco Diaz.

"Get that damn dress off," shouted Johnny as he lumbered over to the table, picked up the ashtray in his fat hands, and snorted one of the three remaining piles. Laura followed Johnny. He passed her the straw and ashtray and she consumed her pile without saying a word and without grimacing. Licking her index finger, she took up the fourth pile with the moist appendage and rubbed it inside her vagina.

Laura went back to the bed and started to slip the dress over her shoulders but, before she could get it off, Francisco Diaz tore at it with a massive jerk and threw it into a corner. The unexpected force caused Laura to wobble slightly, she giggled as her upper body swayed from side to side.

Doped up and drunk, Johnny and Francisco Diaz lay on the bed. Laura strode to the table like a Russian duchess, took a sip from the bottle, and fumbled in her purse for another packet.

"What a couple of flukes," said Laura. "Haven't you got any more friends you can call? We need some rocket experts in here. More men with more missiles ready to be launched."

"Whatcha doin'?" asked Johnny.

Laura began to sing with a slur, "A tootin', a drinkin' and a tootin' . . . a tootin', a drinkin' and a tootin' . . . " She laughed and giggled.

"Shut up," yelled Francisco Diaz as he sat up.

Laura ignored him and kept humming and singing, A tootin' a drinkin' and . . . " She dug into her purse and her handkerchief, compact and lipstick fell out and onto the floor. Reaching down to pick them up, she could not quite make them out but found the bottle instead.

Johnny saw her drinking. "Gimmie dat jug."

"Me too," said Francisco Diaz.

Laura took another swig, then passed the bottle to Johnny. "A tootin', a drinkin' and a fuckin' . . . , " she continued with a happy gaze.

Francisco Diaz sidled over to the table. On the way, he purposely kicked the compact and it went flying against the wall shattering its mirror. Doubting that anything could possibly be funnier, Laura giggled again.

"Where's the white shit?" stammered Francisco Diaz.

Johnny grabbed Laura's purse, dumping its contents onto the table. In the middle was a ball of yellow paper.

"What's dat?" asked Francisco Diaz.

"A tootin', a fuckin' and a tootin' . . . , " sang Laura. "I'm in heaven and I'm not even dead."

"What's dis ting?" wondered Francisco Diaz, as only a drunk can wonder, a vapid look on his face.

"It's nuttin," sang Laura, "a drinkin', a fuckin' –"

"Nuttin's gotta be sumptin," shouted Francisco Diaz.

"It's a wee wee seckert," said Laura coyly, "Sumptin I found at Kelly's villa."

Even though he was drunk, the mention of Kelly's name caught Francisco Diaz by surprise, his eyes blinked and he feigned interest, not knowing why, not fully comprehending what he was hearing.

Because of his uncoordinated movements, it was difficult for him to unwad the ball. With his head rocking back and forth, he slowly read the words, "Whi . . . Whis . . . Whiskey . . . Ho . . . Hot . . . Hotel. What's dis?"

Instead of answering, Laura continued humming and bent down for the bottle again. When the back side of Francisco Diaz's hand caught her on the side of the face, she fell back against the bed. Standing over her, he asked again, "What's dis bitch? What about Kelly?"

Seemingly unfazed by the blow, she got up. She rather liked it and felt herself getting wet between her legs. She said, "Let's ferget nuttin and screw summore. It's only a stoopid piece of paper. Let's screw."

Yes, it was completely logical to Francisco Diaz's drunken brain. Why worry about a stupid piece of paper? Better to screw than worry about a stupid piece of paper.

The two men followed Laura as she dove back onto the bed. Before going, Francisco Diaz crumpled up the yellow paper and threw it back on the table.

When Francisco Diaz awoke, his head was on fire. Laura was sitting at the table toying with the remaining contents of her purse. She slowly moved her comb an inch or so to the left with one thumb and her keys slightly to the right with the other, then picked up a bobby pin and flicked it into the air. Before picking up another bobby pin, she sipped from the half-filled cup of tequila.

The sparkling morning sun beamed in through the windows, forcing Francisco Diaz to shield his eyes.

Seeing him awaken, Laura started with her ditty again, "A drinkin', a tootin' and a drinkin' . . . "

Dizzy from a screaming headache, Francisco Diaz rubbed his eyes, saw Laura, and then the yellow ball still on the table in front of her. She inched her comb to the left and took another drink.

Francisco Diaz rubbed his eyes several more times and thought, *Wow, what the hell am I doin' here? I was goin' to arrange a deal with Johnny without Kelly knowin' and here I am all screwed up. Kelly's goin' to be pissed if he finds out.* He got up and rinsed his face in the bathroom sink. His senses began returning and he decided to take a shower. After letting cold water run in his face for twenty minutes, he stepped out to find Laura and Johnny entangled on the bed.

About to leave, the yellow ball caught his eye. Picking it up, he opened it, read *WHISKEY HOTEL*, and vaguely remembered something about seeing the paper the previous night, about the mention of Kelly's villa.

Walking over to the bed, Francisco Diaz bent over and grabbed Laura by the hair. She did not seem to notice, but Johnny did.

"Get outta here, you dumb spick," growled Johnny disagreeably.

"Laura, what's this?" insisted Francisco Diaz.

"I said out, grease ball," repeated Johnny.

Standing erect, Francisco Diaz let go of Laura's hair with one hand and grabbed Johnny's with the other. Johnny's head snapped when Francisco Diaz jerked it backwards. Staring at the ceiling, eyes agape, his penis fell out of Laura. Francisco Diaz struck with his other fist and caught Johnny just below the eye. Johnny fell off the bed, onto the floor, moaning. The yellow paper fell by the side of the bed.

Going back to Laura, Francisco Diaz slapped her lightly several times.

"What's that yellow paper about, you drunken whore? You *puta*, you *panocha!*"

"Just sumptin I found at the villa," snickered Laura. "I think . . . no . . . wait a moment . . . I don't think . . . I know . . . I know that Kashan has been humpin' Jennie. I was there."

Francisco Diaz was irritated by Laura's comment. "That can't be," he said, "Kelly's girl wouldn't two-time him."

"You wanna bet?" said Laura. "Kashan's humpin' Jennie . . . Kashan's humpin' Jennie . . . " she sang.

Jesus Maria, thought Diaz, *this cunt's been snoopin' around Kelly's villa. What's goin' on? Better tell Kelly. Kelly's gonna be pissed. He's gonna be pissed at me for talkin' to Johnny. He's gonna be pissed at me.*

Francisco Diaz slapped Laura one more time, not gently, and was gone. In his hurry, he forgot to take the yellow paper.

⁂

As he drove away from the villa, Francisco Diaz's thinking was still fuzzy. The cold shower helped, but he needed a few more hours of sleep and some hot coffee. He was not used to the cocaine. Mixing it with the tequila had been dynamite to his body. He felt better after driving around for an hour, but even then could not focus his thoughts on any one thing for too long. He was sure that the previous night had actually happened because he felt so bad. Much of it had a dreamlike quality when he tried to remember specific details. In order to clear his head, he forced himself to think of other things.

. . . now, let's see, what did Momma want? Oh yes, some green chilies and peppers from Hernandez's. Better get those right away. Better tell Momma that I was with Kelly last night. Momma understands. Momma is so beautiful. Momma loves me and Momma loves the hot tamales that I bring home. I love Momma. I had better remember to tell Momma that I love her. Momma loves me. I'm gonna get Momma a nice birthday present this year. Maybe I should take Momma to Ensenada for dinner. Momma and I should go on a vacation. I sure do love Momma. Tonight, Momma and I are gonna . . .

As his mind cleared, Francisco Diaz forgot about having seen any yellow piece of paper or what was on it. He forgot about Johnny and Laura.

15

TIJUANA

"Hey, meestor, you wanna girl?"

The young Mexican pimp was ignored by the tall American dressed in Levis, a loosely-fitting San Diego Charger football jersey bearing a large number "14" on the front and back, and a New York Yankee baseball cap. Undaunted, the Mexican went on with his sales hype. "Hey meestor, hey *amigo,* you wanna fuck my seestor? She is reel virjean. No? OK. You wanna screw my brudder? What you want? I got for you what you want. Cheep. Very cleen." The American continued to disregard the Mexican, but the pimp followed a few steps behind. "I got taxee right here, meestor." Unbeknownst to the American, the Mexican had a master's degree in business administration from UCLA, drove a new Buick sedan, lived on a lavish ranchero just outside Tijuana, and spoke perfect English whenever he chose.

Nothing much has changed in Tijuana, thought Kashan who took in the monologue as he walked past the crowded street corner on Avenida Revolución. As he passed the Mexican, he heard him mutter under his breath, "Cheap son-of-a-bitch."

Dirty busses with cracked windshields and muddy tires jockeyed with pedestrians and dent-riddled taxicabs on the busy main thoroughfare. The noisy vehicles competed with music blaring at full volume from shops selling records, tapes and audio cassettes of drunken Mariachi bands. Kashan passed sidewalk stands offering green chilies, candy, jewelry, sunglasses, raw coffee beans, watermelons, cooked corn on the cob, and fresh papaya and mango juices. He walked by kiosks selling girlie magazines and newspapers and others hawking lottery tickets. People and children were everywhere.

Aggressive and enthusiastic mayors had, in recent years, pushed through numerous projects giving Tijuana the appearance of a facelift. But, it was still the filthiest, toughest, and raunchiest border town along the Mexico-United States border. It was *el culo del mundo* – the asshole of the world. Pimping, fornicating and stripping continued to be its greatest talents.

Kashan strode briskly along the busy avenue. Ahead in the distance he could see the imposing *Jai Alai Palace*. If the building had had at least one or two graceful domes, it could have been a mosque in Iran. Most shops on the main street stocked the same junk which tourists bought by the boxcar – irrefutable evidence to prove they had been brave enough to set foot in a foreign country. Salesmen coaxed pedestrians inside to view real-leather jackets, purses and wallets, silver belt buckles, oil paintings on velvet, an infinite variety of trinkets, chalk statues, onyx bookends and chess sets, cheap watches and jewelry, and large selections of switch-blade knives. An Indian woman, with a baby strapped on her back, sat on the sidewalk selling Juicy-Fruit gum. The baby's sister played nearby with a tattered rag doll.

Kashan left Jennie at one of the few exquisite jewelry stores in Tijuana. If one knew where to go, Tijuana offered some of the finest bargains in certain quality items, rivaling Hong Kong and Rome.

Taking Jennie with him to Tijuana had not been an easy decision. In the end, he felt he'd be less conspicuous crossing the border with her at his side.

Two hours earlier, they had boarded the *Tijuana Trolley* – the red streetcar that runs the fifteen miles from downtown San Diego to San Ysidro on the old Santa Fe Railroad tracks. It was a last-minute choice, a precaution against being followed, but Jennie was unaware of his concern. They walked across the border at San Ysidro and took a Mexican taxi to downtown Tijuana.

When he arrived at *Tijuana Tillie's*, Kashan went directly to the bar. Before he could order, he was greeted by the same *Brother of Islam* who had given him instructions that night at the villa. The *Brother* nodded and Kashan followed out the side door and into an awaiting Chevrolet badly in need of body work and new paint. The other Iranian who had been at the villa sat behind the wheel. Kashan got into the back seat and the two *Brothers* rode in the front.

They drove in silence through the rutted and unpaved back streets, gradually ascending into the Tijuana foothills. Periodically, the driver spoke into what appeared to be a *TELEX* aircraft microphone, but Kashan could not make out what he was saying.

The road dead-ended to an enormous fifteen-foot archway over iron gates with welded bars. This seemed to be the only opening in a ten-foot high wall which vanished into the distance on each side. The wall was barely discernible through bushes and eucalyptus trees planted along its length. The gates swung open and closed as the Chevrolet sped through without stopping.

A dozen Doberman pinschers sat and lay idly along the roadway. Their steely eyes followed every movement of the automobile as it traversed the winding roadway and came to a stop under the portico of a large Spanish manor. It was unlikely that these well-trained, muscular creatures were Mexican dogs. Probably they came from the United States. Armed guards stood on each side of the heavy door with massive hinges dominating the front of the building.

The entry had been paved in Spanish tile and was lit by a majestic chandelier. Kashan was led down a plushly carpeted, arched corridor adorned with bulky Spanish tables and paintings depicting legendary Mexican heroes. The corridor gave way to a cavernous living room furnished with heavy wood and leather chairs. Except for a floor to ceiling bookcase, lavish paintings covered the walls. Antiques and cast sculptures covered the tabletops. A great adobe fireplace kept vigil on the bookcase across from it.

Three men sat about a huge rectangular conference table. The one standing, obviously in charge, had a large stone-like head and was dressed in an Iranian officer's uniform with a full chest of ribbons. Although the two had never met, Kashan recognized him immediately as General Rajavi. Kashan stopped just inside the doorway, the *Brothers of Islam* right behind.

"Welcome, Commander Kashan. I hope your short drive wasn't too mysterious," greeted Rajavi.

Kashan snapped to attention and saluted.

"No need for that," said Rajavi. "Please sit down," he commanded politely.

Still speechless, Kashan took the vacant chair next to Rajavi.

"You're obviously surprised to see me since you weren't forewarned I'd be here. My presence is, I assure you, essential to convey the importance of this operation to you."

"I'm honored to meet you General. Indeed, it's I who am flattered that you would journey half-way around the world to see me."

Rajavi remained standing, leaving no doubt as to who was in charge.

"Don't be flattered, but rather honored your country has selected you to carry out such an important mission."

Rajavi motioned to the *Brothers of Islam* and they left the room, going back down the long corridor. When they were out of earshot, Rajavi continued. "Gentlemen, I present to you Commander Omar al-Kashan. Commander Kashan, I present Colonel Alam . . . Major Muluk . . . and Colonel Badri." Each nodded to Kashan as his name was spoken; handshakes did not seem to be called for and no one made any motion to get up.

"Commander, as you know, *WHISKEY HOTEL* is a very secret project, said Rajavi. "You might be surprised to hear that, aside from some of the ayatollahs, only the five of us in this room will ever know its exact details."

Rajavi's serious mien made Kashan recollect his own stupidity in writing down the name on a piece of paper. He fought showing his uneasiness, resisting an impulse to wipe his brow or drink from the glass of ice water in front of him. Hours of training as a pilot had taught him to not overreact at the onset of an unusual situation. No one had the slightest inclination of the disquiet in his mind.

"All of us are well acquainted with your dossier. We know of your accomplishments as a pilot and your outstanding war record. We know of your devotion to Islam and to Iran. Isn't that right, Commander?"

"Yes, General." Kashan was firm, did not hesitate. "I do love my country and my saint, the Ayatollah, and will do whatever I can to better serve them."

"With your life, if necessary?" asked Muluk before Rajavi had a chance to speak.

"Nothing would bring greater honor to me and to my family," said Kashan. As soon as the words were out, thoughts of Jennie flashed through his mind. He could not help but wonder if he had spoken the truth. As he spoke, he looked directly into Rajavi's eyes.

Rajavi returned the stare, but remained otherwise impassive. "Before we go further, I'd like to ask Commander Kashan to give us a complete briefing about his current stay in the United States. Commander, take all the time you need. You've our undivided attention."

Kashan sat back and tried to relax. Looking around the table, he started relating all events beginning with his flight from Mexico City to Punta Estrella. Then the flight to the private airport fifty miles east of San Diego during which he flew at tree-top level while crossing the U.S.-Mexican border. He described being met by the car and turning the airplane over to the other pilot. In detail, he went over the party in Rancho Santa Fe trying to remember all the people with whom he had spoken. He covered his one week flying in Baja with Kelly and his later flights to various places in the Western part of the United States. He told of Kelly's suspicious dealings with the Mexicans, described the villa on Riviera Drive, and about his meeting with the *Brothers of Islam*.

He didn't tell them everything.

He omitted the confrontation at Punta Estrella with Chicken Bill and the two murders. He did not recount how he had read about Chicken Bill in the newspaper and his subsequent visit to Balboa Naval Hospital to kill him. There was no mention of his flight over Mt. Soledad with Laura. Nor any mention of Jennie or the damned yellow piece of paper. Nearly an hour had passed before he finished.

"Thank you," said Rajavi. "Any questions?"

Muluk edged nervously in his seat. After an extended moment of silence, he spoke in a low voice, "A fine report . . . Commander . . . but . . . why haven't you mentioned the girl? . . . Jennie Ross . . . the girl who's currently awaiting your return . . . at the restaurant in downtown Tijuana."

Kashan was startled.

There was ample reason to omit Jennie. He didn't want them to think he was being frivolous in the midst of an important assignment. They probably wouldn't understand. If they had the slightest inclination he wanted Jennie again and told her he would leave the Iranian Air Force, he and his family would be disgraced. He would face that later.

"She's nothing to me," Kashan quickly lied. He was able to convincingly and with composure.

"Then . . . why . . . why didn't you mention her in your report?" needled Muluk. When Kashan didn't answer immediately, Muluk repeated tenaciously, "Why?"

Looking directly at Muluk, Kashan smiled confidently. "Are Iranian pilots to be denied some of the more pleasurable proclivities of the present life? By the way . . . Major . . . do you ever indulge?"

All eyes turned to Muluk. Alam and Badri laughed at Muluk's expense. Muluk's embarrassment showed in his flushed face.

The ploy had worked.

"I think," interjected Rajavi, "That we needn't further pursue the erotic adventures of our esteemed and very human Commander." Rajavi knew from SAVAK reports that no woman had ever come between Kashan and his duty. But none of them knew of Kashan's earlier involvement with Jennie seven years ago.

"Commander, the exact nature of *WHISKEY HOTEL* is highly secret and you won't be given the details until the appropriate moment." Rajavi failed to add that the specific details had not been fully worked out, but did not want to convey an impression of inadequacy. Instead, he continued with steadfast confidence.

"During the first week of May, on the morning of May 2nd, you'll take a commercial jet from San Diego to Chicago. When your flight lands at O'Hare, you'll be met and taken to a small airport, Meigs Field, which sits in the city center on Lake Michigan. There, at Butler Aviation, will be another Bonanza, like the one you flew up from Mexico City and like the one your devious friend . . . Kelly . . . has been gracious enough to let you fly."

"Kelly's not my friend," interrupted Kashan. "He's an unbeliever."

"Nevertheless . . . with a new engine and new radios, the airplane will be in perfect condition. Further instructions will be given then. If there are any changes in these plans, you'll be contacted by the *Brothers of Islam*."

It seemed foolish they had come all the way to Tijuana just to tell him to go to Chicago. Anyone could have done that. Perhaps their real reason for coming was to personally look him over more carefully. Yes, that must be why.

"I understand," said Kashan, "I'll be ready."

"Good, Commander. Then you can go back to your lovely Jennie." Rajavi almost smiled. Looking in the direction of Muluk, he added, "Civilized Iranians do not keep ladies waiting."

When Kashan got outside, the *Brothers of Islam* were already inside the old Chevy. They drove back downtown, again following a circuitous route.

✈

They silently watched Kashan leave through the corridor. Badri lit his first cigarette since before the meeting.

Rajavi looked around the table. "Gentlemen, you've now met all five pilots and heard a briefing from each. Is there any discussion?"

"I'm concerned about the woman," stammered Muluk. "Have we researched her and their relationship thoroughly enough?"

"Don't be a fool," said Badri, "I'd be concerned if Kashan masturbated every night or took up with young boys."

"But . . . ," started Muluk and then paused. "Shouldn't we pick someone who's, pardon the expression, more fanatical? We need a man who –"

Muluk was cut off by Rajavi. "Enough! I'm satisfied. Kashan is our man."

Kashan waved to Jennie as he got out of a taxi in front of *Caesar's Restaurant.* She sat at one of the outdoor tables. Before sitting down, he kissed her on the cheek.

Jennie seemed radiant and happy. Over a light meal of salad and white wine, she told Kashan about the dress she had found at Tolan's, showed him the gold earrings from Espinosa's, and put a drop of the Joy perfume from *Farmacía Internacional* on her wrist for him to savor.

"How was your meeting with the Mexican Health Authorities?"

"Just fine. Their problems in providing medical services aren't too different from those in Iran. Only Iran's so much bigger than Baja. I'd say, on balance, that our meeting was informative and productive."

"Will you be flying to some of their clinics?"

"Not any more. Kelly took me to some."

The mention of Kelly's name took Jennie by surprise. Kelly had been spending most of every week away from San Diego. She knew it was impossible to love two men at the same time. She could never forget that Kashan had left her once before.

"Do you like Kelly," asked Jennie.

"Sure I do. He's a terrific pilot."

"But . . . I mean as a person."

"Certainly," lied Kashan.

"I'm glad."

After leaving the restaurant, they took a taxi to the border. Kashan had no trouble with American immigration. His forged California's driver's license was convincing. He also carried an altered birth certificate showing he had been born in Los Angeles, but did not need it. The customs official doted over Jennie, almost forgetting to collect duty on her purchases.

A *Tijuana Trolley* was parked in the terminal where it had

pulled in to reverse. They got on and sat down waiting for its departure.

Reflecting back to their earlier conversation, Kashan commented: "Kelly's a very unusual pilot."

"Why's that," asked Jennie.

"When we were in Baja, he insisted I make a landing at the most difficult strip I've ever landed at."

"Which one?"

"A place not on the charts . . . a place called Punta Estrella. He said he goes there all the time," Kashan lied.

Jennie was bewildered.

Kashan felt smug with his clever execution of precision in human endeavor.

All she could think of during the trolley ride back to San Diego was the poor Mexican and the bullet hole in his head.

16

RIVIERA DRIVE

It was not possible for Kashan to get all the flying time he wanted in Kelly's Bonanza because Kelly was away so often. To get around this, Kashan rented a similar Bonanza from Western Sun Aviation at Montgomery Field. Money was no object, but he preferred to fly Kelly's airplane to be less conspicuous. He flew several times a week with the chief flight instructor exclusively doing instrument training. Although Kashan was thoroughly familiar with blind flying, he was unfamiliar with the many specific types of instrument procedures used daily in the United States. When alone, he usually chose a different airport within a day's range and made an instrument landing even in fair weather. Occasionally, he ventured away for several days at a time. He became totally familiar with Air Traffic Control and FAA regulations. When over the desert, he could not resist putting the Bonanza through a series of loops, rolls and spins. Although the Bonanza did not have an inverted fuel system, he would fly upside down anyway until the engine quit. Then, he would let her fall into a gentle spin and restart the engine before two turns had been completed. In one landing at Los Angeles International, the control tower radioed that a jet was following and asked Kashan to keep his airspeed above 180 knots. Over the freeway, he pulled back on the yoke until the nose was at a 45-degree angle to slow down, dropped the gear to add additional drag, and put in full flaps to just barely stop before the end of the two-mile long runway. Every time he flew, he learned something new about the Bonanza.

In the evenings, when not flying, he studied navigation maps and charts and plotted countless make-believe flights, always from Chicago's Meigs Field to other destinations. He memorized airport altitudes, instrument approach fixes, communications and navigation radio frequencies and missed approach procedures. He read everything he could find about weather at various parts of the country during different times of the year.

When Kashan was not flying or studying, he pursued a vigorous physical training program, running for miles along the beach. At times, his own ambivalence troubled him. He was not the same person he had been seven years ago. Neither was Jennie. Jennie would make a good wife, but then, maybe an Iranian woman would make a better one. There was always the family to think of. Maybe he was only kidding himself about Jennie. He reluctantly convinced himself that she was important to him, but, *WHISKEY HOTEL* was more important.

The month of May was rapidly approaching and there had been no contact from the *Brothers of Islam*. Although no contact had been explicitly mentioned by Rajavi, Kashan expected to see them again. They were his only link with Iran and Rajavi, and hearing from them would have eased his impatience. The lack of communication was making him anxious.

Jennie fought an inner emotional battle every day. Although it did not show outwardly, whenever she was alone, she could not help but think of her dilemma with Kashan and Kelly. She did not want to confront Kelly about Punta Estrella. There was always that slight chance there was a logical explanation. Maybe she was making a big thing out of nothing. She had no reason to mistrust Kelly – other than his denial of regularly going to Punta Estrella. Maybe Kashan mixed Punta Estrella up with some other place. A lot of those Spanish names did sound similar and perhaps even more so to an Iranian.

❦

That morning, Kashan made an especially strenuous flight to Santa Monica. When he left, Montgomery Field was socked-in with fog from clouds hovering at ground level. Taking off, he could barely make out the white line down the center of the runway. Surrounded by white mist for over an hour, he broke out to see the twin towers of the Beverly Wilshire Hotel on final approach to Santa Monica Airport. The return flight was easy because the sun had burned off the early morning overcast, but the overall flight left him fatigued.

Back at the villa around noon, Kashan laid on the couch in the living room to rest. Closing his eyes, he dosed into a relaxing sleep with pleasant thoughts of Jennie.

Laura shook his arm. "Is the sheik taking a cat nap?" she asked as if talking to a small child.

Kashan opened his eyes. He knew he was no longer dreaming when he saw Laura's blonde hair. "Laura, what are you doing here?" he asked in a groggy voice.

"Mommy's here to take care of you, baby."

"Go away."

He did not get up. He did not look directly at her. He had not seen her since the morning after their flight over Mt. Soledad and remembered only their unpleasant conversation.

"Want a little drinkee?"

Laura set the two glasses on an end table and half-filled them from a bottle of Dom Pérignon. She sat on the edge of the couch, her body touching Kashan's. He rubbed his eyes.

"No, I don't want a little drinkee. Go away please." His tone was firm but not harsh.

"Where should I go?" Laura was continuing her playful act.

"I don't care. Just go away."

"Do you want me to tell Kelly a little secret?"

"Do whatever you want."

"A little secret about you and the princess?"

"What?"

"You know what I'm talking about."

Kashan was now wide awake, aware Laura's playfulness was taking on a sinister note. She remained sitting, bending over him with her arms around his waist.

"No. I don't"

"Yes, you do."

Laura strutted around the room, humming to herself and smiling wryly. She waved her head from side to side and her hair waved back and forth in unison with the rest of her body. Kashan did not say anything, but sat up with a perplexed look on his face.

Laura went on, playful again, "I know something that –"

"What is it? What are you talking about?"

"Don't you remember?"

"Remember what?"

"Remember you are *fucking* Jennie. Was she so lousy you've already forgotten?"

"That's nonsense." There was strength in Kashan's voice.

"It may be nonsense. It is *non-sense.* It sure as hell isn't common *sense.*"

"You can't be serious."

"Yes, damned serious."

Laura sat on the couch.

"What do you want, Laura?"

"Laura doesn't want anything . . . Laura just wants to take care of the sleeping baby boy."

"I'm not asleep anymore."

"That's even better."

"Go away, Laura, and leave me alone."

"OK. I'll tell Kelly."

"Tell him what? He'll never believe anything you say."

"Oh, I don't know," Laura teased, "Maybe that I found Jennie's panties and bra in your bed last week and . . . "

Kashan suddenly became angry, angry with himself, with Laura, and with Rajavi. He blamed himself for being in this vulnerable position. He wished he were back flying his F-4 over the blue waters of the Persian Gulf. Laura sat smugly, hinting at wiggling her breasts towards Kashan. As always, she was impeccably dressed with an alluring feminine smell about her.

Laura continued, " . . . and maybe I was here at the villa last week . . . and maybe, just maybe I saw you and Jennie . . . and –"

"You're making something out of nothing."

"Maybe I am . . . maybe I ain't . . . it all depends."

Kashan tried to maintain his dignity but was visibly disturbed. He picked up the glass of champagne, thought about drinking it, and set it back down.

"Why you're starting to come around," said Laura. "You're not such a bad guy after all."

"Be reasonable, Laura."

"I am."

"What do you want?"

"We'll see." Now Laura was sportive. She cupped Kashan's face in her hands and kissed him lightly on the cheek.

His mind was in a thousand places. He tried to think clearly, but everything was muddled. He wondered what his options were. *WHISKEY HOTEL* flashed through his mind and he remembered the meeting in Tijuana and Muluk's insinuations. He was to do whatever necessary for the operation. Having no other choice did not keep him from being infuriated.

"You're a slut, Laura."

"Oh yes," she laughed, "But didn't you know? . . . Sluts have more fun! Good girls go to heaven but sluts go *everywhere!* Do you want to take Laura to heaven?"

"Not especially."

"But, you might, right?" It was more a statement of fact than a question.

"I'm not interested."

"But, you might make an exception. Right?"

"No . . . possibly . . . I might . . . I –"

"Kelly will kill you if he finds out."

"Finds out what?"

"Ha . . . ha, ha, ha . . . ho, ho, ho," she howled back and forth in laughter.

"It's not like you think –"

"Laura doesn't think anything, sweetie. Laura *knows!*" I didn't tell you to go and dip your wand into Snow White."

Kashan had no desire to face a confrontation with Kelly over stupid lies. He felt it was necessary to placate Laura in some way.

"Let's talk this over."

"Sure. I've got lots of time."

Kashan thought of the yellow paper and wondered if Laura found it. Maybe Laura saw the *Brothers of Islam* at the villa too. Maybe Laura knew more than she was saying. He would have to proceed carefully to find out. He picked up the bottle of Dom Pérignon and refilled Laura's glass.

"Do you want money, Laura?"

Laura became enraged and slapped Kashan's face. "Hell no! I may be a slut, but don't you dare ever think that you can buy me off. I'm not a whore."

"I'm sorry, I didn't mean it that way."

"We'll see."

Her rage passed as quickly as it had come. She kissed Kashan again on the cheek. He was not totally cooperative, but less reluctant than earlier. She rubbed her hand on his leg and on his chest.

Laura kissed Kashan behind his ear and whispered, "I want you, right here."

"Well . . . I . . . I need to ask you something first."

"You want to know if I'm an Arabian princess? Well, I'll be goddamned."

Kashan saw no humor in Laura's attempt at wit. He could not afford to make another mistake. Laura was certainly no fool and was in the driver's seat – at least temporarily. He had to play along to find out her intentions. Getting up from the couch, he poured her another glass of champagne.

Kashan looked back at Laura and carefully chose his words. "I had some . . . some notes . . . a piece of paper that was here in the villa that day . . . did you by chance . . . by chance pick it up?"

The question caught Laura by surprise. *So, there is more to it than just Kashan and Jennie sleeping together. Kashan wants something. Notes? What notes? Could he be thinking of that yellow ball of paper? Now, let me see. I did find it here that night in front of the fireplace. That's right. I did. Maybe it is something important. It has to be important if he wants it. What did I do with it? Damn, I can't remember. I had it at the motel with Johnny and the Taco. I must have put it back in my purse.*

Kashan could see Laura's mind clicking away like an old adding machine. Maybe he was too direct in asking the question. Maybe he should have taken her to bed first. Her answer did not surprise him.

"I might have."

"Did you, dammit?"

"Maybe I did."

"Tell me!" Kashan was becoming impatient.

"OK, so I did."

"Where is it now."

"I've got it."

"Please give it back."

"In a bit."

"Now!"

"In a bit, I said."

"In my country, men have authority over women. It says so in our holy book, the Koran."

"We're not in your country now, sweetie."

"But –"

Kashan lost his composure and groped for words. Laura's self confidence seemed to grow in proportion to his loss. She cunningly noted his movements. He was not standing as tall as he could and his voice was wavering. It was time.

In one quick coordinated motion, Laura picked up her skirt and pulled her panties down around her ankles, sat on the edge of the couch and spread her legs.

"If you want the notes," she said smugly, "Then show me how much!"

Momentarily, Kashan was astonished It did not take him long to realize she was serious. What could he do? He wanted the goddamn piece of paper. He could not afford to jeopardize *WHISKEY HOTEL* over a dumb blonde. Maybe Muluk was right. Maybe he wasn't the right man for the operation. He should have been more careful. He must do whatever necessary to correct his blunder.

Slowly, he got up and, slowly, he knelt down before her.

Laura leaned back on the couch and closed her eyes.

"Do a good job, camel fucker," she said quietly.

Then she remembered throwing the yellow ball out her car window going over one of the bridges in Mission Bay.

17

LA JOLLA CANYON

The *Baja Vagabundo* cut effortlessly through the rolling swells of the cold Pacific. A quarter moon cast enough light so that the shore line was just perceptible. A biting breeze chilled the air with dampness, and scattered low clouds covered the entire California coastline. There were no other craft out on the ocean at this late hour. Occasional lights in houses along the coast were the only signs of life in the otherwise dark abyss. Kelly ran the *Baja Vagabundo* on one of the two Volvo engines and it purred almost silently. The only sounds came from the sloshing of the black water against the hull. A mile off shore, the *Baja Vagabundo* cruised without navigation lights. She had left Mission Bay twenty minutes earlier and would soon be abreast of La Jolla Cove. The fifteen story condominium on Coast Boulevard in downtown La Jolla stood out like the Empire State Building.

Less than a half mile from the coastline, there were two deep ocean canyons which originated in La Jolla Cove. Scripps Canyon started about 900 yards north of the pier at the Scripps Institute of Oceanography, and La Jolla Canyon a little further south of the pier. Both canyons dropped off steeply to depths in excess of 500 feet. Two miles off shore, the single canyon formed by the juncture of the two went down more than 1000 feet. This was a perfect place to dispose of a body.

The lights at the end of the Scripps Pier were visible starboard and a little ahead of the *Baja Vagabundo* as Kelly cut the engine. He checked the Raytheon depth finder and the reading was off scale indicating the bottom was more than 600 feet down. They were somewhere over La Jolla Canyon.

"We're here, Pachuco," shouted Kelly towards the back of the boat.

Gagged and bound, the *Brothers of Islam* sat on the deck of the aft stateroom.

A smile came across Francisco Diaz's face and he replied, "Hot doggie!"

Earlier that afternoon, Francisco Diaz was called by one of the Mexican *peons* working across from Kelly's estate in Rancho Santa Fe. When the wetback previously saw the two foreigners snooping around, Francisco Diaz wisely gave him a twenty-dollar bill, his home telephone number, and the promise of a second twenty for information about any other suspicious activity near Kelly's house. The investment paid off. The *peon* saw the same two foreigners he had told Francisco Diaz about earlier, and they were back at the estate.

A lucky phone call found Kelly at his hangar, which he sometimes used as an office. They agreed to meet right away at Quimby's Restaurant in the Rancho Santa Fe Village. From there, they took one of the old horse trails and slowly made their way on foot to the estate, keeping hidden in the rolling sage of the canyons and the eucalyptus trees. Kelly helped Francisco Diaz up the six-foot adobe wall surrounding his property and then scaled the wall himself with ease. When in view of the house, they could see the *Brothers of Islam* peeking into the windows.

"I'll kill both a the fuckers," whispered Francisco Diaz.

"No, Pachuco! We don't kill! Let's find out what they're up to," answered Kelly.

Preoccupied with sketching the floor plan of Kelly's house, the *Brothers of Islam* did not hear Kelly and Francisco Diaz come up from behind. Each of the *Brothers* was in his mid-thirties, had a full head of deep black hair which went far down the back of the neck, and each wore the same dark-blue pin-striped suit. There was no struggle when Kelly and Francisco Diaz stuck the barrels of their .38's into the *Brothers'* backs.

Francisco Diaz attempted to persuade the *Brothers* to talk with a fair amount of punching and kicking, but they answered none of Kelly's questions. They had bloody noses and cuts above their eyes. The *Brothers* reacted to all questions with amazement and incredulity. They were either good actors or did not know anything, but that did not dissuade Francisco Diaz in his zealousness. The Iranians carried no forms of identification, although their wallets were stuffed with fifty-dollar bills. They were unarmed. From their clothes, Kelly could tell they were upper class and, by the way they spoke, that they were college educated. Drying blood was beginning to cake on their black moustaches and white shirts.

Kelly relaxed in the living room reading a newspaper while Francisco Diaz continued the interrogation in the family room. After he finished the paper, he went to the refrigerator for two bottles of beer. He took a sip out of one and gave the other to Francisco Diaz who was sweating profusely.

"Looks like they're not going to say anything," said Kelly.

"We don't know anything," said one of the *Brothers*.

"You mother . . . ," started Francisco Diaz.

"Wait a minute, Pachuco," interrupted Kelly. "There's no sense in banging them around anymore. I've got a better idea."

"What's that," asked Francisco Diaz.

"Let's take these two for a boat ride. Maybe they'll be a little more friendly and talk to us on the *Baja Vagabundo*. Let's get them into the back of my pickup. I've got four sacks of concrete in the garage. Get them and put 'em into the truck with a couple of large buckets. There are some plastic ones out there. Tie these two to the bed of the truck and put some carpet over them."

⁂

The pickup pulled up to the villa just after dark. Kelly drove into the garage and Francisco Diaz quickly closed the garage door. They took the *Brothers* in through the villa, down the stairs to the pier and onto the *Baja Vagabundo*. Kelly was thankful Kashan had taken the Bonanza on a practice cross-country flight to Albuquerque and would not be back until the next day.

As soon as they boarded, Francisco Diaz began mixing the quick-setting cement. At gun point, each *Brother* carried a bag from the truck. Kelly carried one and made a second trip to the truck for the fourth. Each bucket was large enough to accommodate both feet of the Iranians as well as two 90-pound sacks of concrete.

Holding their heads high, the *Brothers* endeavored to maintain arrogance. When they attempted to speak to one another in Farsi, Francisco Diaz slapped them.

Francisco Diaz sat with his gun pointed at the *Brothers* while Kelly drove the boat from the lower station.

The gun was hardly necessary since the *Brothers'* hands were tied behind their backs. The concrete was setting around their feet and the men were virtually immobile. The gun felt good in Francisco Diaz's hand and he enjoyed holding it. He enjoyed more having something to point it at. The gun represented potency and force, but he would have preferred a knife.

Kelly turned off the engine and joined the others on the rear deck.

"Well, I suppose we ought to get them into the water, Pachuco," said Kelly.

"Sure nobody'll find them out here? Like maybe a diver?" asked Francisco Diaz.

"Not likely. Most SCUBA diving is done to depths much less than a hundred feet. Even Navy divers rarely ever go below three hundred."

The *Brothers of Islam* watched Kelly intently as he spoke, and Kelly let his eyes go from them to Francisco Diaz and back as if holding a conversation with all three. The *Brothers* were still gagged.

"Why not?" asked Francisco Diaz.

"For several reasons. First, it takes a hell of a lot of air. Two hours worth at the surface lasts less than fifteen minutes when you're down two hundred feet. And that doesn't even take into account the air needed to go down and back up. Then, there's the risk of the bends and the need to decompress while coming back up."

"That must take extra air too," commented Francisco Diaz.

"That's right. And the longer a diver stays below, the longer it takes for him to decompress. For real deep dives, the Navy uses special mixtures of gasses which the ordinary diver can't even get."

"Did you dive in the Navy?"

"No, but I knew a number of guys who did. The biggest problem at greater depths, aside from the cold, is that visibility is poor – it's only a couple of feet or so down three hundred feet."

"So, if we're gonna send these turkeys down six hundred feet, somebody'd have to be rubbing pricks with them before they would ever see them."

"Yeah. But don't worry for a moment. There won't be any other humans down that deep. Only saltwater, cold fish, and whale shit."

The *Brothers* listened with wide open eyes, they scarcely blinked. They did not know that Kelly and Francisco Diaz had rehearsed a very similar conversation earlier in the cab of the truck.

"Are there any sharks out here?" asked Francisco Diaz.

"You bet!" Kelly lied. Sharks were seldom seen in the La Jolla Cove except maybe once or twice a year during the summer months.

"So, maybe they'll be ripped in half before they drown."

"There's a good chance of that."

Francisco Diaz undid the gags and the *Brothers* gasped the fresh air, sucking in mouthfuls and exhaling.

"Are you motherfuckers ready to talk now?" asked Francisco Diaz.

"We don't know anything," said one.

"What're you guys dealin' in?" asked Diaz, "Diamonds? Are you spies? Who do you work for?"

"We've told you that we don't know anything. Please believe us."

"We'll make you a deal," said Kelly. "You tell us what we want to know and we'll let you go. That's a promise."

"We don't know anything. Don't kill us. We've got wives and children."

"Who do you work for?" asked Kelly.

Neither *Brother* was ready or eager to talk.

"Have it your way. Die now and avoid getting bumped off later," said Francisco Diaz.

"We're wasting our time," said Kelly. "Let's get them into the water. We'll show them we're not bluffing."

With two ropes tied around each *Brothers'* chest, they were lowered feet first into the water. It took both Kelly and Francisco Diaz to manipulate their bodies and concrete-bucket covered feet over the side. One set of ropes was tied to a cleat about half way between the bow and stern of the *Baja Vagabundo*. Francisco Diaz held the other two ropes. The Iranians were at the side of the boat and enough tension was maintained in the ropes to keep their heads well above the water. The water was cold and they immediately began shivering. Kelly held a flashlight and shined it on the two heads, side by side in the water, close enough to the rear deck that conversation was possible in normal voice.

It did not take long for the *Brothers* to become more responsive.

"If we t-tell you who we w-work for, you p-promise to l-let us go?"

"That's what I said," answered Kelly. "You tell us that and a little more."

The *Brothers* were shaking and their voices quivering. One or the other began talking rapidly in the hope of a quick end to their ordeal.

"We are w-with the *B-brothers of Islam*."

"What's that?" asked Kelly.

"A Moslem s-sect. W-with connections t-to Iran."

Kelly pondered this for a moment. "So . . . I see . . . so you guys really aren't into smuggling. But . . . obviously . . . then there must be some connection between you and Kashan?"

"It's very co-cold in this w-water. We were t-told to watch h-him. We d-don't know anym-m-more. Please b-believe us."

"You sure exaggerate watching Kashan when you were snooping around my place." *So . . . there is something deeper in Kashan's visit to the States than some phony medical program. That's pretty clever. I take my hat off to him . . . leading me around by the nose and me supposedly teaching him how to fly my airplane,* mused Kelly "Why is he here?"

"Honest, w-we d-don't know. That's the t-truth."

"Bullshit, you must know more," said Francisco Diaz.

"Please . . . p-please don't k-kill us. All we k-know is that there's s-some sort of op-operation in progress . . . w-with the c-code n-name *WHI-WHISKEY HO-HOTEL*."

The mention of *WHISKEY HOTEL* startled Francisco Diaz and he abruptly remembered the yellow piece of paper in the motel room with Johnny and Laura. He became excited and spoke rapidly in a loud voice, "Kelly! . . . my god! . . . Kelly! . . . Sometin' funny is goin' on! . . . I saw them! I saw them! . . . I saw those words! I saw those words *WHISKEY HOTEL!* I saw them written on a piece of paper! Jesus Christ! *Jesus Maria*! I saw them!"

Instinctively, Kelly spun around to face Francisco Diaz. The flashlight in his hand automatically followed his body motion and he inadvertently shined the light in Francisco Diaz's eyes, momentarily blinding him. "What?" he asked with incredulity.

"Yeah. I saw them and forgot to tell you! Jesus Christ! God-damn! I'm sorry! Jesus Christ! I forgot!"

"What the hell –" started Kelly. He put his hand to his fore-head and rubbed his chin. Too much was happening too quickly. It all started when Kashan showed up. Now the mention of Kashan's name. What the hell was Kashan up to? Was the Iranian government planning some covert acts against the United States? Kelly felt uneasy. He sure as hell did not want to get involved in any way with clandestine government matters. The FBI and the CIA would be all over his ass. He wouldn't be able to say "twat" without them asking how to spell it. They would be watching his every move and start asking too many questions. Once the Pentagon got wind, everybody would be running scared. He had to know more.

Kelly whispered to Francisco Diaz so the Iranians could not

hear, "This is serious, Pachuco."

Francisco Diaz did not know what to say. He remained silent.

Kelly turned the light back on the two heads in the water. He spoke in a calm and businesslike tone. "Alright. We're going to quit playing games. Just tell us the rest and we'll haul you out. And that's a promise."

"Honest t-to Allah, that's a-all we know," said one of the *Brothers*.

"Please b-believe us . . . p-please!" pleaded the other.

Kelly turned again to Francisco Diaz. "What do you think, Pachuco? Do you believe them?"

"Yeah, Kelly. They're tellin' the truth. I can tell."

"OK," Kelly said with enthusiasm. "Pull 'em out."

They heard the sound of a boat engine at about the same time. Its running lights shown off in the distance.

"Goddamn, another boat," said Kelly in disgust.

In the darkness, Francisco Diaz panicked and threw the two ends of the ropes into the water. It happened so quickly there was scarcely time for a scream before the two heads disappeared. Kelly held the flashlight on the water and watched in disbelief as the ocean filled in the short-lived voids in the surface. There was still tension in the other two ropes attached to the cleat.

"Goddamn!," said Kelly with urgency. "We've got to get them out! That boat's two miles away. We've got to get them out! Hurry!"

Without waiting for Francisco Diaz, Kelly quickly made his way to mid-boat holding on to the aluminum railing to guide him with both hands. The ropes, having been attached to the cleat with Francisco Diaz's massive strength, were difficult for Kelly to undo. The tugging of the bodies did not help. Finally, they were free. Kelly pulled feverishly, slowly, the *Brothers* emerged from the emptiness.

It was too late. The *Brothers of Islam* had been in the cold water too long. Their eyes were closed, their lips blue, water gurgled from their mouths. They had either drowned or died from hypothermia. Kelly did not need a doctor to tell him they were dead.

Dejectedly, Kelly threw the ropes into the water, the *Brothers* began falling towards the bottom. On the way down, they hit a ledge, hesitated, stopped, then continued the journey to their watery graves.

Francisco Diaz sat across from Kelly in the galley.

"They didn't have to die, Pachuco. What the hell have we gotten ourselves into? We've got to think. There's no turning back. Son-of-a-bitch. We've got to think and start asking the right questions. First of all, Pachuco, tell me all about how you saw that piece of paper with the words *WHISKEY HOTEL* written on it. Take your time. We can sit here for the rest of the night if we have to."

Francisco Diaz told about the night in the motel with Johnny and Laura and about how he tried to put it out of his mind. He recalled drinking too much tequila and how the cocaine screwed up his brain. With reluctance, he gave some of the sordid details of the three-some. Kelly listened with patience.

After over half an hour, Francisco Diaz came to a long pause, he was nearly finished. "That it, Pachuco?" asked Kelly.

Francisco Diaz seemed troubled. "What's the matter, Pachuco?" asked Kelly.

"Kelly . . . I . . . I, ah . . . there's sometin' more . . . just one more thing . . . ah . . . Laura . . . ah . . . she was prob'ly just talkin' through her hat . . . she . . . she . . . ah . . . she . . . ah . . . said sometin' else –"

"What?"

"That, ah . . . that –"

"What did she say!"

"That, ah . . . ah . . . Kashan and Jennie . . . ah . . . ah . . . they got a thing goin'."

"What the hell! Jennie wouldn't do that!"

"I'm sorry . . . Kelly . . . I'm sorry . . . that's what the cunt said."

Kelly stood over the stern of the *Baja Vagabundo* looking towards the lights of La Jolla. Francisco Diaz sat quietly, waiting for Kelly to sort things out and come up with a plan. Kelly always did and he would now. Francisco Diaz was confident.

Kelly was morose when he came back to where Francisco Diaz was sitting. He was dejected and his face ashen. He looked into Francisco Diaz's eyes and said forlornly, "Go to the villa and bring Kashan to *The Ranch* at midnight. I'll be waiting. Whatever you do, don't hurt him. We need to question him. Don't hurt him."

18

RIVIERA DRIVE

Francisco Diaz had no aversion to killing.

He liked it and rather thought of himself as a physician – a giver and taker of life. He took life by killing. He *gave* life by *not* taking it. His scalpel was his knife, a garrote, a razor, or whatever sharp instrument was handy at the moment. Although some people thought shooting was necessary, he found it abhorrent. Doctors did not *shoot*, they *cut*. He once thought that if he could live his life over again, he would become an M.D. However, that required more intellect than he possessed and probably more hard work than he was willing to do. Realistically, it could not possibly have been as interesting as working with Kelly and he certainly could not have made as much money.

Death was a part of Francisco Diaz's life growing up in a *barrio* of Los Angeles. Before he was ten, one of his brothers was shot by a policeman during a robbery and an uncle was stabbed in a quarrel with another Mexican over a woman. Neither lived. When she was not in the final stages of pregnancy, his mother operated a sewing machine in the garment district for twelve hours a day, and his father, when sober, worked as a janitor. That was not often. They lived in poverty and frequently did not have enough to eat or shoes to wear. As a child, he thought, from watching his uncles and father, that laughter was something poured out of a tequila bottle. He was sixteen when he plunged an ice pick into the chest of a black during a high-school gang war. From then on, it was easy. His first job was as an enforcer for a loan shark. The first person in his life to show him love and affection was Momma. With the exception of her, their children, and perhaps Kelly, he regarded all living things with equanimity. A man's life had the same value as a mosquito's.

Francisco Diaz parked several blocks from the villa. He opened the trunk and took out a machete wrapped in brown paper. His knife was in his pocket and a garrote attached to the inside of his leather belt. He bent into the trunk a second time, found the stiletto, and shoved it into his boot. He was prepared.

As he walked through the dark alleyways of Pacific Beach towards the villa, the final words of his conversation with Kelly on the *Baja Vagabundo* in the early morning hours rang in his ears.

"Don't hurt him."

But, Kelly was wrong. In that motel in Ocean Beach Laura had said Jennie and Kashan were involved. How could Kelly ever get Jennie back unless Kashan was dead? Surely, after it was all over, Kelly would see it his way and agree. Yeah, Kelly was pissed about the deaths of the two Iranians. But, this was different. This would be the last one and only then would it be over. Kelly would see it his way. There was no reason to question Kashan. Kelly would surely see it his way when it was all over. Kelly was usually right, but this was different. Kelly was his friend and he owed it to him to get rid of Kashan. Kelly would never agree, Francisco had to take it upon himself to do what was right.

It wasn't difficult for Francisco Diaz to convince himself that Kelly would be pleased when he brought Kashan's head to him in a box. Being a little psychopathic made it easier. This was a side to Diaz Kelly had never seen.

He smiled when he thought of the words "head in a box." He had never cut off a man's head before, and was looking forward to it. Like any qualified surgeon, he should be able to perform a procedure for the first time. After all, *most* did not do *all* types of operations in medical school. There had to be a first time for everything. If one knows and understands the basic fundamentals, then one should be able to apply them successfully. This was going to be his greatest killing. They were all *good*, but this one was going to be *great*. He was anxious and could hardly wait.

When he got to the villa, he took out the key Kelly had given him months earlier. Instead of going up the stairs, Francisco Diaz went under the deck out into the sand which formed the shoreline of the bay. He laid in the soft sand and looked back towards the villa less than twenty feet away. Through its plate glass windows, he could see Kashan talking to Jennie. Francisco Diaz was puzzled. He had not expected Jennie to be there. Kelly had checked at the hospital and she was scheduled to be on duty that night. He glanced at his watch. Nine-seventeen. No wonder. It was still early. She would probably leave soon. He put the key back into his pocket, laid back and closed his eyes. His apprehension faded away.

Inside the villa, Kashan sat talking with Jennie on the couch. She wore her nurse's uniform, ready to go on the night shift at the hospital. Kashan was on edge, especially when he thought of what Laura had tricked him into doing on the same piece of furniture, and especially more so when he realized afterward that he did not know with any certainty whether or not Laura actually knew anything. As in the meeting with Rajavi in Tijuana, Kashan was good at hiding his nervousness from Jennie.

Jennie had called earlier in the afternoon with some urgency. She had a remote idea of the pressures facing Kashan but never dreamt for a moment she was one of them. She knew nothing of *WHISKEY HOTEL*, and how it was tearing at Kashan's insides. Neither was yet aware that the *Brothers of Islam* swayed at the bottom of La Jolla Canyon. Neither suspected Francisco Diaz lay outside in the sand only yards away waiting to kill Kashan.

"Are you sure Kelly said he doesn't go to Punta Estrella anymore?" Kashan asked.

"Yes. I told him a Mexican with a gunshot wound was brought into the emergency room, and that the Mexican had been found by the American Coast Guard at Punta Estrella in Baja."

"And, do you remember what Kelly said?"

"He said he hadn't been there for years."

"Jennie, I hate to be the one to say this, but Kelly is undoubtedly involved in some sort of illicit operations in Baja. I'm sure it's not too serious. He wouldn't hurt anybody," lied Kashan.

"What'll I do?" pleaded Jennie. "What if he and Francisco Diaz did kill the Mexican? It's hard to believe Kelly would do a thing like that. But, what if?"

"Maybe it's best to forget about that day in Mexico."

"I can't," said Jennie.

"Tell you what I'll do."

"What, Kashan?"

"I'll tell Kelly I saw an article about the Mexican in an old newspaper and ask him if he had seen the man recently."

"I was confident you'd think of something. I couldn't go to the hospital without getting this off my mind."

She did feel relieved after sharing her burden. Little did she know though, even at that very moment, that Kashan was planning to lie to her and say he had been mistaken and he and Kelly had never gone to any place called Punta Estrella, but to a different field called Punta Estoria. That lie would come later. It was too soon for it to be credible now.

"I have to go to Chicago in the next couple of days to pick up an airplane. I'll tell you all about it later when we have more time. I'm flying commercial so how about being a good sport and taking me to the airport?"

It was shortly after ten o'clock when Francisco Diaz heard the *click, click, click* of ladies' high-heels descending the steps from the deck of the villa. Jennie didn't wear heels when she worked but always kept a pair in her trunk. Moments later, a car started, headlights flashed on, and it drove away. His heart began to beat faster and his eyes bulged. Soon, very soon, he would be inside the villa – alone with Kashan and his machete.

Waiting a good quarter of an hour after the lights went out, he stood and brushed the sand from his clothes. He unwrapped the brown paper from the machete and let it fall. He stroked the flat blade of the magnificent instrument for several minutes, running his stubby fingers back and forth, and slightly slivered his skin causing a drop of blood to ooze out.

The door from the villa to the deck was unlocked. Francisco Diaz carefully opened it and let himself in. There was enough light from the moon to see Kashan lying on his back on the couch in the living room. Francisco Diaz slowly inched his way over. *I don't think Kelly will mind a little blood on his couch,* he thought. *He can well afford to buy a new one.*

Inhaling a deep breath, he lifted the machete high over his head with both hands.

Sweat formed on his temples. His eyes focused on Kashan's bare neck, undulating up and down. The Adam's apple would be the target. He'd split it in two like a pea before the machete continued its journey through to the pillow. Quickly severing the larynx would keep Kashan from yelling. Kashan's breathing was deep and regular.

The more he watched the more the motion of Kashan's throat had a mesmerizing effect. It was difficult to concentrate on starting the downward swing. His subconscious compelled him to delay the moment as long as possible to heighten the final climax. In the meantime, his mind began to wander.

He wondered what it would have been like to have been an executioner a long time ago, to cut off heads every day before breakfast, just like he had told the *niños* at the orphanage.

He began to breathe more heavily, the machete still raised high over his head. Normally, he wasn't one to fantasize, but, then, he had never cut off a man's head before. There was no quivering in his arms. No blinking of his eyes. More beads of sweat appeared on his forehead.

Kashan stirred slightly after a drop fell on his cheek. Although staring directly at him, Francisco Diaz did not seem to notice.

Instead . . . *Francisco Diaz heard a clock a long way off strike three times. The soldiers laughed and drank all night long while the workmen hammered to complete the scaffold some twenty-feet high next to the town fountain. The wagons loaded with criminals made their way through the cobblestone streets inching toward the wooden framework topped by a blade that gleamed in the afternoon sunshine. Seated in the front row of chairs were a number of women busy knitting. None looked up at the statue of La Guillotine standing boldly before them. None looked down at the wine-red street below stained by countless streams of blood from countless heads. There was talk of the crimes which must be paid for with heads – talk of the sixteen-year-old girl who took a loaf of bread, of the unlawful opener of a letter. On the platform, the executioner, daintily dressed in a gold-laced coat, bellowed orders. The load from the first wagon ascended the steep stairway in single file. All was ready and suddenly there was a loud crash. The crowd stirred and the women kept knitting as the first head was held up. The process was repeated sixty-seven times in the next sixty minutes . . .*

Once again Kashan stirred as larger drops of sweat fell on his face and neck. This time Francisco Diaz saw the movement and his arms trembled. The tip of the blade of the machete traced an oval like the path of an erratic planet. In a split second, it would be over. The blade raced downward towards Kashan's neck.

The machete nearly sliced the couch in two. The blade became stuck in the heavy wooden framework under the upholstering. Francisco Diaz struggled to free it, grunting and groaning like an ox.

The blade missed Kashan by only a fraction of an inch.

Finally awakened by the dripping sweat and seeing Diaz holding the machete, Kashan rolled off the couch in a lightening quick move that almost knocked Francisco over. Kashan scrambled to his feet and lunged back at Francisco Diaz but Diaz beat him off with a powerful elbow to the head.

The sole object of Diaz's attention was the machete and his compulsion to free it from the wooden frame. Pulling with all his strength, he swore in Spanish, but the machete would not budge.

Dazed by Diaz's blow, Kashan recovered, picked up a heavy table lamp and smashed him over the head from behind.

Kashan was far away by the time Francisco Diaz regained consciousness.

19

QOM
May 1st

"Gentlemen," began Rajavi, "I'm most happy to announce that today I can reveal the details of *WHISKEY HOTEL*. As we talk now, in fact, the plan is being implemented. As we discussed in our first meeting, our vague objective was to consider the destruction of one of America's most cherished symbols of national pride with a minimum loss of life. We all owe a deep sense of gratitude to Major Muluk who conceived the final idea and planned it down to its most minute detail. The plan is bold. If I may be so brash, I personally see no way in which it can fail.

"In a few minutes, I'll let Major Muluk tell you of his remarkable concept, but first some background material.

"The plan was conceived before we met with our pilots in Tijuana, but lacked several essential details. For that reason, I chose not to release it then. We did know enough to give our pilot his next instruction and begin making preliminary arrangements.

"The idea struck Major Muluk when he remembered reading of the young West German pilot who flew across The Soviet Union and landed his Cessna in Red Square. Now you'll hear *WHISKEY HOTEL* in its entirety.

"Americans call us fanatics because we take our religion seriously. They fail to see how fanatical they are in the eyes of the rest of the world in some of the things they do daily. Americans are fanatics about traveling and the possessing of freedom to travel anywhere and at any time. They own more automobiles than the rest of the civilized world combined and are the world's major user of petroleum. In the same vein, they fly more than anyone else in the world, and they have more private aircraft than all other nations of the world combined. Any American can drive his personal automobile on any road in the United States and, by the same token, any American who flies a private airplane can fly into any airport in the U.S. Such freedoms are unknown even in other highly democratic countries. Often, we hear of collisions between airliners and small aircraft in America. The fools don't have enough sense to realize the airspace around their major airports is a national resource which should be controlled by the government for the benefit of the most, and not for indiscriminate use by the wealthy few who can afford their own private airplanes.

"This is the combination that struck Major Muluk. America's obsessions with travel and freedom. I'll let Major Muluk continue."

Muluk got up and walked around to the front of the table while Rajavi walked the other way around the table and sat down. Muluk appeared confident and at ease.

"Thank you, General Rajavi," he began. "Many of the major airports in America are located in the middle of cities. I remember flying many years ago into Washington, D.C. on a commercial flight. Out of my window on the left side of the airplane, as we landed, I could see the Capitol, the Mall and the Washington Monument, and the Reflecting Pool and the Lincoln Memorial. I assume all of these are now familiar to you."

Muluk paused and walked over to the end of the table where there were a number of large charts. He selected one and placed it on an easel where it could easily be seen.

"This chart shows the location of Washington National Airport and landmarks in the Washington area. Traffic landing at the airport usually lands on Runways 15 and 18 and, as you can see by extending imaginary lines along the centers of the runways,

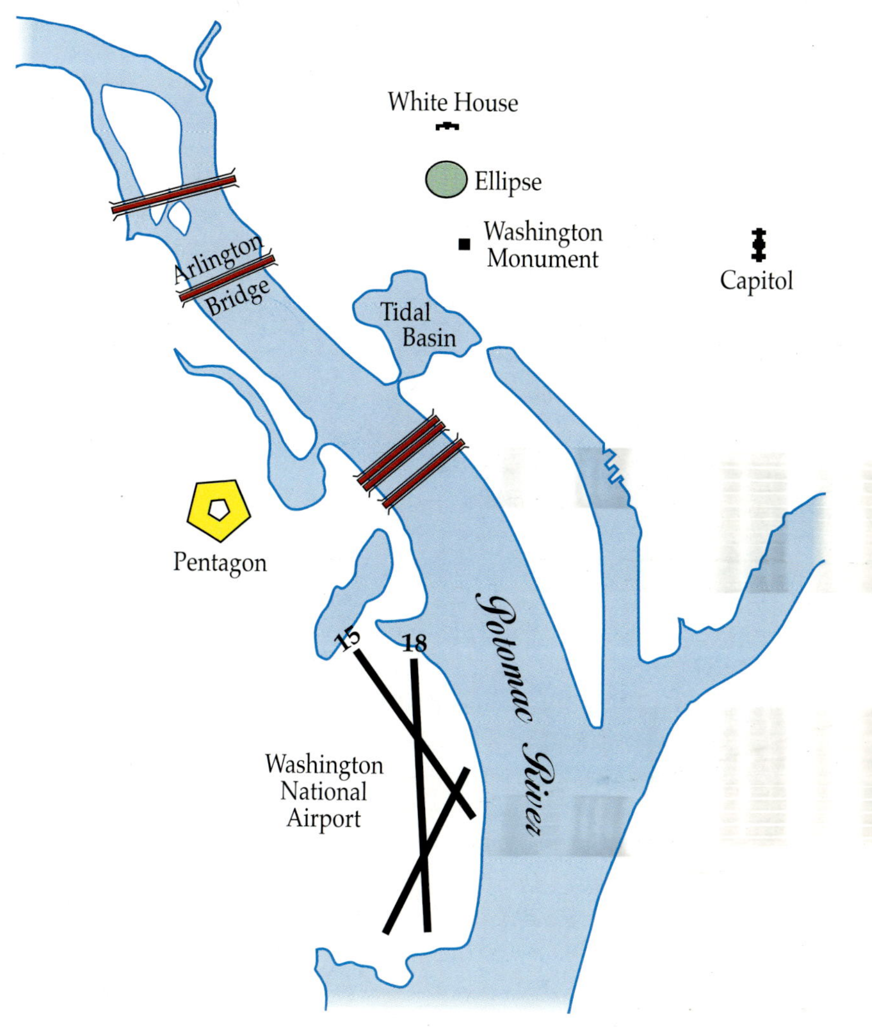

Muluk's chart showing Washington National Airport and landmarks in the Washington, D.C. area

Rajavi's slide of garden inside the Pentagon

approaching traffic to these comes in from the north along the Potomac River. In fact, there is one approved landing pattern in which a landing aircraft follows along the Potomac River from ten miles away all the way to the airport. This has the official name of *River Visual Approach*. This particular flight pattern lines planes up with Runway 15. However, even when Runway 18 is in use, planes still follow along the river, but make a 30-degree turn about a mile away to line themselves up before landing. This is done to keep planes from flying over their sacred monuments.

"Because of their insistence on freedoms of air travel, a private aircraft has the same landing rights as commercial jetliners at all airports in the United States. I propose that a private airplane piloted by one of our men request permission to land at Washington National Airport from the northwest. He will assuredly be instructed to fly down the Potomac River. About three miles from the airport, the plane will pass over Theodore Roosevelt Island, located in the middle of the river and easily discernible. A bridge goes across the south end of this island and spans the river. The next bridge is called Arlington Memorial Bridge. At this point, the pilot turns off his radios, pushes the throttle full forward, starts a diving turn over the Tidal Basin, and heads directly for the Washington Monument. The monument, pardon my expression, looks like a six hundred foot tall penis, and is very easy to make out from the air."

Muluk paused and there was laughter in the room. Even the stoic Rajavi cracked a slight smile.

"Sixteenth Street is just before the monument. The street does not actually go through at this point because of the large grassy area called *The Ellipse*. The pilot gets down low and flies where Sixteenth Street would be, above the grassy area at ten feet altitude at full speed of two hundred and sixty miles per hour. He passes over drunks and bums sleeping on the grass. Two blocks away, he can see the WHITE HOUSE! Between the trees on the lawn, he sees the American Flag on the roof and the six ionic columns which form the South Portico. He passes between the large evergreen tree to the right and the large sycamore to the left. He goes over the fountain so low that he gets spray on the belly of his airplane. He flies the airplane, which is loaded with a thousand pounds of high-performance plastic explosives, towards the White House and crashes into the first floor, destroying the entire building."

Muluk was enjoying his performance on center stage. He had full command of the small group.

"Bravo, bravo," yelled Badri.

"Praise be to Allah," shouted Alam.

Rajavi grinned from ear to ear. Badri and Alam shook Muluk's hand, hugging and kissing him on the cheek. Rajavi did nothing to call order to the room, but let them relish the moment. After a few minutes, he arose and walked around to the front of the table. The others took their chairs, still whispering congratulations back and forth.

"The plan is a masterpiece," said Rajavi. "Major Muluk is to be highly commended. I salute him. There're a few details he neglected to mention, so I'll fill you in. When the pilot begins his turn from the accepted course along the river, he'll be approximately one mile from the White House. At a speed of two hundred and sixty miles an hour, it'll take him thirteen seconds to cover this distance. Even if the Americans know that something is awry, they'll have only thirteen fleeting short seconds. However, there's no radar in the world that can track an airplane flying below the tops of the trees around it. For the last five seconds, the plane'll be no more than ten feet above the ground. The Americans may think something has gone wrong with the airplane and may think it's going to crash. In fact, we might have the pilot radio in that he's lost control. That way the stupid Americans will be totally confused. Flying at such a low altitude and such high speeds demands an extremely capable pilot. Iran has such a man in Commander al-Kashan.

"The foolish Americans have been erecting barricades in front of their precious White House to keep trucks from crashing into it. They never thought of a private airplane below tree-top level. It's a perfect plan. It cannot fail to succeed."

Badri said: "General, it's difficult for me to believe that no plans have been made for the defense of the White House. Don't they have missiles or something?"

"Good question," said Rajavi. "Muluk thought of that too. He learned that the Stinger missile, the hand-held version, has been deployed on the roof of the White House. With a little research, he found two articles in the *New York Times*." Rajavi paused while he dug through his papers. "One, dated February 10, 1984, is entitled 'Navy's Defenses for Attacks By Suicide Pilots Questioned.' The second, dated July 22, 1986 is an editorial called 'The Stinger Is No Stinger.' Both of these clearly show that the Stinger is over-rated and is not an effective weapon, especially against low-flying aircraft."

Badri seemed quite satisfied. Rajavi took a slide from his briefcase and inserted it into the projector. The slide showed the garden inside the Pentagon. Diagonally across the picture was the wing strut of an airplane.

"To further demonstrate the feasibility of his plan, Major Muluk had our pilot at Andrew's Air Force rent a small Cessna and land at Washington National Airport. When he was on final approach to land, the tower told him a large commercial jetliner was on his tail and ordered him to execute two complete turns so the jet could land first. Gentlemen, the plane was right over the Pentagon at less than two hundred feet altitude! The pilot banked and his passenger took the picture you are looking at. He could easily have bombed the Pentagon!"

The slide caused quite a stir. Alam and Badri again congratulated Muluk.

"For obvious reasons, the plan's been assigned the code-name *WHISKEY HOTEL* using the international phonetic alphabet for the first two letters of *White House*," said Rajavi. "It would, of course, be a simple matter to destroy either the Washington Monument or the Jefferson Memorial since these are closer to the river. But, we are going to go all out and get the White House.

"A thousand, two thousand, even ten thousand years from now, our descendants will speak of this fantastic feat in the same way we talk of the Martyrdom of Hussein, son of Mohammed. It will become a part of Islamic tradition.

"As we know, the leader of Islam is called *The Shadow of God*, and since our Air Force is, figuratively speaking, our wind, this momentous occasion will go down in history as *Wind of the*

Shadow.

"The Japanese word *kamikaze* literally translates into *divine wind*, but there will be no comparison between their reckless suicidal missions and the wondrous accomplishment of *Wind of the Shadow*.

"Our goal is not to kill, but to destroy America's most treasured symbol. If we should, by accident of course, kill the President and his wife, that would be a happy coincidence. But the primary goal of *WHISKEY HOTEL* is to destroy the White House.

"At precisely the 5th second of the 5th minute of the 5th hour of the 5th day of the 5th month, the White House will cease to exist except as a pile of rubble. May 5th, gentlemen, is the date of the beginning of the future glory of Islam.

"Mohammed will be proud of us."

Wallowing in glory, it never occurred to Rajavi that the *Brothers of Islam* had not reported in.

20

THE RANCH
May 1st

When Francisco Diaz failed to show up at *The Ranch* by midnight, Kelly called Momma who said she had not heard from him. He told her they were working on a project, not to expect him that night, and not to be concerned. Momma had learned to trust Kelly, she would not ask any questions. He next dialed the villa and there was no answer. Kelly began to worry and the lines appeared on his forehead. He thought about calling Jennie at Balboa Hospital, but quickly dismissed the idea. Impatiently, he paced back and forth.

As Kelly waited for word from Francisco Diaz, he tried to make sense out of the events which had transpired since Kashan's arrival. Admitting he believed Kashan's story about setting up a medical program in the remote areas of Iran, he despised himself for having been so gullible. He thought about how he relished the danger of flying off the carrier in Vietnam and conceded personal greed had partially led him to resign his commission. But, Kashan was not driven by greed. He should never have believed Kashan's lies. Kelly thought back to their conversations around the campfire in Baja – about how an intelligent man like Kashan could not see Khomeini was a fanatic. He should have realized Kashan had to be a fanatic too. He had let himself be fooled by Kashan's flying abilities, although he did have suspicions then. "You can always tell a man's character by the way he flies an airplane," he had said to Jennie. The words haunted Kelly now. How could he have been so wrong?

Kashan was definitely in the United States on some sort of an operation for Iran. The *Brothers of Islam* had said so. There was an operation in progress with the code-name *WHISKEY HOTEL*. *Damn!* He questioned how he had been responsible for the deaths of the *Brothers*. *That was stupid!* He could have learned more from them. *What does WHISKEY HOTEL mean? It's an unusual name and has to have some meaning attached to it,* he thought.

Finally, Kelly wondered about Jennie. He had been neglecting her. *Was it true she was seeing Kashan?*, he pondered. It sure made sense. She had seemed troubled by something the last few times they were together. *Maybe Jennie knew Kashan from his earlier days at Miramar,* thought Kelly. But then, Francisco Diaz said he had heard about Jennie and Kashan from Laura. Why should Kelly believe anything the drunken slut had to say? The best thing, he concluded, was to confront Jennie. Maybe Jennie knew more about what Kashan was up to. Maybe Laura did too. He would find out.

The minutes ticking away, Kelly became increasingly restive. He tried to read the newspaper and then a flying magazine, but was unable to concentrate. He kept looking at his watch and out the windows.

It was almost two o'clock in the morning when Francisco Diaz stumbled into the front door at *The Ranch*. Laura was only a few steps behind. She had found Francisco Diaz unconscious at the villa in a pool of blood. She had a difficult time arousing him partly because she was more than a little inebriated. But she did the right thing in listening to his insistence and drove him directly to *The Ranch* instead of to the emergency ward at some hospital.

The back of Francisco Diaz head was covered with dried blood and some had spilled down the back of his neck and onto his shirt. Kelly took him into the kitchen to clean off his wound.

Laura, who kept mumbling "Wowiee," followed along. Laura's pink wool outfit was splattered with blood and her usually impeccable blonde hair was matted in several places with reddish brown blotches.

Kelly was furious. He wanted to lash out verbally at Francisco Diaz but contained himself. He got a bottle of tequila from a cabinet over the sink and forced Francisco Diaz to drink some followed by hot coffee. Then Francisco Diaz started to babble.

"He got away, Kelly. I don't know how . . . I had him and he got away . . . Don't know how . . . He hit me with sometin' from behind . . . He got away . . . Sorry . . . Kelly."

"Take it easy, Pachuco."

"Sorry, Kelly. I fucked up again . . . Sorry . . . He got away."

"Do you know where he went?"

"No, no. Don't know nothin'. Was out like a lite."

"Think, Pachuco, think! Did he say anything?"

"No."

"Tell me everything – everything that happened from the time you went to the villa till the time you got here. I want to know everything you can remember."

"When I got there, Jennie was talkin' to Kashan. Never thought she'd leave . . . "

Francisco Diaz related the events of the previous night, but left out his own decision to kill Kashan. Francisco Diaz even remembered some parts of the visions he had while standing over Kashan with the machete held high in his hands, although he was not positive he thought these things before or after the blow to the head. He still experienced dizziness and probably had a slight concussion, but he was remarkably coherent.

Laura sat on a kitchen chair. Attentive, she quietly sipped from a glass of tequila while Francisco Diaz talked. Every once in a while, she added another "Wowiee" but did not distract him.

Kelly was too busy thinking about Jennie to hear all that Francisco Diaz said. When Diaz finished, Kelly merely asked, "Are you sure that Jennie was there when you got there?"

"Yeah," answered Francisco Diaz.

"I think she's fucking him, Flyboy," said Laura.

Kelly heard Laura's comment but chose to ignore it. Right

then, it was more important that Kashan was gone and they didn't know where he was. Much as he tried to avoid the inevitable conclusion, there was only one way to turn and that was to Jennie.

⚜

Jennie was surprised when Kelly called her at Balboa Hospital and asked her to come to *The Ranch* as soon as she got off work at 7:00 a.m. It was about 8:00 a.m. by the time she got there, still wearing her nurse's uniform. She appeared tired from the long night as she walked from her car to the house.

Kelly had sobered up Laura with coffee, two hours sleep, and made her take a cold shower and wash her hair, but he could do nothing about her stained clothes. Francisco Diaz was still dizzy. He lay on a couch in the living room with a large white bandage around his head.

During the time they were waiting for Jennie, Kelly tried to figure out what was going on. After her shower, Laura was surprisingly helpful, although reluctant, in recalling her episodes with Kashan. They agreed to make no mention to Jennie of the deaths of the two Iranians or of Kashan's sexual encounters with her. Those, Kelly rightly felt, would only serve to make Jennie apprehensive. At this point, they needed her since she was their last lead. They'd have to be careful because Jennie was not easily fooled. Kelly would do most of the talking and Laura none.

Jennie kissed Kelly on the lips in the foyer before she saw Laura and Francisco Diaz in the living room. Seeing the other two made her wonder why they were there. Indeed, she wondered why she was there. Kelly had not been definite, but did insinuate he wanted to see her for personal reasons. That meant only the two of them.

Before Jennie could speak, Kelly did. "Please sit down, Jennie." His voice was kind and gentle. "Something has happened and we need your help."

"Something to do with Kashan?" asked Jennie. Her eagerness gave away the uneasiness she was feeling and the urgency in her question left no doubt she was alarmed.

"I'm afraid so," said Kelly.

"Is he all right?" pleaded Jennie. Her eyes had not drifted from Kelly's.

"We don't know where he is. He cold-cocked Francisco last night and then took off."

Surprised, Jennie glanced over at Francisco Diaz.

"That's right," said Francisco Diaz.

"He's mixed up in something," went on Kelly, "Something to do with Iran."

"Yes, that's right," said Jennie without hesitation. "You know about his medical work for Iran."

"Jennie, that's a cover," said Kelly.

"I don't believe you," Jennie said defensively.

"Jennie, please believe me." Kelly's manner was still gentle but there was a new firmness to his voice.

"Why?"

"It could be very important."

"Why should I believe you? Didn't you already lie to me about having been at Punta Estrella when the Mexican was shot?" asked Jennie angrily.

"Jennie, I *did not* lie. What makes you say that?"

"Kashan told me"

Kelly walked over to Jennie and took her hands in his. Contritely, he begged, "Jennie, Jennie, Jennie. Please believe me and please listen carefully to me. I have *not* been to Punta Estrella for years. If Kashan told you differently, he was lying to you."

"What about all those trips you make to Arizona and Baja," asked Jennie. "What are you involved in?"

"I probably should have told you a long time ago. Francisco and I visit several orphanages in Mexico. We take supplies for them. On the way back, we bring medicines that are overpriced and hard to get in this country. I'll tell you all about it when this mess is over."

At first Jennie was bewildered. Orphanage? Medicines? It took several seconds for the meaning of Kelly's words to register.

Before she could respond, Francisco Diaz said: "That's right, Jennie. That's the way it was."

"You're throwing an awful lot at me, Kelly," said Jennie. "I need some time to digest all this. If what you say is true, you can't imagine how relieved I am to hear those things. I want to believe you. In my heart, I just knew you couldn't have been involved in killing the Mexican. It's not like you."

"What do you know about *WHISKEY HOTEL*?" asked Kelly.

"With a perplexed look about her, Jennie answered. "That's the name of a race horse Kashan's friend wanted him to bet on. He told me so." Then she added, "In all honesty, though, I didn't quite believe him."

"Jennie, we have reason to think it's the name of a secret Iranian operation against the United States and Kashan's in the middle of it."

"No. That can't be! He wouldn't do anything like that. It can't be!"

How could Kelly have been so stupid to not have seen it before. Probably everything Laura had said was true.

"You do love him, don't you?" he asked.

"Kelly, of course I do. In a way that maybe it's hard to understand. Call it love or call it deep affection. There's little difference. We were very much in love when he was here seven years ago. I didn't know to explain it all to you. I was wrong in not having come right out and said it the first time you mentioned his name. But I don't love him as I love you. I can't simply put aside my past feelings for him. I had to see him to make sure it was over. If I hadn't, I could never have been honest with you again. We talked a few times and spent a day in Tijuana together. Old friends don't just ignore one another. There *is* nothing more."

"How do you explain your panties and bra in his bed?" Laura snickered.

"Kelly! She's got it all wrong! We went for a swim in the ocean and I changed into a bathing suit in the bedroom at the villa. He wanted me, I'll admit. He even asked me to marry him."

Laura snickered again.

"Jennie, you've got to help us before it's too late. Maybe we can stop this whole thing before it goes anywhere."

"He seemed . . . seemed so involved with his medical program.

Are you sure this whole thing isn't just some ugly mistake? I thought he was so dedicated. He had a meeting with the Mexican Health Authorities that day in Tijuana and is planning another with the International Red Cross. It can't be just . . . just a front. Can it?"

"Jennie, dearest, I'm afraid it is."

Taking pleasure in Jennie's befuddlement delighted Laura. She felt like celebrating with a drink or two, maybe three.

Kelly continued. "Jennie, there were a couple of Iranians snooping around here. Francisco and I caught them. They told us Kashan was involved in this operation called *WHISKEY HOTEL*." Kelly did not bother to add that the *Brothers of Islam* were now at the bottom of La Jolla Canyon. "They said they didn't know anything else. Other than that, we don't have any real facts to go on – except Kashan's disappearance. We can't go to the authorities with such a flimsy story. The only thing we can be reasonably sure of is his need for an airplane for whatever it is he's up to."

Kelly also didn't admit the real reason for not going to the authorities was that they would want to know more details about the *Brothers of Islam* and, once started, would ask too many questions. *Yes,* he thought, *letting them die had been a stupendous blunder.* It wouldn't be easy, but he'd have to tell Jennie about this too.

"The most important thing right now is for us to locate Kashan," said Kelly.

"I'll do what I can to help," said Jennie. "But, only if you promise you'll help him in any way you can."

"Of course I will, Jennie. Do you have any idea where he might be? Did he say anything to you?"

Jennie thought about her conversation the previous evening with Kashan, about him asking her to take him to the airport for a flight to Chicago. Now, she wished she had taken the time to have asked more. Her lingering doubts about Kashan made her hesitate before answering. She didn't want to accept the facts, or what appeared on the surface to be facts. She could not. There had to be an explanation for everything.

"I know where he is," said Jennie. "But, I'm not going to tell you until you convince me you're interested in helping him."

21

CHICAGO
May 2nd

The new terminal at O'Hare Airport in Chicago was a refreshing sight to Kashan. The backbone of the building was formed by exposed steel columns which raced over a hundred feet straight up before bending over to culminate in an asymmetrical, glass-enclosed arch. Save for the antlike creatures scrambling around on the main floor, the cavernous dome contained over a billion cubic feet of mostly empty air.

Kashan hurried past the waiting areas and the dozens of super-market-style check-in counters to the escalator which took him down to the baggage area. The events of the past several days occupied his mind.

The vision of Francisco Diaz standing over him with the machete came back each time he tried to close his eyes. He could still feel Francisco Diaz's warm sweat dripping on his forehead, hear Francisco Diaz's hollow panting, and sense the rush of cold air past the back of his head from the blade of the machete.

After leaving the villa, he had spent the night at the Hilton Hotel in Mission Bay Park. Initially, it was difficult to put aside a burning urge to go to Jennie, but then much easier when he realized it would have been an obvious mistake. He spent the day buying new clothes and checking on his flight to Chicago.

Francisco Diaz's attempt to kill him could only mean he was

ordered to do so by Kelly. *Damn that bitch Laura.* There was, Kashan thought, no reason for Kelly to know about *WHISKEY HOTEL*. Kashan had never mentioned it to anyone – except for the damned piece of yellow paper. *But, even if Kelly knows some things;* Kashan wondered, *he wouldn't know WHISKEY HOTEL was in progress. Besides, even I haven't been told the exact nature of the operation yet. How can Kelly know more than I? Only Jennie knows I am in Chicago. She won't tell Kelly.*

The man who sat in the back of the plane on the flight from San Diego was not noticed by Kashan, nor did he pay any particular attention when the man edged by and got off the plane before him. Now, he was ahead on the escalator down to the baggage area. The man stopped at the bottom and waited for the other passengers to get off.

When Kashan stepped off, the man removed his hat and sun glasses and spoke in Farsi, saying, "Good afternoon, Kashan."

Kashan was expecting to be met by someone, but was taken aback when he realized the bald-headed man with glasses standing before him was Major Muluk. He remembered him from the meeting in Tijuana, especially from the inquisition Muluk tried to wage over Jennie.

"It's a pleasant afternoon," replied Kashan, also in Farsi. "Are you going my way? Possibly we can share a taxi?"

"Yes, that is a possibility."

Muluk replaced his hat and sun glasses as they began walking to the ramp to await their baggage. Muluk chatted about his long flight from Qom on a Lear jet operated by the Iranian Air Force, but disguised to look like an Egyptian corporate plane. Without the advantage of the eleven-and-a-half-hour time difference between Iran and California, he would not have been able to be there to board Kashan's flight. After their baggage came, they went outside and found a taxi. Muluk told the driver to take them to Butler Aviation at the Meigs Field Airport near downtown Chicago.

⁂

There was little conversation during the forty-five minute taxi ride along the John F. Kennedy Expressway through the northwest part of Chicago. The new multi-story hotels, office buildings, and world corporate centers surrounding O'Hare Airport soon gave way to small, ancient two-story homes, crumbling red-brick apartments, old factories, dilapidated stores and boarded-up offices which covered Logan Square and the Near North Side. Once near the Loop, the driver took the Eisenhower Expressway ramp and the West Congress Expressway. A right on Michigan Avenue and a quick left brought them to Lake Shore Drive. In a few minutes, they passed the Shedd Aquarium, the Field Museum of Natural History, the Alder Planetarium and were on the service road to Meigs Field.

The airport was built on a man-made island in Lake Michigan and existed to serve only the rich, the super-rich, and the Chicago and down-state politicians. The single service road provided the only access to the island. There were no commercial flights into Meigs Field and the city regularly picked up the tab for running it. Few airports in the world offered the spectacular view of a major downtown area, seemingly passing inches away when landing and taking off.

City-invoked curfews and high landing and tie-down fees discouraged use of the airport. Small planes could go to Pal-Waukee or to Schaumburg or to one of the other airports in the outskirts of the city. The City Fathers did not want them near the downtown area. In spite of its premiere location, Meigs Field was one of the best kept aviation secrets in the United States and was hardly used by the general aviation community. It bordered upon being deserted.

✈

The taxicab pulled up in front of Butler Aviation and Muluk paid the driver. Just as Rajavi had said during the meeting in Tijuana, inside the Butler hangar was a V-tail Bonanza identical to Kelly's except for red trim. The registration number that Rajavi had picked, N555AK, was lettered on the side of the fuselage instead of following the more modern trend of using smaller letters and putting it on the vertical tail.

Whatever had to be done, he would do in this beautiful machine. He sat inside the cockpit for a few moments while Muluk was occupied with one of the people from Butler Aviation.

The new instrument panel held a full complement of the latest radio and navigation equipment. Unconsciously, Kashan's hand reached out, his fingers grasped and gently turned two or three knobs slightly one way and then back the other.

He dug into his pocket, finding the small gold filigree locket. Opening it, he lost his thoughts in Jennie's picture before reading the inscription opposite the photo aloud, "Love is splendor," and added, "My dearest Jennie. Our love *was* splendor. Now thoughts of it will help me complete this last mission."

Kashan put his hand into his pocket again and took out his knife. Carefully, he loosened a screw on the instrument panel and used it to attach the gold locket where he could see it from the pilot's seat.

Late that afternoon, they flew the Bonanza for two hours and checked all the instruments, radios and navigation equipment. Everything worked flawlessly. Twenty miles out over Lake Michigan, Kashan did a power dive from 1000 feet altitude down to within ten feet of the water and flew for several miles at full throttle. Once back at altitude, he could not resist doing several snap rolls. It was evident to Muluk, sitting in the right hand seat, that Kashan had complete control of the airplane.

After landing at Meigs, Kashan and Muluk went to a private conference room and discussed the maps and landing charts for Washington National Airport. While they talked, two men drove up in a black limousine. From its trunk, they took out five large suitcases and stowed three into the back seat of the Bonanza and the other two into the baggage compartment. All were secured with canvass straps and nylon ropes. Kashan did not see them, but Muluk knew they were there and what they were doing.

Kashan was curious as to what *WHISKEY HOTEL* entailed, but Muluk did not offer any details. Kashan would wait like the good officer he was until Muluk was ready.

⸙

At first, it greatly surprised Kashan when Muluk made no mention of *WHISKEY HOTEL* during dinner. And it also surprised him to find Muluk far more worldly and sophisticated than he had acted around Rajavi. Their conversation ranged over a wide variety of topics but usually, one way or the other, drifted back to the Holy War between Iran and Iraq. Although Muluk was not a pilot, Kashan was impressed by his knowledge of aviation. He was puzzled by Muluk's intense interest in the United States. Muluk was a good conversationalist and the early evening passed quickly. Kashan could not help but conclude Muluk possessed a sensitive and adventurous spirit tainted by some mixture of cruelty. A touch of romanticism came through from time to time.

Throughout dinner, Kashan kept thinking *WHISKEY HOTEL* was some sort of smuggling or kidnapping operation. He was convinced he would be ordered to fly somebody or something from some place in the United States to a foreign country – probably to Mexico. After the mission was over, he would go back to San Diego. Maybe then he could smooth things over with Jennie.

After dinner, Muluk did not waste time in getting down to business. As soon as the dishes were cleared and coffee served, he started, "As you know, Kashan, General Rajavi and I have been working closely on the *WHISKEY HOTEL* operation . . . "

Muluk patiently gave Kashan a rundown on the meetings in Qom. Even before Muluk was done, Kashan had a pretty good idea as to what he was going to be asked to do. Long before Muluk finished, he began thinking about what he was going to say.

" . . . and so, Kashan, your country is asking you to give up your present life for it. We both know the Koran teaches that the next life is the important one."

After what seemed like an appropriate pause, Kashan answered in carefully measured words, "Major, I have always been prepared to give my life for my country and to my saint, the Ayatollah Khomeini. I will do as you ask."

Kashan gave the correct response demanded under the circumstances. Being a well disciplined military officer, he was expected to obey orders. It was no different from leading a bombing run into enemy flak or dogfighting when outnumbered. He had often put his life on the line when the odds seemed against him. He would obey orders.

But, there was something odd about Kashan's reply. It was too perfect. Only another Iranian could have detected it. The reply lacked fanaticism. There was no far-away look in Kashan's eyes. His breathing was too regular and there was no hint of perspiration on his brow. His voice was too controlled. Muluk noticed.

Out of the clear blue sky, Muluk stated sympathetically, "You do love Jennie."

The sudden switch from *WHISKEY HOTEL* to Jennie startled Kashan. He could not help but admire Muluk's perceptiveness.

Muluk continued in a kindly voice. "You might be surprised to hear I was once very much in love. I was much younger then and not marred by cynicism as I am now. The world was glorious when we touched and painful when we parted. It was paradise to be near her. We were married less than a year when she died. My heart died with her, but my body continued to live. Without a heart, I became cruel and insensitive. I began living like an automaton."

Muluk paused, expecting a reply from Kashan. But, there was none and so he went on in the same vein.

"I think I do understand your feelings for Jennie and your inner struggle in having to choose your country and your religion over her. It's not the first time that higher principles and causes had to be put before love. You could never be happy if you turned your back on your country. You would be labeled a traitor, hunted and murdered. There is no place you can hide. You really do not have a choice. You cannot alter destiny. It's best to simply accept your role in history."

They sat silently looking through one another for what seemed like an eon.

When he finally spoke, Kashan was sullen, his face a cobweb of anxiety. He was resigned to his fate, but his voice strained with agony, "Yes, Major, you were right all along. I love her dearly . . . I don't want to complete this mission . . . But . . . I will . . . I have no choice."

Kashan was defeated. Soon he would be destroyed.

❧

After dinner, they went over the maps and landing charts for Washington National again. They discussed the alternate plan in the event the wind was from the north so that the *River Visual Approach* would not be in use at Washington National on the morning of May 5th. In this case, Kashan would fly the ILS for Runway 36 and execute the standard missed approach procedure. This would also take him over the Potomac River in view of the Tidal Basin. Muluk continued to impress Kashan by his total familiarity with all facets of standard flight patterns. Muluk knew it would be impossible to precisely time the crash to occur at the 5th second of the 5th minute of the 5th hour. If it happened to within five minutes, they would be lucky. The ayatollahs would never know the difference and no one in the world would care anyway.

Before parting for the night, Muluk told Kashan about the 1000 pounds of high explosives set to detonate on impact. He also revealed his plans to photograph the last several seconds of the flight. Finally, he said he would notify Rajavi that night that everything was proceeding according to plan and gave Kashan a rundown on their schedules for the next three days.

"Tomorrow, May 3rd," Muluk said, "We will repeat the checks of the aircraft and go over the maps and charts again. One can never make too many checks or be too careful.

"On the morning of May 4th, I will take a commercial flight to Washington, D.C. You will fly the Bonanza to the airport at Frederick, Maryland, fifty miles from Washington. On the morning of May 5th, you depart the Frederick Airport and fly a one-ninety-seven degree course to intercept the Victor-eight airway which heads straight into Washington National. This will bring you over the Potomac River about twenty-five miles northwest of Washington. From there, weather permitting, you begin the *River Visual Approach* or, if necessary, follow the alternate plan.

"We will go over all this again several times tomorrow. Good night, Kashan."

❦

Midnight had long passed before Kashan got to bed. A stickler for detail, Muluk did not let Kashan go until every element of *WHISKEY HOTEL* was covered thoroughly.

Kashan could not get Jennie out of his mind as he lay in bed tossing and turning. His thoughts would not let sleep take control of his body.

. . . Jennie made me feel fulfilled. There was no emptiness and there was no void. For the first time in my life, I now know and understand what true love is. I know it now because I am going to lose it. When I left Jennie the first time I was confused and did not fully understand what I was doing. I should never have gone. I had love in my grasp and let it fall away like sand through my fingers. Why didn't I cup my hands? Why didn't I see what I had? How could anyone expect or want anything more than what Jennie had given me and the life she offered to share in the future? I was a fool.

Most causes and principles are not as important as two people in love. If I were a true believer, I would not question the call to die gloriously for Iran. And, I would not consider leaving Iran for Jennie. No. Religion is for ignorant peasants. Muluk is wrong. What is one more life in a long string of meaningless deaths? To defend against aggression is one thing but to be an aggressor is another. Kelly was right all along. The jihad is going nowhere. It's one fanatic killing another fanatic and not brother killing brother. To think that I have been a fanatic for all of these precious years. WHISKEY HOTEL is little more than an act of terrorism crudely contorted and enshrouded as a deed of honor by fanatical rhetoric. I see that so clearly. I should have seen Rajavi's madness.

Although I no longer believe in what I am doing, I must go through with it. I cannot alter destiny. If only I could. If only there were a way . . .

The realization that he would soon be dead made Kashan despondent. He got up and frantically paced the room, stopping periodically to gaze out the window at the downtown Chicago skyline. His mind searched in vain for a way out, but it was hopeless. He always had control of situations, but now felt a lonely surge of inadequacy. Rajavi and Muluk were in control. He was a sacrificial pawn in a lunatic game of chance and there was nothing he could do. His chest tightened and his head felt as if it were in a vise. The situation was out of control.

He sat on the edge of the bed and picked up the telephone. Slowly, he dialed Jennie's number. He had to hear her voice one more time. He had to let her know, above all, that he loved her. He had to say good-bye. The phone rang several times before the ringing stopped.

"Hello," said Jennie sleepily.

Kashan ached to talk to Jennie. He could see her sitting up in her bed and longed to hold her in his arms one more time.

"Hello," she repeated.

Gently, Kashan placed the handset back into its cradle before she had a chance to speak again.

22

SAN DIEGO
May 3rd

Jennie had more than a faint recollection of the telephone call. Deeply asleep, the ringing at first seemed part of a dream. She had not seen nor heard from Kashan since he had asked her to take him to the airport for his flight to Chicago two evenings earlier. She had agree to take him, but he had never called. It was probably him now.

But, there was only silence.

Please speak Kashan, she thought. *Please say something! I know it's you. I know it! Please, dear God, please make him say something. Make him tell me where he is so we can go to help him. He needs us. If he's in as much trouble as Kelly says, then he surely needs us. Please speak!*

Jennie turned on the light, sat up, and ran her fingers through her hair.

The silence persisted.

It must have been Kashan.

After a few seconds, the silence was eradicated by the dial tone.

Frustrated, she fell back asleep.

When she awoke late that morning, bright sunshine streamed through her bedroom windows. It was perhaps the most beautiful time of the year in San Diego – that time between the sometimes heavy rains of winter and early spring and the weeks of overcast in June.

❧

Kelly wiped his hands with a red rag. There was complete quiet in his hangar at Montgomery Field and little traffic at the airport, typical for a mid-week morning. A student pilot practiced touch-and-go's on the right runway, Runway 28R, but the Cessna's engine could scarcely be heard this far away in the hangar. The environment of the airport, where he felt most at home, was the best place for Kelly to think things out.

Kelly was torn between his desire to know the facts and his reluctance to get too involved in clandestine matters. The driving factor, though, was his nagging feeling of not being in complete control. Perhaps, if he had a clearer understanding of the facts, he would be better able to make a wise decision when the time came.

Francisco Diaz perched atop a small step-ladder with his feet on the bottom rung and watched Kelly tinker with the Bonanza's engine. The spark plugs had already been changed. He had installed a new type of plug which claimed to give increased performance by running hotter. The cost was shorter engine life and wasn't recommended by the factory or the FAA. Kelly also had made some unapproved modifications to the fuel injection system and the turbocharger. He quietly crowed that his Bonanza could peak out at thirty miles an hour faster than any other in the country.

Time passed slowly as they waited for something to happen. Francisco Diaz was content to sit around and do nothing but Kelly had to keep busy. As the hours dragged by, they both became edgy, and found themselves rehashing the same points.

"Pachuco, I'm convinced Kashan is going to use an airplane somehow in this *WHISKEY HOTEL* operation. I feel certain because he flew my plane so much. But, where do we go from there?"

It was a rhetorical question Kelly had asked often the previous day and so Francisco Diaz did not bother to reply. Sooner or later, Kelly's tenacity would lead him to an answer. It was only a matter of time.

"Pachuco, we've got to start thinking like Iranians. If we were fighting krauts, we'd think like Germans. If we were up against the gooks, we'd think like Vietnamese. We've got to think harder . . ."

While he checked and rechecked bolts, wires, screws, clamps and hoses, Kelly kept up his monologue.

"We need to know two things, Pachuco. Where and when? Once we know where and when, everything will fall into place. Where and when?"

"Don't know 'bout where, but I do know when," interrupted Francisco Diaz.

"You do! Well, for chrissake, tell me."

"Soon, Kelly. It's gotta be damn soon."

"Yeah, Pachuco. You're right about that. It's got to be soon."

Francisco Diaz alit from the step-ladder and walked to the hangar doors for a look about outside, an old habit. While he was gone, Kelly kept talking to himself.

"Soon . . . yeah . . . soon . . . It's got to be soon . . . Let's see . . . this is May 3rd . . . five-three . . . tomorrow is May 4th . . . five-four . . . the next day is May 5th . . . five-five . . . five-five . . . hmmm . . . five-five . . . hmmm . . . wait a minute . . . wait a minute! . . . wait a goddamn minute! . . . son-of-a-bitch! –"

"Pachuco!" he yelled. "Come here!"

Francisco Diaz ran back from the hangar door.

"Pachuco, I think I might have something. Listen to this."

"OK, Kelly. Shoot."

"Did you know that the 1918 Armistice to end World War I was purposely set up to go into effect at precisely the 11th hour of the 11th day of the 11th month?"

"Nope."

"And that D-Day in 1944 took place on the 6th day of the 6th month?"

"No. What's that got to do with Kashan?"

"Columbus set sail in 1492 on the 9th day of the 9th month. Don't you see it?"

"No, I don't see nothin'."

"In two days, it will be the 5th day of the 5th month."

"So what?"

"My God, Pachuco! Five is a sacred number to all Moslems because of their Islamic religion. They pray five times a day, have five holy men, conduct their daily lives by five special rules, and they probably shit five times a day too. The number five is magic to them. Surely, if they were planning something, they'd pick the 5th day of the 5th month. It's too much of a coincidence to pass over."

"Kelly, I'm not too smart, but that sounds nutty."

"Maybe it does at first. But, remember, we're not dealing with ordinary people. It's no more nutty than the Armistice beginning at 11 o'clock on November 11th. Or any more nutty than D-Day on June 6th. Or Columbus sailing on September 9th. The people who are in positions to make history think in such bizarre ways. It's incredible, but after sacrificing hundreds of thousands of lives, the assholes who lead armies to the brink of destruction revert to such childishness to worry about inane things like dates. In fact, in ancient times, kings would not make important decisions or lead troops into battle without first consulting their astrologers. Every king had his own personal astrologist. There's a rumor that Reagan's wife Nancy has one."

"No shit!"

"That's right. Countries are and always have been run by abnormal people . . . by the kooks of the world. And all nuts, it seems to me, are taken in by crap like astrology. Their superhuman egos lead them to think they are above and beyond ordinary mortals and to believe in superhuman forces."

"Kelly, you don't really believe all leaders are crazy? Do you?"

"In a way, yes. If any sane man were elected President of the United States, the very first thing he would do, in my opinion, is to resign. That's what a sane man would do. No sane man can possibly want all the troubles and responsibilities of the world on his shoulders. It's too much for any one man to bear. How the hell could he ever sleep at night?"

Francisco Diaz nodded silently.

"So, it may initially sound strange to sane people like us, but I feel certain the fanatics of Iran would pick the 5th day of the 5th month if they were planning something on a big scale. Something epic. All leaders are a little superstitious, especially those who believe they act with divine guidance from above."

"Maybe you're right."

"Bet your sweet ass I am. Jesus Christ, Pachuco, it's got to be something really big and we don't know what it is. At least we've made some progress as to when it will happen. The next question is, where?"

⁂

Jennie mechanically went through the motions of washing and drying her hair, putting on her make-up, and getting dressed to go to the hospital for the afternoon-evening shift. All the while, she kept thinking of the telephone call during the middle of the night and blamed herself for not having said more than just, "Hello." It must have been Kashan reaching out for help. She let her one opportunity slip by.

Reluctantly, she concluded there was only one thing she could possibly do. Her only hope was to put her faith and trust in Kelly.

In desperation, she picked up the phone and dialed the number of Kelly's hangar.

⁂

Kelly hung up the phone and then turned to Francisco Diaz.

"Pachuco, that was Jennie."

"What'd she have to say?"

"We're in luck. She said she thought Kashan was in Chicago. She's decided to play along with us. She was supposed to take him to the airport a couple of days ago so he could go there to pick up a plane for, as she put it, his last assignment. But, she didn't hear from him then. She also said she had a call in the middle of the night, but the caller didn't say anything. She thinks it was Kashan and she wants us to help him."

Francisco Diaz laughed. "What's he doin' in Chicago?"

"That's for us to find out."

Kelly was deep in thought for several minutes.

"Pachuco, go home and pack a suitcase. It's two o'clock now. Meet me back here in three hours. Chow up before you come back. We're going to Chicago. Shouldn't be too hard to find an Iranian with a Bonanza, but we can't do it sitting here on our asses. And, when we find him, I want him alive. No more foul-ups. Understand?"

"Hot doggie!"

ᛋᛏ

Kelly drove to *The Ranch* and hastily packed a small suitcase with several changes of underwear and a shaving kit. He had extra shirts and Levi's at the hangar. He went into the family room and took two .12 gauge shotguns and a half dozen boxes of shells from the gun case. From a drawer at the bottom of the case, he withdrew a .25 caliber Beretta automatic, a .38 caliber Detective Special Colt revolver, and several boxes of ammunition. The Beretta was small enough to fit easily into his back pocket, the Colt he stuck into his belt, and the shotguns he threw into the back of the Ferrari.

He went into the garage and opened the padlock on a large metal cabinet. Inside were plastic explosives, coffee cans filled with TNT, sticks of dynamite, blasting caps, and assorted hand grenades – a collection he had amassed surreptitiously during his years in the Navy. Kelly selected a dozen sticks of dynamite and as many hand grenades.

While loading up the car, he brewed a large pot of coffee. It would be a long flight and the coffee would be welcome later. He quickly made some ham sandwiches which, he knew from experience, would taste great somewhere over Kansas.

ᛋᛏ

The first thing Francisco Diaz did when he arrived home was inspect his machete. Then he made love to Momma.

The machete was delivered that morning by the Mexicans, friends of Francisco Diaz, who repaired and reupholstered the couch in Kelly's villa. They also cleaned the villa and replaced a piece of carpet stained by Francisco Diaz's blood.

He carefully scrutinized every inch of the blade and was happy it had not been damaged. Then he put it into the trunk of his car while Momma waited in the bedroom.

Lest he forget, Francisco Diaz retrieved his .38 caliber Colt, a match to Kelly's, from his dresser drawer before sitting down to a meal of *chili rellenos* and *enchiladas*. These he washed down with a bottle of *Carta Blanca* beer.

He kissed Momma and told her how much he loved her before leaving.

⁂

Back at the hangar, Kelly thought about calling Jennie, but decided against it. He would call her from Chicago. Instead, he called Laura and asked her to keep an eye on Jennie.

When Francisco Diaz returned to the hangar, he heard the air compressor running. Two cans of quick-drying acrylic paint were open on some newspapers spread on the hangar floor. Kelly had already changed the registration number on one side of the rudder from N77BK to N878KR and was working with a small spray gun on the other side. Francisco Diaz had seen him do this once before and was not surprised. It was a simple matter to alter the first "7" to an "8," alter the "B" to look like an "8," and add an "R" at the end. There was little danger of the switch being noticed since the FAA virtually never checked aircraft registration numbers.

It was nearly 7:00 p.m. before they lifted off from Runway 28L at Montgomery and took a left downwind departure. The dark night loomed to the east ahead and, as they gained altitude, looked like an enormous tidal wave waiting to engulf them. With a stop for refueling in Dalhart, Texas, Kelly estimated about ten hours for the flight from San Diego to Chicago. Because of another two hours lost in going from Pacific to Central Time, they did not expect to see Chicago until 7:00 a.m. the following morning.

"Just like old times, eh Pachuco?"

"Sure feels good," answered Francisco Diaz.

Kelly leveled off at 11,500 feet. Except for the lights of Phoenix and Albuquerque, the flight to Dalhart would be over the mostly open, lonely, mountainous wastelands of central Arizona and New Mexico. After Dalhart lay the flat farm country of Oklahoma, Kansas, Missouri and Illinois with no shortage of small towns to pinpoint the way.

There were no clouds in the sky and Kelly hoped it would stay that way. The flight would take longer if he had to file and fly on instruments – especially if they were put into a holding pattern before landing, which was not at all unusual in the Chicago Terminal Control Area.

Flying was effortless by the light of the full moon. The horizon was visible and terrain features were easily discernible. But, it really did not matter that much to Kelly, who let the Bonanza's autopilot do all the work. He sat back and listened to Miles Davis play classic ballads on his golden trumpet, the first of which was *Bye Bye Blackbird*.

23

QOM
May 4th

There was one empty seat around the mahogany table but, otherwise the room had not changed – unless a smile on Rajavi's face was to be regarded as a change. Instead of assuming his normal rigid stance in front of the table, he was absentmindedly gazing out one of the arch windows almost enjoying the activity at the nearby mosque. He was so overjoyed he could have been riding on a magic carpet and it showed. He scarcely noticed Colonel Alam and Colonel Badri come in and take their seats at the table minutes earlier, for his mind was thousands of miles away in another continent. Daydreams of smoke and fire occupied his thoughts as he stood by the window luxuriating in the sun. It was time for the meeting, time to cease the foolishness he had this once permitted himself, but he savored a last few seconds. Finally, he turned away from the window and sauntered over to the table.

"Good morning, gentlemen. I do hope you are as happy as I today," beamed Rajavi in a mellow, but jubilant voice.

Broad grins came to Alam's and Badri's faces. Rajavi's unusual cheerfulness was contagious. Spearheaded by it, they answered "Yes, General," almost in unison.

"I've received word from Major Muluk who met yesterday with Commander Kashan in Chicago. *WHISKEY HOTEL* is proceeding according to plan."

There was a slight stirring in the room and the two colonels gleamed with excitement. They smiled at each other and Rajavi's return smile acknowledged approval of their minor indulgence at the expense of military formality.

"As the loyal and dedicated Iranian I knew he was, as the lover of his country, his religion, and his ayatollahs, he will follow orders and complete the mission as directed. Commander Kashan checked the aircraft awaiting him at Meigs Field in Chicago and found all in order. A thousand pounds of high explosives were loaded onto the plane.

"Incidentally, the aircraft registration number is N555AK. The "N" designation refers to the United States, and it was necessary to include it to avoid arousing undue interest. The number "5" has, of course, special significance to all Moslems because of the five pillars of Islam, the five persons of the *ahl el-beit*, our five daily prayers, and so on. The "AK" refers obviously to our saint, Ayatollah Khomeini. Nothing could be more appropriate."

This added touch of sophistication greatly pleased Rajavi. Abstract concepts were important to Moslems. Rajavi was in the process of making history and everything had to be perfect. He'd forget nothing.

Rajavi continued, "I am sure you understand why we have selected the 5th second of the 5th minute of the 5th hour of the 5th day of the 5th month to destroy the White House. After *WHISKEY HOTEL*, the number "five" will become as significant to the rest of the world as it is to Moslems. The infidels are under the misconception that "seven" is a lucky number. They'll learn and we'll be their teachers.

"The ayatollahs have given their blessings to *WHISKEY HOTEL* and its success is begged for in their daily prayers to Mohammed. They personally studied our plan for five days and found no fault in its conception, planning, or ultimate impact upon the rest of the world, and referred to it as brilliant. They agree, the destruction of America's most cherished edifice by the forces of Islam will show the world the power of our religion – it will prove our religion is the true religion – it will show we are not barbarian terrorists."

Badri lit a cigarette and Rajavi did not seem to notice or care. Both Alam and Badri sat motionless listening attentively to essentially the same preaching they had heard for many years. Only this time it was Rajavi who was doing the preaching and not one of the ayatollahs. It would not last much longer.

But, Rajavi did not want it to end. He planned to be giving speeches like this long into the future. This was a dry run of sorts, a kind of prototype. He was going to be in the limelight and it was necessary that he speak well.

The order to have Muluk killed before he left the United States was already issued. Rajavi expected to grab all of the credit for *WHISKEY HOTEL.* Muluk was too smart to let him. With Muluk out of the way and Kashan dead, that left only Alam and Badri. They would not be a threat. They would surely be a lot easier to manipulate and control than Muluk. Muluk definitely had to go and he would as soon as he completed his role in the operation. Alam and Badri would be dealt with as need be.

Rajavi smiled when he thought of the glory and prestige awaiting him. In less than twenty-four hours, by this time tomorrow, he would be a national hero.

Rajavi put his thoughts aside and went on, "The ayatollahs have suggested a huge celebration all over the country once *WHISKEY HOTEL* is completed. They want constant anti-American propaganda on radio and television. We are to do all in our power to encourage massive crowds and let the religious leaders give speeches. The Army will stage a large parade and the Air Force will have a constant stream of fighters in the air over Teheran. Leaflets will be dropped by the millions. Fires will be started at the old American Embassy and prisoners set free. The ayatollahs are preparing three hours of speeches which will be delivered before a million Iranians and telecast to the rest of the country. This will be the greatest celebration since the ousting of the Shah and the return of Khomeini from France."

Rajavi envisioned himself before the television cameras and reminded himself he must later prepare a formal speech and answers to likely questions. Surely he would be awarded a decoration by the ayatollahs. Getting a dozen new uniforms made right after the meeting crossed his mind.

"Major Muluk will be in Washington to film the destruction of the White House from the grassy area just to the south. He'll film Kashan's plane approaching from the Washington Monument and its spectacular crash into the South Portico and the resulting fires and explosions. This film will be flown at supersonic speed to Iran and shown on television and in the movie theaters twenty-four hours a day for the next several weeks, or months, or maybe even years."

Rajavi failed to mention he would do all in his power to see Kashan received the minimum publicity. Kashan would be moderately praised and his family name mildly honored. But, after all, *any* pilot could have carried out the mission. The real genius lay in the concept and in the planning. Pilots, like soldiers, were a dime a dozen and expendable. Everyone knows the great military strategists of history received all the credit. No one cared or thought much of the lives that battle consumed. The end result was what mattered to historians. Iran had already lost 300,000 lives in the Holy War with Iraq. One more life could not possibly be of significance. Yes, he would play down the publicity Kashan received and direct as much attention as possible to his own strategic genius. The point would be made that the Iranian Air Force has many outstanding pilots, any one of them could have done what Kashan did. Besides, a dead hero isn't nearly as attractive as a live one. Muluk must not be mentioned in any way.

Other matters requiring immediate attention began to filter into Rajavi's mind. The ayatollahs would demand a detailed report. This could not be entrusted to Alam or Badri and he would do it himself. An address before the National Assembly would be expected. Finally, it would be necessary to brief foreign ambassadors and the delegation to the United Nations. A lot of difficult work lay ahead and he was not expecting to get much sleep in the next several days.

Alam had something on his mind and did not hesitate in speaking out. "General, there's one point which hasn't yet been mentioned, a point troubling me. Do you think the Americans will retaliate in any way?"

"I'm glad you brought that up, Colonel Alam. This is the one point to which the ayatollahs gave more thought than any other. I am pleased to say it's their consensus that world opinion will not permit any retaliation. The Americans will be embarrassed that a single small airplane was allowed to penetrate their defenses and cause such destruction. It would not sit well with the rest of the world if America sent squadrons of bombers over Iran. The Soviets will be on our side. World opinion will blame the Americans for having been so lax in protecting their precious White House. It was proposed, at one point, that we use Commander Kashan as a scapegoat and say he acted without authority, but this was quickly abandoned. First of all, even if it were true, no one would believe it. Secondly, it is highly preferable for Iran to take complete credit for bringing the most powerful nation in the world to its knees. Even if there were retaliation, Iranians would gladly sacrifice themselves for the glory of Islam.

"Past experience has shown there's little the Americans will do. Just as when one of their presidents is assassinated, they'll create special commissions to investigate the matter endlessly. Their news media will have a field day reporting the event. Months and months will go by before any action is taken. Their democratic form of government does not function well in coping with new situations. Half of their politicians will blame the other half and their own government for being at fault. There will be some firings and resignations. But, all in all, they'll spend most of their time blaming themselves for their own vulnerability. The rest of the world will do likewise. There will be no retaliation.

"The Americans did retaliate against Libya, but, in reality their air strike was little more than a slap on the wrist. However, world opinion was against Libya because it openly supported terrorism. That will not be the case with Iran. The world will see this more as David against Goliath and the United States will be the laughing stock of the world when it becomes known that Commander Kashan was taught to fly by the Americans, that their system permitted him to fly one of their own airplanes, to get so close to the White House as to destroy it. The American system will be found at fault and there will be no retaliation."

Rajavi knew that Muluk did not accept or believe these arguments in the least, but instead foresaw an immediate and sizable military retaliation. It was just one more reason for getting rid of him. Muluk was probably right, but it was just as wise to tell the ayatollahs what they wanted to hear. Whether or not there would be retaliation really did not interest Rajavi. Handling the honor and prestige to be bestowed upon him will be a full time job. He decided to let someone else worry about matters like retaliation.

Rajavi patiently waited for more questions. Fidgeting about in his seat, Badri was timid about the subject, but it finally came out. "General, we all realize *WHISKEY HOTEL* will be a great thing for Islam . . . Alam and I were wondering . . . well . . . we were wondering how we're going to be rewarded . . . Will we be given promotions . . . or commendations . . . and bonuses . . . for the important work we've done? Major Muluk conceived the idea, but surely it couldn't have been carried to fruition without our assistance . . . our brainstorming during many sessions must have been of immense help to him . . . maybe only indirectly . . . but nevertheless . . . we feel we helped considerably . . . "

Alam nodded in obvious agreement as Badri spoke. It was evident they had planned this together.

Deep in thought, Rajavi did not answer immediately.

Rajavi's silence disconcerted Badri. He wondered if he'd asked the wrong question and, sheepishly, began digging himself into a hole. "We're not greedy or anything, General . . . or that we expect too much . . . of course, we care more about serving our country . . . than we do about silly rewards . . . maybe you should forget that I ever asked the question . . . " There was a worried look on his face and his voice trailed off obsequiously.

Rajavi smiled broadly. "Not at all, not at all. Of course, all the members of this committee will be handsomely rewarded for their outstanding work. Neither of you will ever have to worry about working again. All of Iran will be eternally grateful to you for all you have done."

Alam and Badri were openly delighted by Rajavi's reply. Badri sighed relief, wiping his brow with his handkerchief. He fumbled for another cigarette and clumsily lit the end with the filter. He snuffed it out in the ash tray and lit another in its place. These antics did not go unnoticed by Rajavi.

Both Alam and Badri must die, Rajavi thought. *I had better take care of it personally. I can't afford to give them the opportunity to claim some of the credit for the operation. I can't let them tell anyone it was Muluk's idea. All the credit belongs rightfully to me. I was in charge of this operation and deserve all the credit. All of it! I was captain of the ship.*

Maybe I should kill the Brothers of Islam too! For a fleeting second, he wondered why they had not reported. But, his mind quickly returned to the honor soon to be his.

Rajavi focused his attention once again on the two men. "It won't be long now, gentlemen, not long before *Wind of the Shadow* becomes a part of Islamic history. Tomorrow morning!"

24

CHICAGO
May 4th

The bright sunshine belied the dark empty night left far behind in the other world of Dalhart, Texas. Passing over Joliet, Illinois, Kelly decided to follow Interstate 55, the Adlai Stevenson Expressway, to downtown Chicago. In about ten minutes they would be landing at Meigs Field. From twenty-five miles out, he contacted the tower at Meigs. Instead of following the interstate, Kelly was instructed to fly directly to Lake Michigan to avoid traffic at Midway Airport and follow the shoreline with a straight-in approach to Runway 36.

The tower cautioned Kelly to watch for birds in the vicinity of the airport. The controller in the tower was not a pilot. Had he been, he would have known birds are virtually impossible to see until it is too late to avoid them. Kelly paid no attention to the warning.

An hour and a half earlier, when passing over Kansas City, Missouri, Kelly decided to play a long shot. O'Hare was the world's busiest airport with almost exclusively jet traffic and Midway handled mostly air cargo. That left Meigs Field as the only other airport within the city limits for use by general aviation. Primarily though, the general aviation community preferred to stay out of the high traffic of Chicago and use Pal-Waukee or Waukegan Airports in the northern suburbs and Schaumburg or Du Page Airports in the west. If Kashan were at all trying to be discreet, he would shy away from O'Hare or Midway. The last time Kelly flew into O'Hare, he had to get a reservation five hours earlier and then was put into a holding pattern over Round Lake for nearly an hour. Air Traffic Control was prevented by law from banning small plane traffic at O'Hare but, they had their ways of making it inconvenient.

Kelly called Kansas City Center and asked for a telephone patch to Chicago Approach Control.

"Chicago Approach, this is Bonanza eight-seven-eight-kilo-romeo over Kansas City at seventy-five hundred. I need some information."

"Eight-kilo-romeo, Chicago Approach. Go ahead."

"Chicago Approach, eight-kilo-romeo is attending a meeting of the *Bonanza Society of America* and requests registration numbers of Bonanzas flying the past couple of days in the Chicago area." The *Bonanza Society* was one of the oldest organizations of private pilots in the United States.

It was a blatantly unusual request. The air traffic controller was puzzled by it and did not quite know how to respond. Usually, the weather was what most calls were about. Once in a while, there might be a question about radio frequencies or runway repairs, but never about other air traffic.

Being one of the most authoritarian agencies in the government, the FAA wielded unlimited power with a complex system of rules, laws, policies, and regulations – seemingly devised to hamper aviation. Each was strictly enforced in a tyrannical way. Whenever a doubt arose, the FAA automatically assumed the position of righteousness. Anything a pilot wanted had to be literally begged for.

The controller decided to play it safe.

"Eight-kilo-romeo, Chicago Approach cannot comply. That information is confidential." He spoke with a tone of authority designed to command awe and respect. No one would have guessed he was barely over five feet tall and weighed nearly 200 pounds.

Goddamn, thought Kelly. *I'll have to use a little friendly persuasion.*

"Chicago Approach, eight-kilo-romeo. That information essential. If necessary, I will go through General Candy at the Pentagon. Do you want his number?" *And your ass will be in a sling,* Kelly wanted to add but did not. Kelly was more than a close friend to General Candy. Candy had arranged the medicine operation in Baja and was at the party for Kashan at *The Ranch.* Kelly knew Candy would back him in anything.

Jimmy Wilcox, the controller, was even more perplexed. Pilots did not make demands of Chicago Approach. Who the hell did he think he was and who the hell did he think he was talking to? But, there was always the chance this was somebody important. Wilcox did not want to risk making a wrong decision and decided the safest thing was to make no decision at all. "Eight-kilo-romeo, Chicago Approach. Wait five please."

Wilcox called out to the shift supervisor, Randall Peters, who strutted over to his station. "What's up baby?" asked Peters.

"Randy, some buffoon wants to know about air traffic over Chicago for the past couple of days. He's got a hard-on for Bonanzas."

"What?"

"Yeah, he say's if I don't tell him he's got an inside line with some General Goddamn Candy at the Pentagon."

"Sounds like a smart-ass," said Peters.

"All pilots are smart-asses," answered Wilcox with disdain.

"Why can't the fly-boys just let us do our job of keeping them from running into one another? Don't they know we're busy here asshole deep with jet airliners?" Peters took a sip from his coffee mug.

"Should I tell the bastard to go piss up a rope?" asked Wilcox.

"I don't know. Jesus Christ, maybe he wants to know if I got laid last night too. Where is he?"

Wilcox stroked the black beard growing out of his pudgy jowls. "Just east of KC."

"Let me see the log first."

"Fuck 'em. Let's not tell him anything," Wilcox dared as he

punched some commands into a keyboard. His computer monitor displayed lists of data with each line beginning with an aircraft registration number. Peters stepped behind Wilcox and bent over for a better look.

"The last thing we want around here is for some jackoff to raise Cain in Washington. What'd you say the general's name was Wilcox?"

"Candy."

"Oh shit. I know that name. He's on the Joint Chiefs of Staff. He's a real prick."

"B.F.D. So what?"

"Now wait a minute, Wilcox, let's be a little diplomatic. We don't need any trouble. Washington has been getting hot on our asses lately because of the big increase in near misses this year. We don't want Candy pissing and moaning to some senator. There hasn't been much traffic the past couple of days. Maybe we should just tell him and get him off our back. Sam Candy is a mean ass. I read about him in *Time Magazine*. A nasty prick."

"You're the boss."

"Tell him what he wants."

Visibly disgusted, Wilcox stroked his beard with one hand and picked up the telephone with the stubby fingers of the other as Peters walked away. "Bonanza eight-kilo-romeo, Chicago Approach."

"Chicago Approach, eight-kilo-romeo with you."

"Eight-kilo-romeo, Chicago Approach. Our log shows only three Bonanzas with activity in the Chicago Terminal Control Area the past two days. Bonanza one-five-seven-four-sierra has been flying out of the Waukegan Airport. Niner-seven-eight-five-yankee and five-five-five-alpha-kilo have been doing practice approaches out of Meigs Field. We don't have data on operations outside the TCA."

"Chicago Approach, eight-kilo-romeo thanks you, and General Candy thanks you too from the bottom of his heart." Grinning, Kelly hung the microphone on the tab between the seats and turned to Francisco Diaz.

"Did you hear that, Pachuco?"

"Yeah, but what about it?"

"Those goddamn fives again. Five-five-five-alpha-kilo. These Iranians are nuts. It's Kashan's plane. Three fives and alpha-kilo. The alpha-kilo surely signifies Ayatollah Khomeini. It was stupid for them to draw attention to the plane with such an obvious numbering, but fanatics aren't logical. Three fives and 'AK.' We're going to Meigs."

While taxiing off the runway to transient parking at Meigs, Kelly and Francisco Diaz scanned everything in sight for any sign of Kashan. They did not want to be seen first. But, there were no Bonanzas on the tarmac and no sign of human life except for two heads moving around in the control tower.

Rather than inquire at the tower, they went to Butler Aviation, the only fixed base operator on the field. A white-haired, distinguished looking man in his sixties was busy leafing through a stack of receipts on top of a glass display case containing maps and assorted flying manuals.

"Howdy," said Kelly.

"Hi. You just land in the Bonanza?"

"Yeah. How about having the gas truck top off the tanks with hundred octane?"

"Nice looking airplane. Where're you from?"

"Thanks. San Diego."

"Long way from home. Anything else I can do for you?"

"We're supposed to meet a guy in a Bonanza – an Iranian."

"Oh yeah. Been three or four of them around here last week. They pay all their expenses with new hundred-dollar bills. I like that. Nice doing business with them. We kept a plane here for them for a week or so. It was a nice spiffy looking thing – a V-tail like yours."

"Can you tell me where they are now?"

"Nope, 'fraid not. Paid all their bills and the Bonanza left about twenty minutes ago."

"Oh hell. Did he say where he was going."

"No. But he asked an awful lot of questions about landing at Washington National in D.C. so I figure he's gone back that away."

"Thanks. Was his plane number five-five-five-alpha-kilo?"

"Yeah, that's right."

⁂

In spite of Major Muluk insisting it was perfectly safe, Kashan felt uneasy flying with the explosives on the plane the previous day. Before the explosives could detonate, Muluk explained, each suitcase had to be activated by turning a key in its lock. Kashan would do this on the morning of May 5th before his last flight.

Kashan took off from Meigs to the north towards Navy Pier. Making a tight turn with the John Hancock Building as a focal point, he headed east over the southern tip of Lake Michigan. The Chicago skyline slowly melted into the horizon behind him. He intended to stay low and enjoy the scenery. The manifold pressure was set to 21 inches and the propeller pitch adjusted for 2200 rpm. The Bonanza hummed along quietly. Scattered clouds over the lake thickened to a broken sky as the Bonanza crossed the shoreline in Indiana over the Indiana Dunes State Park in the general direction of Fort Wayne. Kashan estimated his ground speed at 180 mph and figured to be in Frederick, Maryland in just over three hours. He was amazed how crowded the Eastern part of the United States seemed in comparison to the openness of the Western states.

An hour before leaving Meigs, he had bid Muluk a warm last farewell. Kashan was now resigned to his fate. He tried not to think of Jennie and what might have been.

⁂

Vending machines dispensing soft drinks, cigarettes, candy and coffee took up one wall of the pilot lounge at Butler. The opposite wall was dominated by a five-foot by seven-foot contour map of the United States used for flight planning. A length of cord, held by a thumbtack through Meigs Field, dangled from the map and concentric circles, centered at Meigs, were drawn in

India ink at 100-mile intervals. Mounted next to the map were two wall phones with direct lines to the Chicago Flight Service Station. A dozen metal folding chairs surrounded the two long Formica-topped tables in the center of the room. One of the tables held a stack of tattered flying magazines and on the other were scattered pads of blank flight plan forms. Framed prints of WWII fighters filled the empty walls not occupied by the lone window which looked out onto the runway. It was a typical pilot lounge.

Francisco Diaz sat on one of the chairs with his feet propped up on one of the tables sipping coffee from a plastic cup. Kelly stood in front of the wall map gazing at the area between Chicago and the east coast.

"Kelly, how does this alpha-kilo stuff stand for Ayatollah Khomeini?"

"Simple, Pachuco. Alpha stands for 'A' and kilo stands for 'K' in the international phonetic alphabet and those are his initials."

"That's what I thought. Well, then why can't the 'W' and the 'H' of *Whiskey Hotel* stand for somethin' else?"

"They can."

"Like maybe . . . White House?"

Turning from the wall map, a look of wonder filled Kelly's eyes. He smiled and said, "Pachuco, did I ever tell you that I love you because you have the brain of a mathematical wizard?"

Kelly went out to his Bonanza and returned with a briefcase full of maps and charts and the paper bag of ham sandwiches which they had not eaten during the night. While Francisco Diaz busied himself with the sandwiches and the pile of flying magazines, Kelly pensively studied the maps and charts. Occasionally he would get up to refer to the wall map and at other times he would do some quick calculations on a small pocket computer he kept in the briefcase. He made several calls on one of the wall phones to the Chicago Flight Service Station. Finally, he seemed finished, carefully folded the maps and put everything back into the briefcase.

"Pachuco, there's little doubt about it in my mind. Kashan is going to try something funny at the White House. My hunch is he might try to drop a bomb. We've got to stop him."

"*Jesus Maria!*"

"A few days ago, Pachuco, things were different. I was more interested in Kashan for selfish reasons. But, now, my God, we've got to stop him. We can't let him bomb the White House. Do you know what turmoil that would throw the country into? Besides, I really do love this country in spite of the crap I sometimes say."

"Shouldn't we tell somebody – like the FBI or the CIA?"

"No. We can handle it."

"How're we gonna do that?"

"I've got some ideas. He didn't file a flight plan when he left Meigs because it's not required in good weather. Washington Approach hasn't heard from him yet. He'll probably spend the night in some out of the way place and head for D.C. in the morning. There are just too many airports within a hundred miles of D.C. and most of them don't have control towers. There's no way we can hope to find out where he is. We've been lucky so far."

"What's next?" asked Francisco Diaz.

"We're going to the D.C. area – to a small airport called Bower near Oxon Hill in Maryland. It's a private field but, they accommodate overnighters. It's on the Potomac River just south of Washington National Airport. We'll be in the air tomorrow morning waiting for Kashan."

"OK."

"Let's get going. We can make some more checks later when we're airborne."

25

SAN DIEGO
May 4th

Laura sat at a corner table at *The Top of the Cove* restaurant nursing a cup of coffee. Her table commanded a sweeping view of the Pacific waters off La Jolla. Several small fishing boats, anchored in the cove, hoped to catch some of the yellowtail tuna running in close to shore.

At first, Jennie thought of meeting Laura at Kelly's villa, but after reconsideration decided neutral ground would be better. She did not know how Laura would respond to her suggestion of a meeting. "You had better goddamn well be sober," Jennie said when she called Laura that morning. "And, I mean it!"

Jennie walked over to the table and sat across from Laura.

"Hiya toots," beamed Laura.

"Cut the nonsense, Laura." Jennie was determined, not angry. She added, "Have you heard from Kelly?"

"Yes. He called and asked me to keep an eye on you . . . I don't know why he would do that . . . I don't even like you."

"You don't like anybody, Laura. Not even yourself."

"Well –"

Jennie interrupted, "This isn't the time for asinine quibbling. Can't you see something is going on that overrides your childish likes and dislikes? Cut the pretensions and get serious. Now, tell me about that call. If there is anything we can do to help

Kelly and Kashan, let's get our heads on straight and do it. No nonsense, Laura. Please."

Laura sat up in her chair. "Kelly said he was going to Chicago with Francisco Diaz."

"And?"

"They went in Kelly's plane. He said he'd call when they got there but I haven't heard anything."

Once Laura accepted Jennie's resoluteness, the conversation flowed smoothly. There was little one knew that the other did not, but Jennie methodically forced herself and Laura to go over everything that happened in the past few days. As far as Jennie was aware, only Laura and she had any inklings something amiss was going on. All along, Jennie knew what she was going to do. First, she had to make sure there were no important pieces of information she lacked. After the better part of an hour, they were finished.

"Laura, I will admit to you I have been a fool in believing just about everything Kashan told me. He has been obviously shading the truth to cover something up. I don't know exactly what, but I intend to find out and get to the bottom of this. Perhaps it's all innocent and perhaps it's not. We can't simply sit around and drink coffee while Kelly and Kashan are flying all over the country. Grab your purse."

"Where are we going?"

"To see an old friend, Ben Crawley. He runs the FBI in San Diego. I need your help, Laura. I desperately need it."

Suddenly, Laura felt a glimmer of admiration for Jennie and began to think that some day she might even like her.

Instead of meeting in his office in the Federal Building downtown, Crawley decided to meet with Jennie and Laura in an unmarked office he kept on West Point Loma Blvd. As far as he knew, there was nothing extraordinary about the meeting; however, experience had taught him less formal surroundings put people at ease. He sat on one of the sofas and Jennie and Laura on the other with a coffee table separating them. Brass lamps on the end tables cast a warm glow.

Laura sat like a mannequin while Jennie did the talking. She told Crawley about Kashan's sudden reappearance after his long absence, about Kashan's medical mission for Iran, about Kelly and Kashan's trip to Baja, about Francisco Diaz being hit over the head. She told how Kelly thought *WHISKEY HOTEL* was a cover name for a suspected secret mission and about Kelly's frequent trips to Mexico. She repeated what Kelly said about finding the *Brothers of Islam* on his estate at *The Ranch.* She left to the end her future plans with Kelly and her previous romantic involvement with Kashan. But, Jennie knew nothing would be gained by omitting anything and she was as candid as she could be.

"So, as far as you know, they are both in Chicago now," summarized Crawley. "I hate to be so blunt, but we hear stories pretty much like this every day. Most of them turn out to be nothing. But, we can never be too careful. It is possible that there is an explanation for everything. I'll admit things look suspicious, but people do go around hitting each other over the head more than the general public would care to admit. Although Kashan's story about being here on a medical mission smells rotten, it could be true."

Crawley was doing his best to be tactful.

"What puzzles me most," said Crawley, "Is why Kelly didn't come to us. He was an officer in the Navy and he knows better."

"Ben, if you knew Kelly," answered Jennie, "You would know he is one of the most self-reliant men God ever created. He is self-made and doesn't know the meaning of the word 'help.' It is a part of his personality others admire most, including me. Kelly is usually the one people go to for help and advice. I know he means well."

"Another thing, Jennie, why would Iran let one of its top pilots leave the war with Iraq?"

"Kashan is a compassionate man," said Jennie. "He hated flying combat missions and directing his energies to killing. He finally decided he had enough and chose to do something positive for humanity."

"That may be," said Crawley. "But, you must admit, it didn't take him long to abandon his noble cause and propose to you."

"Ben, you're not being fair," argued Jennie.

"Yes, I am being totally fair," insisted Crawley. "And, you had better accept it. Your involvement with Kashan, whatever it was, has perhaps kept you from the obvious. You didn't come here seeking blind sympathy. You want the answers to troubling questions. You know me well enough to know I don't beat around the bush."

"You're right . . . Ben. Yes . . . you are. I suppose the important question is what we do next?"

"You're not going to like this, but there is nothing you can do at the moment. Leave everything up to me. I'll do all I can. I'll find out if they went to Chicago. I'll make some other checks too. If there is anything unusual, I'll turn it up. Go home and relax the best you can.

"You must put complete faith in me. I won't ask for your word, but I know you will call me as soon as you hear anything from either Kashan or Kelly."

After a few more words of encouragement, Laura and Jennie left. On the way to the car, Laura said, "Jennie, it may not sound like much coming from me, but I respect what you are trying to do. It must have been a difficult choice for you."

"Yes, it was," answered Jennie softly. "Very, very difficult."

Crawley drove back to his office downtown. It would be easier to conduct his investigations from there.

26

WASHINGTON, D.C.

May 5th

Kashan spent a restless night in a motel a mile from the Frederick Airport. In the early morning, he decided to offer prayers. He asked himself what difference it would make in a couple of hours, but prayed anyway.

Staring at the piece of paper, he checked his calculations for the last time. Flying the dogleg, he estimated 45 miles to the White House. With six minutes for the climb to 3000 feet at 120 mph and cruising the remaining 33 miles at 200 mph, it would take a total of 15.9 minutes. He wondered if he should take off a few seconds for the final dive. No, he decided to just call it 16 minutes. He would start his takeoff roll at 4:49 a.m. That would be close enough.

⁂

"Rise and shine Pachuco."

"*Jesus Maria,* Kelly, what time is it?"

"Three a.m. Get movin'."

"OK, OK. You still think Kashan is gonna try somethin' at five this morning?"

"Yep! And we're gonna be ready!"

Thomas J. Duncan, head of the FBI, cursed several times, but it did not stop the phone next to his bed from ringing. Finally, he reached over and picked it up.

"What son-of-a-bitch would wake me during the middle of the night?" he growled angrily even though such calls were not uncommon.

"Tom, Ben Crawley here in San Diego."

"What the fuck time is it?"

"A little after midnight here."

"This had better be goddamn good."

"A couple of dames came to see me late yesterday and I've spent the entire evening checking out their story . . . "

It took a good fifteen minutes for Crawley to condense everything for Duncan and answer questions. Yes. There had been an Iranian at Meigs Field during the past week. Yes. Kelly had landed there too. No. The Bureau had not been keeping tabs on Kashan. That was Agency territory. No. He did not know where the two planes were now. Yes. He knew Jennie and she was reliable.

"Sounds like you may be onto something, Ben. I'll get some boys here and in Chicago on it right away. Don't say anything to the Agency until I give you the word. Thanks for calling."

Duncan hung up the phone.

"Got to go, Margie," he said to the shapely blond in bed next to him. "Got some action in Chicago."

By that time, she had her hand on his groin and began to stroke him. He responded immediately and decided ten more minutes wouldn't make any difference.

There was plenty of light from the four-day-old full moon and Kashan did not need a flashlight. He opened the baggage door of the Bonanza and inserted the key into the lock of one of the two suitcases. After hesitating for a moment, he turned the key. There was no hesitation with the second suitcase. He closed and locked the baggage door and stepped up on the wing to open the cabin door on the passenger side. Kneeling on the passenger seat, he reached over and, one by one, inserted the key and turned it in the lock of each of the suitcases. *Maybe I could throw the suitcases out the door,* he pondered. *No, that's a stupid thought. I might get one out but not all five, and the one would hit the wing anyway and detonate. No way.*

Sitting down in the pilot's seat, he reached over and closed and latched the door. After fastening his seat belt, he flipped on the battery and alternator switches. Closing his eyes, he thought of Jennie, trying desperately to put her out of his mind by concentrating on the mission. It was useless, when he opened his eyes the filigree locket was watching.

⁂

Kelly sat on the front passenger seat with his feet out the door, heels resting on the wing, and undid the last bolt holding the door hinge. Standing in front of the right wing, Francisco Diaz reached out and held the door while Kelly worked with the wrench.

When Kelly finished he said, "Just latch it down in the baggage compartment, Pachuco. We can stop at some small airport later and put it back on."

"I've never shot down a plane before," said Francisco Diaz.

"Normally, you need five to qualify as an ace, but if you get this one, I'll personally see to it that you get the DFC, the Victoria Cross, the Croix de Guerre, the Knight's Cross with Oak Leaves and Swords, and all the tacos you can eat for the next hundred years. But, remember, we want to take him alive if we can."

Francisco Diaz retrieved the two shotguns and shells from the baggage compartment and set them on the floor in front of the passenger seat. He was proficient with shotguns as with most types of weapons – the loan shark had seen to that.

"Remember, Pachuco, don't shoot until I tell you. I'm gonna get so close that it'll be like shooting fish in a barrel."

"Yeah, but it still seems to me it's gonna be awful tough to hit a movin' target like that."

"Don't forget, I'm his teacher and I know what moves he'll try to make. I'll get you so close you'll be able to read the time on his watch and count the rivets in his wing. Don't worry. Just let me do the flying. Once he sees us shooting, I can probably force him down."

"OK. If you say so."

Suddenly, Kelly remembered telling Jennie what a good pilot Kashan was; it made him uneasy.

"I've also got another surprise for Kashan. I had Allison piston rods put into the engine and a supercharger installed to increase compression. The mechanic added a pump to squirt a blend of alcohol and distilled water to cool the mixture. I picked these tips up over the years from pros at the Reno Air Races, but never used them before. We'll be able to fly circles around any other Bonanza."

"Yeah. But I still think it's gonna be tough."

"And remember, for chrissake, we want him alive so don't throw any grenades unless we absolutely have to, unless we're banked real steep and high enough over him. We don't want to blow our own asses up."

"I'll let you tell me when. I'm not crazy about these fuckin' pineapples."

"We're going to take off about four-thirty and circle a couple of miles north of the White House. We can circle there under the TCA as long as we stay between a thousand and fifteen hundred feet. We'll listen to Washington National Tower and to Washington Approach Control on our radios. If anybody asks us what we're doing, we'll say we're taking aerial photographs."

Major Muluk stayed at the Crystal City Marriott Hotel on Jefferson Davis Highway, a short distance from Washington National Airport. The previous evening, he treated himself to the swimming pool and sauna and a dinner of veal cordon bleu. He thought about celebrating with a bottle of wine, something he had never tasted. No. He decided against it. Alcohol was expressly forbidden by Islamic law.

Because of the early hour, special arrangements had been made for breakfast to be served in his room. The two Iranians who met him at the airport occupied the adjoining suite but, Muluk kept his door locked and had little to do with them. He was grateful they had brought the right video camera – the one he spent so many hours using the past two weeks in Iran. During the night he charged the battery pack and its spare.

He placed the battery packs and video camera into the specially designed black suitcase and set it by the door. Before leaving, Muluk made one last time check with the telephone operator.

It was still dark when his Hertz limousine emerged from the hotel underground parking garage. Muluk preferred to drive. The Washington Monument was a short distance away over the Rochambeau Memorial Bridge. He would be early – very early – as he had intended. That would give him more than enough time to find a parking space and a good spot for taking pictures. Muluk believed in being early.

Confident everything was going to work out well, Muluk could not help but wonder if the cherry blossoms would be in bloom this time of the year.

⁂

Kelly and Francisco Diaz circled over the northern part of Washington, D.C., occasionally straying as far as Silver Spring and Bethesda. The gear was down and full flaps in. There was no conversation, the atmosphere was tense. They kept searching the sky, but there was nothing. The minutes at first ticked by slowly, then speeded up rapidly as 5:00 a.m. approached. Soon it was 5:00 a.m. and five after and quickly ten after.

Time could not be stopped, it was five-thirty and the first smattering of light began to creep over the Eastern horizon.

There was no sign of Kashan.

"Maybe we screwed up Pachuco," Kelly said.

"What're we gonna do now?" asked Francisco Diaz. "It's past five-thirty."

"Don't know. Grab the *Farmer's Almanac* from the glove compartment and see what time sunup is."

Francisco Diaz opened the glove compartment and got out the *Farmer's Almanac*. He shined his flashlight on the page for the month of May.

"Let's see . . . sunup for May 5th is four-thirty-five."

"That's in Boston," said Kelly. "You'll have to look in the time correction tables and get the correction for Washington."

Francisco Diaz looked in the table. "Have to add thirty-five minutes for D.C.," he said.

"That makes it ten minutes after five," said Kelly. "Add one hour for daylight savings time and –"

Kelly abruptly stopped talking in the middle of his sentence. Francisco Diaz was quick to notice and quick to catch the reason for it.

"Kelly, am I thinkin' what you're thinkin'?"

"Yeah, Pachuco. Maybe Kashan isn't using daylight savings time."

"That's right."

"That's our last hope. With standard time, he'd be an hour behind. Keep your fingers crossed."

Kashan was *not* using daylight savings time.

The point had been considered in detail by the ayatollahs and at the meetings in Qom. The ayatollahs were opposed to daylight savings time which they regarded a capitalistic corruption of natural phenomena. More pragmatically, Muluk could not take video pictures unless standard time were followed.

There was no traffic at Frederick and no tower to worry about. Kashan sat in the run up area until 4:48 a.m. Eastern Standard Time before calling Unicom on 123.0 and announcing he was taking off. He taxied into position and, at exactly 4:49 a.m., eased the throttle all the way forward and began his takeoff roll.

The city lights of Frederick glowed off to his right and behind stood the Blue Ridge Mountains – foothills by comparison with the Rockies or the lofty peaks of Iran. At 1000 feet, Kashan could make out the peak of Sugar Loaf Mountain and headed directly toward it. He leveled off at 3000 feet, the published altitude for beginning the *River Visual Approach* into Washington National, then called Washington Approach on 119.85 for permission from Air Traffic Control to fly through the Dulles Terminal Control Area, and inform them of his intention to fly the *River Visual Approach*.

Except for Kashan, there was no other traffic on the radar screens at the Air Traffic Control Center. It was too early in the morning. The controller responded to Kashan's request, "Five-five-five-alpha-kilo is cleared for the *River Visual Approach*. Intercept Victor-eight and fly heading one-three-seven degrees. Maintain three thousand. Contact National tower ten DME northwest on one-one-niner point one. Squawk zero-three-six-six."

Kelly and Francisco Diaz did not hear Kashan's call to Washington Approach but picked up the call back to Kashan loud and clear.

"He's coming in from the northwest, Pachuco, along the Potomac River. We'll hear him report in when he's ten miles away from National. We'll be closer than that and maybe see him by then."

Francisco Diaz picked up one of the shotguns and cradled it in his arms.

It was light enough for Kashan to make out the rolling hills, the snaky rivers and streams, and a small lake here and there which composed the farm country of Virginia and Maryland. The pastoral landscape gradually gave way to city lights, freeways and shopping malls. The white marble of the Washington Monument dominated the Washington skyline, standing out like a lone pine on a vast desert.

Kashan passed Great Falls and, in front of him, could see the Capital Beltway crossing the Potomac River near the Naval Ship

Research and Development Center.

He would call Washington Approach when over the beltway.

Major Muluk was early. Parking his rental car on one of the side streets nearby, he found an empty park bench in The Ellipse that seemed an excellent spot from which to capture Kashan coming from the south, an overhead pan would catch the belly of the airplane, then the flames and explosions to the north. It would be perfect.

Muluk was so early he decided to take a stroll to pass some time. Heading down Constitution Avenue, he ended up at the Lincoln Memorial. The Washington Monument stood majestically at the end of the Reflecting Pool, whose water bounced off rays of gleaming moonlight. Muluk decided to go over to it. The first faint streaks of light appeared in the sky as he arrived, nearly time to unpack the camera from the black suitcase.

His eye caught sight of a pamphlet lying in his path with a picture of the Washington Monument and he bent over and picked it up. Perusing it as he walked, the pamphlet gave the history of the Washington Monument. What caught his eye immediately were the physical dimensions:

> *"The Washington Monument is 555 feet 5 inches all and is 55 feet square at the base . . . "*

All those fives!

All those fives!

All those fives!

This had to be more than just a coincidence, perhaps a divine message from God. Obviously, the fives were a sign from Mohammed who intended for them to destroy the Washington Monument all along. They had been too ignorant to see it. It was too late now. There was no way Kashan could be reached to change his target.

It was a bad omen.

Racked by despair, Muluk wanted to scream out, "The Washington Monument is 555 feet 5 inches tall and is 55 feet square at the base!" Then, he thought of the picture he had sent to Rajavi. "The Pentagon has five sides!" and wanted to scream it as well.

As soon as Kashan passed the beltway, Kelly and Francisco Diaz saw him near Langley and the CIA Building. It was two-and-a-half minutes past the hour. With his landing gear up, Kashan began a high speed descent. Kelly rightly guessed he had no intention of landing. Several layers of clouds had formed during the night but were well high in the sky.

Totally preoccupied with his flight, Kashan did not see Kelly's Bonanza slightly below and off to his left. Kelly purposely tried to stay under Kashan and in his blind area blocked out by Kashan's left wing. Kelly and Francisco Diaz arrogantly grinned as Kelly rapidly closed the distance between the two aircraft. Finally, he nudged Francisco Diaz with his elbow. Francisco Diaz smiled and raised the shotgun, pointing it out the open door. He fired two quick blasts but missed.

Not being able to hear the reports above the sounds of his engine and propeller, Kashan did not notice the shots.

Deciding he had to get closer, Kelly motioned to Francisco Diaz to get ready. Kashan's sudden dive caught them by surprise. Wingtip to wingtip, Kashan's head spun sideways. His eyes opened wide in disbelief. It seemed Francisco Diaz was sitting on Kashan's wing, pointing a gun straight at him. Francisco Diaz's daunting smile elicited an unpleasant memory of the night at the villa. Kashan could not see Kelly, but knew Kelly's airplane and sensed Kelly's presence.

Shocked, Kashan wondered where they had come from. *How did they know? Am I hallucinating? How did they know? No one knew. Rajavi said so. So did Muluk. It just can't be. They're not only here, they're shooting. I didn't even tell Jennie my final destination. But, wait. maybe . . . just maybe . . . maybe Kelly was sent by Allah . . . maybe Kelly is the answer to my dilemma . . . maybe!.*

Kashan began formulating a plan.

Banking precipitously to the right, Kashan did not see Francisco Diaz pull the trigger. The shot caught the underside of the fuselage but did virtually no damage. Immediately, Kelly followed Kashan's steep bank. This time he would stay with Kashan.

With the first shotgun empty, Francisco Diaz felt around the cockpit for the other and the extra boxes of shells. Everything was happening quickly – he would not get a chance to use the hand grenades.

If Kashan continued turning, his course would take him away from the planned approach over the Tidal Basin. He snapped the Bonanza into a bank in the opposite direction and pushed forcefully on the yoke to increase the angle of dive. For a brief moment, Kashan was totally exposed and Francisco Diaz had a clear shot from only feet away. But, by the time he sighted and pulled the trigger, Kelly started a reverse bank and the shots went wild.

Kashan's Bonanza screamed over the Tidal Basin at 260 mph, diving frantically to get low with Kelly practically on top. Kelly looked ahead and saw the White House. He had guessed correctly. Kashan was headed there. Kelly rammed the throttle all the way forward and felt his airplane jump with a new surge of power. Slowly, he inched in front of Kashan and turned into Kashan forcing a bank or the risk of a collision. Less than ten feet over the grass, Kelly angled in even closer. Kashan at last gave in, swerving to the right. The Washington Monument passed between them.

Kashan was out of position for the approach to the White House, with Kelly quickly closing the gap. Francisco Diaz fired again and this time the blast knocked out one of Kashan's side windows. Kashan tried twisting and turning, finally he pulled back on the yoke to gain altitude. Kelly followed, Francisco Diaz's body rocking back and forth, from side to side, trying to keep pace with the gyrating motions of the airplane.

After a sharp right turn over the dome of the Capitol, Kashan headed back toward the Potomac River and the Tidal Basin. Then he entered a mad dive, beginning a series of evasive maneuvers. Once his airspeed built up, Kashan pulled all the way back, starting the first half of a loop. At the top, Kelly suspected he would execute an Immelmann by doing a half roll, pull back on the yoke again to stall and go into a spin. Kashan might have forgotten that Kelly taught him the sequence years ago.

Francisco Diaz fumbled for more shotgun shells, some of the boxes had fallen under his seat. Unlatching his shoulder harness and seat belt, he bent forward until he had a firm grasp on one box, still holding the shotgun firmly in his other hand. He did not notice that Kelly had started the first half of the loop.

Although the loop was initiated at 250 mph, by the time the Bonanza reached the top inverted, the airspeed had bled to 80 mph, the lost velocity being converted to altitude.

Centrifugal force kept Francisco Diaz in his seat, but as Kelly executed the half roll at the top of the loop, Francisco Diaz tumbled out the open cabin door, landing on the rotating wing. As if an enormous paddle, the wing slapped his face once ferociously, breaking his nose and knocking out his front teeth. Instinctively, he dropped the shotgun and a box of shells, one extended arm stretching for a handhold on the wing's leading edge, the other grabbing the frame of the door. The extra boxes of shells sailed past and the other shotgun sped by.

The thump on the wing and the accompanying buffeting drew Kelly's attention. Looking over, he was awe-struck at the sight of Francisco Diaz thrashing about outside the airplane, one hand clutching the door frame. His first impulse was to release the controls and lunge over to help, but there was no time.

His bloody face contorted by the angry wind, his hair straining to rip free from his scalp, Francisco Diaz slid off the back edge of the wing.

For a while, he seemed suspended, motionless in midair, his eyes locked on the Bonanza, pleading helplessly, pleading in vain. His arms reached out as the Bonanza sped away, his fingers grasping at molecules of empty sky.

He kept yelling "Momma, Momma, Momma," over and over as he plunged the 1000 feet straight down into the Potomac River.

"Aw, c'mon Dunky, just one more time?"

Thomas J. Duncan slipped into his pants, sat on the edge of the bed and began putting on his socks. "For Christ sake, Margie, I've got a job to do for the FBI. You know better than to ask now. I'll be back later."

"Then tell me you love me, Tommy-Tommy."

"OK, OK. I love you," said Duncan dispassionately. "Help me find my shoes."

"Are we going out for din-din tonight?"

"I don't know. Where are those goddamn shoes?"

"Here's one, baby, right here under the bed-bed," said Margie, naked, on all fours, peeking under the bedspread.

Duncan finished dressing hastily, put on his shoulder holster, quickly kissed Margie, and left.

By the time Kashan entered his spin, Francisco Diaz was in the river. Kashan did not see him fall.

Oh my God, thought Kelly, stunned by the empty seat next to him. *Poor bastard! When's it going to end?* But, there was no turning back. He clenched his fist and his jaw tightened. Now, he has to stop Kashan. But, how? With Diaz gone, he had no way of reaching the dynamite or grenades. Even if he had them, he couldn't fly the Bonanza and throw them out at the same time, the Bonanza's only door being on the passenger side.

Kashan completed two turns of the spin, pulled out fifty feet above the water and headed for the Tidal Basin again.

Kelly followed a fraction of a second later.

As the distance between them narrowed, Kelly thought of chopping off a piece of Kashan's tail section with his propeller. He had heard of that having been done during WWI when machine guns had failed.

Just a little, tiny nick, that's all it'll take, thought Kelly. *I just need to barely touch Kashan's tail. I'll ease her forward ever so slowly, and get a tiny little nick. That will be enough to send him out of control. I've got to stop him. If he'll just stay in one place long enough, I'll get him.*

Kelly's Bonanza inched closer.

Kashan's mind was racing as fast as the airplanes. *Kelly's no fool, but if I can trick him into crashing into the White House, I'll be home free. I'm a better pilot than he,* smiled Kashan. *I proved that years ago in Yuma when I was his student. If Kelly crashes into the White House, Rajavi will think it was me, even if the Americans say otherwise. WHISKEY HOTEL will be a success. Kelly'll be gone and I'll have Jennie all to myself. I'll get low and pin Kelly under me. He won't be able to move. I can do it. I did it before. I know I can do it. Maybe my prayers have been answered. Praise be to Allah!*

Less than a foot separated Kelly's whirling propeller from Kashan's V-tail. *Here we go,* thought Kelly, *time for some rough play!*

"Banana Peel calling Blue Banana."

Hearing his radio spark to life startled Kelly. The thought of calling Kashan on it never occurred to him. He eased back on the throttle, permitting several feet separation between the Bonanzas. After switching radio channels to the one used years ago in Yuma for unofficial conversations, Kelly answered, "Blue Banana with you."

"Where are you?" asked Kashan.

"Right behind you. What the hell are you up to, Kashan?"

"I want to see what the White House looks like from the air. Are you going to try to stop me?"

"You're damned right! Why don't we talk this over?"

"That's what I'm doing. Pull up alongside so I can see you while we talk."

"OK. But, let's head downriver."

Both turned south, flying in formation.

"You're making a mistake, Kashan. Why don't we land and kick this around before it's too late?"

"There is no mistake, Kelly. I'm going to take out the White House. Do you want to go with me?"

"Kashan, be reasonable!"

He's playing right into my hands, thought Kashan.

"I am reasonable, Kelly, but I've got a job to do."

"You're nuts! Think of Jennie. She cares about you. Stop this crazy stunt. Think of her."

"I think of her all the time, but there are more important things in life."

"Why not knock this crap off, Kashan? You know my plane can fly circles around yours. Up here, it's our machines that count. Without them, we don't have any definition or much in common. We're like naked strangers."

Kashan executed a steep turn, heading back upriver and Kelly followed. Kashan dove for the water, letting Kelly get below.

"See you in heaven," said Kashan.

"Not if I have anything to say about it, you bastard," said Kelly.

They raced towards the Tidal Basin, Kashan gradually descending, forcing Kelly lower. Kelly's only choice, thought Kashan, was to stay below so he could keep Kashan in view. If he let Kashan get ahead, he would have no way of stopping him.

"Kashan!" called Kelly.

There was no answer.

I'll time this just right, thought Kashan. *At the last possible moment, I'll pull up and Kelly will hit the White House.*

Kelly again thought of nicking Kashan's tail with his propeller. Staying under Kashan was not going to work. He eased back ever so slightly on the throttle, letting Kashan sail past, then jerked the yoke to gain altitude.

Kelly almost got too close.

His propeller cut out a large chunk of Kashan's V-tail but the blades of Kelly's propeller were damaged by the impact.

Almost immediately, Kashan tumbled out of control. Kelly pulled up, barely in time. With a bent propeller, his Bonanza reacted more slowly and he almost crashed into Kashan.

The tumbling of Kashan's Bonanza detonated at least one of the suitcases of explosives creating a large white ball which emanated rays of red and blue fire like a small exploding star. The center ball engulfed his plane with a flash and sporadically spit bits and pieces of aluminum and plastic and rubber and pieces of singed human anatomy; arms, legs, and feet. Secondary explosions from either the gas tanks or the remaining suitcases rocked the sky. The fires died as quickly as they had begun like a spent Fourth of July firework. Numerous sparks accompanied what was left of the airplane as it fell in a smoldering lump of scrap metal into the Potomac River.

Muluk had seen the entire duel through the lens of his video camera from his park bench in The Ellipse. He had been too captivated to activate the camera and had missed the opportunity to record the explosions and flames.

The sun was several degrees over the horizon and its bright rays illuminated the drops of dew still clustered on the blossoms on the cherry trees.

The phone rang just as Thomas J. Duncan sat at his desk. An airplane had exploded over Washington.

27

QOM
May 5th

General Rajavi stared out one of the arched windows on the second floor of the mini-palace. A look of disbelief dominated his stony face. He did not hear the television set blaring away on the mahogany table amidst the piles of papers and charts. As usual, the guard stood outside caressing his Uzi submachine gun.

The holy man in the minaret was finishing his evening call to prayer:

> *Come to security.*
> *God is most great.*

Minutes earlier, a telephone call had informed Rajavi that the ayatollahs were waiting to see him. Neither Colonel Alam or Colonel Badri knew about the call. Each lay on the floor next to the mahogany table in a pool of his own blood with a small hole in his temple.

For the first time, it became clear to Rajavi why he had not received a scheduled report from the *Brothers of Islam*. Distracted by dreams of glory, he had overlooked the omission. He was solely responsible for the failure of the operation. He was in charge. He was captain of the ship.

Rajavi lifted the 9 mm Beretta automatic to his head and slowly pulled the trigger.

28

LANGLEY
May 5th

Early that morning, the Director of the Central Intelligence Agency had called an emergency meeting with representatives from the FBI, the Joint Chiefs of Staff, the FAA, the Secret Service and the State Department. They surrounded the large oak table in the 7th-floor conference room. Armed guards stood by outside the door.

The DCI began the meeting. His question was aimed at no one in particular although his eyes were focused on the Administrator of the FAA. "How the hell can two planes have an air duel over the Washington Monument?"

"Yeah, what's goin' on? We'd like to know too," said the Chairman of the Joint Chiefs. Our guys on the roof of the White House almost blasted the fuckers out of the sky with their Stingers."

"The controllers at Washington National saw a couple of blips on their radar screens," said the FAA Administrator defensively. "It was early this morning and nobody else seems to have gotten a birds-eye view except some drunks."

"How's that possible?" asked somebody.

"Ever been to the Capitol in the early morning hours. It's like a morgue. Most government people get snockered every night and nobody gets up early. How about you guys at the Bureau?

Did you hear anything?" asked the DCI.

"Yeah," answered Tom Duncan. "One of our boys saw the planes and called me. Nothing else came our way," lied Duncan. He'd have to call Ben Crawley. Then, he decided to add, "We had a flimsy tip about a couple of planes in the Chicago area, but didn't attach too much to it."

"How come the Service wasn't in on this sooner?" asked the Head of the Secret Service.

Nervously, the DCI scanned the table. "We've picked up one of the two pilots. A former Navy jet-jock named Burton Kelly. His prop was badly bent but he managed to make it back to the Bower Airport near Oxon Hill. He called us after he landed. He claims there was a plot to blow up the White House by some Iranians."

"That's crazy," came back the head of the Secret Service without hesitation. "We would have known about it."

Tom Duncan didn't say anything. He was wondering how he was going to get out of this mess.

"Probably just a couple of nutty private pilots flying airplanes they don't know much about and trying to be cute," quipped the FAA Administrator.

"I doubt that," said the DCI with apprehension. "Before we go any further, tell me, *could* a small plane fly over the White House and get away with it?"

"That airspace *is* restricted and small planes are *not* permitted in there," answered the FAA Administrator. "But, short of closing down National and keeping all air traffic outside of a twenty-five mile radius, there's little we can do. We've never had a problem before. In fact, when Nixon was in office, we used to let planes fly right over the Western White House as long as they maintained two thousand feet altitude. Even now, planes fly over the Pentagon every day since it's under the landing pattern to National."

The Chairman of the Joint Chiefs was quick to add: "We can't very well position anti-aircraft guns all around the goddamn White House. The president would never go for it. He did agree to have some Army guys on the roof with Stingers. But, if some turkey came in low enough, we'd never have enough time. It's just something we have to live with."

"What?" came back the DCI. "We've spent millions erecting barriers in front of the White House to keep a vehicle from ramming through. We've spent more dough on bullet-proof glass in the House and Senate to keep terrorists from shooting our crooked, fat-assed politicians. Now, you are telling me that some shitty fuckin' little airplane can just pop over the White House whenever it wants to."

"That's about right. Just remember to say your prayers every night," said the FAA Administrator.

"Oh fuck," said the DCI gloomily.

Silence dominated the room, allowing time for the impact of the FAA Administrator's words to sink in: the White House was vulnerable under current flight rules. There was nothing that could be done.

"We'll keep you posted," said the DCI. "Once we've had a little more time to check out the story this Mr. Kelly has given us."

EPILOGUE

La Casa de Niños de Agua Prieta

On the way over, Jennie flew the Bonanza. She had passed the flying examination for her pilot's license after taking lessons for several months.

They were married in the small chapel at the orphanage. Father Miguel performed a simply ceremony. Ellen was Jennie's maid of honor. Each of Kelly's thirty-one "best men" took great pride in affixing his signature to the *certificado*. Those of some of the smaller boys were barely legible.

Father Miguel offered prayers in memory of Francisco Diaz before the wedding. The day before, he had convinced U.S. Immigration authorities to issue thirty-two visas so they could all go to visit Momma in San Diego. This was highly irregular, especially since few of the children had birth certificates. It would be difficult to fit all of the kids on the truck. They'd manage somehow. They would probably need a second truck. But, it would happen. After all, who was Father Miguel to question the mysterious ways in which the Lord sometimes worked?

Meigs Field, Chicago, Il.

The white-haired, distinguished looking man in his 60's was again busy leafing through a stack of receipts on the glass display case at Butler Aviation. It might have been the same stack he was leafing through when Kelly and Francisco Diaz landed at Meigs the previous week. He was only half-heartedly going through the stack and appeared deeply in thought. Finally, he seemed to have completed some mental calculation and he spoke.

"With your general knowledge of aviation, we can have you flying a Bonanza with about 40 hours of training - that's if you're willing to work at it and apply yourself. We can probably do the whole thing in a couple of months. Your flight instructor will be younger than you and some folks take offense at that. It'll cost you about $7000 - give or take. If you want to give me a deposit now, say $500, we can get started whenever you want."

With that, he looked directly into the eyes of the baldheaded bespectacled man standing before him.

Maj. Muluk reached into his pocket, took out his billfold . . .

AUTHOR'S NOTES

This book is fiction and all characters with the exception of historical figures are the product of the author's imagination. Any resemblance to living persons is purely coincidental. Most of the locations described have been visited by the author and are real.

The photograph of the inside gardens of the Pentagon was taken by the author while William Clay piloted a Cessna 172. We were on final approach to Washington National Airport when the tower gave us instructions to execute a 720-degree turn to make room for a commercial jet to land before us. If there is any doubt in anyone's mind that such a flight is possible, let him or her go and land at National Airport.

I am indebted to the many who had faith that this novel would be completed. Special thanks go to Elizabeth Garrow, Ann O'-Connell, Laila the Belly Dancer, Burt Reynolds and Gerald and Sarajean Harwood.

POSTSCRIPT

In the early morning hours of September 12, 1994, a small plane did indeed crash into the White House. The pilot, reported to be mentally ill, died and we will never know what motivated him to embark on his disastrous flight.

Later that same day, I sent letters to The *Los Angeles Times, The New York Times* and *The Washington Post* (see Appendix I). And to *Peter Jennings News, Paula Zahn,* and Mike Wallace of *60 Minutes.* The letters pointed out a gaping hole in the White House defenses and suggested a means whereby this hole could be plugged. There was no reply from any of these letters. *60 Minutes* had been previously contacted in 1991 and, at that time, chose to disregard my letter.

Slowly, I began to feel paranoid, to feel that my book was being censored. Although we celebrate freedom of the press, censorship is not new in America. I understand that when Reagan was President, that it was almost impossible to rent one of his movies called *Bedtime for Bonzo.*

A more concrete example is given by Ben H. Bagdikian in his book *The Media Monopoly.* He gives the example of the book *Countercoup: The Struggle for the Control of Iran* written by Kermit Roosevelt. Bagkikian claims that the book was published, copies were on sale in bookstores, and reviewer copies were in the mail when British Petroleum persuaded the publisher to recall all the books, the ones from the stores and the ones from the reviewers. Evidently, BP wasn't too crazy about the publicity exposing their politics in the Middle East.

The only publicity my book received was an interview on the local television news station on September 12, 1994 and mention in Kathleen Allen's column "**People/About Town**" in the *Tucson Citizen* newspaper on September 17, 1994:

> Tucson writer **Robert Powell** wasn't too stunned about the recent plane crash into the White House's well-manicured lawn.
> His book, "Naked Strangers," has a similar scene in it. Unfortunately, the book, in manuscript form, is sitting on the desks of two New York publishers. Maybe we'll get a chance to read it before the mystery of the real crash is solved. . .

At that time, I was living in Arizona. Later that same day, the letter reprinted in Appendix II was sent to the President.

With this letter and with the publication of my book, I feel I have done my part as a good citizen in bringing to light a potentially dangerous situation.

It is entirely possible that the idea for this book could have come from conversations in a back-street bar in Tijuana with a bald, bespectacled man or a drunken blond masquerading as a Russian princess. It could have come from similar conversations with and ex-Navy pilot or his beautiful wife in some classy restaurant in Rancho Santa Fe. Maybe some thoughts were exchanged over a few shots of tequila and maybe a little money bought a photograph. It is not beyond the imagination to think that such things are possible. The only people who know are the ones who possibly partook of the free booze or sold the photograph. I am not going to tell.

Flying small airplanes is one of the tremendous pleasures of living in a free society. There is nothing suggested here to put any restraints on this freedom. All freedoms are balances between the rights of the individual and the rights of his fellow men and women. Once in a while one or the other needs to be slightly compromised. Hopefully, the government will not go overboard.

I still cannot help but wonder about a few things. If I had this idea a long time ago, or got it from someone else, surely it has occurred to others. Or, did the guy who slam-dunked his small plane into the South Portico somehow see an advance copy of this book? Can it happen again? Is our First Family safe? Should some steps be taken to insure that they are? Maybe this whole area needs some reevaluation.

APPENDIX I
Letter to the Media

Robert Powell
7777 N. Santa Anna Drive
Tucson, AZ 85704
(602)555-1212

September 12, 1994

Editor-National News
The New York Times
New York, NY

Dear Editor;

I feel I know something about small planes crashing into the White House. I predicted yesterday's scenario almost perfectly in my novel *NAKED STRANGERS*. I was off a little since I said the pilot would have 13 seconds whereas the news media has been reporting 14 seconds from the time he was picked up on radar until the crash. Otherwise I foresaw the flight would start in Maryland, come in from the north, head for the Washington Monument, fly below the radar screen, avoid the Stinger Missiles, and crash into the South Portico.

I am submitting the enclosed editorial entitled "Crash of the Cessna into the White House" as an exclusive to the *New York Times*. I expect to be compensated at your normal rate.

If you are interested, please let me know ASAP. I intend to submit this editorial elsewhere if you are not.

I think it is ironic that I could predict almost exactly the pilot's actions as if I had been in the cockpit myself. I cannot help but wonder why the Secret Service or the FAA could not or did not do likewise.

Sincerely,

Robert Powell

Robert Powell

APPENDIX II
Letter to the President

Robert Powell
7777 N. Santa Anna Drive
Tucson, AZ 85704
(602)555-1212

September 17, 1994

President Clinton
THE WHITE HOUSE
1600 Pennsylvania Avenue
Washington, D.C.

Dear President Clinton;

I feel I know something about small planes crashing into the White House. I predicted last week's scenario almost perfectly in my novel *NAKED STRANGERS*. I was off a little since I said the pilot would have 13 seconds whereas the news media has been reporting 14 seconds from the time he was picked up on radar until the crash. Otherwise I foresaw the flight would start in Maryland, come in from the north, head for the Washington Monument, fly below the radar screen, avoid the Stinger Missiles, and crash into the South Portico.

I think it is ironic that I could predict almost exactly the pilot's actions as if I had been in the cockpit myself. I cannot help but wonder why the Secret Service or the FAA could not or did not do likewise.

Enclosed is a copy of my book. Take a look at pp. 168-172 in Chapter 19.

I tried to call all this to the attention of the previous administration but my letter was never answered. I also tried to call it to the attention of *60 Minutes* in 1991 but, again, there was no reply.

What can be done now to avoid a repeat, to avoid another small plane from blowing up the White House? Absolutely nothing if the policies of the FAA at Washington National Airport are not changed. Prayers are not going to work. I recommend that all air traffic be kept out of a 25-mile radius of the White House unless they make a reservation 24 hours in advance. This will surely inconvenience some of our legislators and businessmen in Washington. However, what price must be ultimately paid for the convenience of a select few?

Sincerely,

Robert Powell

Robert Powell